Daughters of Pengollan

ELAINE SINGER

Grosvenor House
Publishing Limited

This book is published by
Grosvenor House Publishing Ltd
Link House
140 The Broadway, Tolworth, Surrey, KT6 7HT.
www.grosvenorhousepublishing.co.uk

This book is a work of fiction. Any resemblance to
people or events, past or present, is purely coincidental.

A CIP record for this book
is available from the British Library

ISBN 978-1-80381-796-5
eBook ISBN 978-1-80381-797-2

For my mum and dad, May and Norman Reed,
who would have been so proud. Miss you.

Elaine lives in Cornwall with her husband,
Adrian, and two Labrador dogs.

Also by Elaine Singer
Sisters of Vellangoose

Daughters of Pengollan

1

Shannon hit the accelerator, roared up the narrow farm track and in through the gateway, then squinted out of the windscreen at where her dilapidated caravan stood parked against the hedge. Something hung there, nailed to the door, its end flapping in the wind.

She braked. Her knuckles whitened around the steering wheel. Only a handful of people knew she lived in this godforsaken spot, and they didn't leave things on her caravan door. She glanced across at Carnmarth Farm, grey and stark against the skyline. There was no one about.

She got out.

A black cat stood in the middle of the rutted track that led towards the farmyard. Its piercing yellow eyes glared at her before it slunk under a gate and darted off, a mouse dangling from its mouth.

She walked a few paces and yanked the flapping object free.

A photograph.

Or, more accurately, half of one, torn down the middle.

Her heart raced. A mix of emotions rolled through her as she stared at the snapshot. Her mum looked back at her, so young and so beautiful. Next to her stood a much younger Shannon, dressed in tight shorts and a top that only a fifteen-year-old would dare wear.

'Hello.'

She jerked around.

A stranger – not much older than her, forty or so? – stood in the gateway, hands in pockets, a big grin on his face.

She stomped over and waved the photo in the air. 'Did you put this on my caravan door?'

A gust of wind whipped the picture from her hand, and the man chased it along the ground. Shannon ran after him, but he reached it first and picked it up.

She lunged for it. 'Give me that.'

After glancing at the photo, he burst into laughter and handed it back to her. 'What are those people wearing?' His laughter died away, and he frowned. 'Sorry, is that you?'

'What are you doing here? What do you want?'

Before he could answer, Trevor appeared on the corner of the lane, his thick farmer's hands wrapped around a shepherd's crook and a woolly hat pulled down over his ears.

'Hold up there, Shannon.' Trevor hunched his shoulders and sucked in a deep breath. 'Bloody hell, Zach, I told you not to go rushing ahead.'

Shannon glared at her landlord. Unshaven, grumpy, and dressed not much better than a tramp, he seemed old, but she suspected he was still in his forties. 'You know this idiot?'

'Calm down. What's put you in such a foul mood?'

She shoved the picture deep into her jacket pocket before Trevor could see it. 'Been at Mrs Martin's all morning,' she said. 'You know, cleaning her greenhouses and about a million pots and trays, fun stuff like that.'

'Ah, well, 'tis the way it is when you need the money. Gotta do what you gotta do.' He waved towards the other man. 'Talking of which, Zach's taken the caravan next to Vic's. I wanted to introduce him so you didn't rip into him when you saw him around the place,' he grunted. 'Bit late for that now. It's like I said, Zach, you'd best stick to the yard area. This one likes her privacy, she does.'

'She accused me of putting a photograph on her van or something,' Zach said.

'What photo?'

'Nothing for you to worry about, Trevor.' Shannon's hand moved protectively over the snapshot in her pocket.

Zach stepped forward. 'I think we should start again.' He held out his hand. 'Hello, Shannon. Nice to meet you.'

She hesitated momentarily, then took the offered palm and gave him the once over. Well-spoken and from somewhere in the home counties, if she had to guess.

Her gaze shifted back to Trevor. 'Didn't think you were taking on any workers. You know I–'

'Yeah, yeah,' Trevor butted in. 'You've still got first dibs on any work that's going here. Zach's renting the van, that's all.'

Zach grinned. 'I got chatting to Vic in The Wheatsheaf. Told him I was looking for a place to stay and that I was a bit short on cash. And, hey, here I am.'

'Come on, Zach, enough chatting.' Trevor strode back towards the track. 'Leave her in peace.'

Zach hesitated and then followed him.

Through half-closed eyes, Shannon watched their retreating backs. Something about Zach didn't sit right with her. He might be all dressed up in cheap jeans and a black and gold Cornwall rugby shirt, but his expensive haircut, easy swagger and posh accent told another story. Why did this man, who whiffed of money, want to slum it at Carnmarth Farm in the middle of winter? Hiding from something or someone, maybe? She shrugged. Weren't they all?

The icy February wind stung her face. In the distance, a fragment of silver-grey sea shimmered on the horizon. She could imagine the welcoming lights and warm houses of Falmouth tucked in the bay below.

With a sigh, she pushed the caravan door open. Shack would be a better word for the place she called home. Paintings and sketches dotted the walls. A shelf, which ran below the roofline, held all she owned: books, a few items of food, a small selection of clothes.

She sat on the single bed-cum-sofa, kicked off her boots, pulled the patchwork quilt over her legs and stared once more at the image of her mum. Her thumb ran over the jagged edge. Her head throbbed with memories and questions. Why this photograph? Why now? It looked like an original, but how could that be possible? Butterflies tumbled in her stomach and formed a tight knot. Where was the missing half, with the smiling faces of her best friend, Rosa, and her mother? She'd never seen the photo before but remembered when she'd posed for it on the beach at Marazion like it was yesterday. Twenty-three years, six months and four days ago. Shannon and Rosa's joint fifteenth birthday celebration.

For several minutes, Shannon continued to gaze at the image. Then, she lifted a rucksack onto her lap and pulled out a sketch pad and pencil. She flicked to the next blank page, studied her mother's face for a moment and started to draw. When she'd finished, she added the date and a short narrative in the corner before closing the pad. The knot in her stomach had disappeared. She took a deep breath and again peered at the snapshot, then kissed her finger and pressed it to her mum's face.

That day at Marazion had been the best day ever.

Before everything changed.

2

Even after six months, a mixture of distaste and pleasure pulsed through Rosa's body every time she turned into the driveway and caught sight of Curlew House. Distaste at the sight of the ultra-modern glass monstrosity that dominated the landscape and stood out like a sore thumb from the other Cornish cliffside properties. Pleasure because the building was a physical symbol of her and James's obvious wealth and status.

She'd never felt the instant love for the multi-million-pound house – that look that estate agents dream of seeing in their clients' eyes – but James had, so he'd bought it. Bought it without telling her.

The immediate riverside scenery and the distant sea views of Falmouth Bay were the property's best features. Regardless of her feelings towards the house, she knew she would never tire of living on the Helford. She glanced at the water as she followed the drive past the lawned area in front of Curlew House and parked her BMW in one of the two double garages at the back of the property.

Her diamond ring glinted in the winter sunshine as she pushed the door open to the utility room, walked across the slate floor and stored her boots and coat in their allotted places. James would be home in forty-five minutes. She walked into the open-plan kitchen and touched the smart panel. Lights flashed on. Blinds dropped in slow motion, closing off the emerging darkness. The meal was cooking; the automatic timer had done its business. She double-checked the label on a bottle of red wine and uncorked it.

Next, she lifted the pudding for the evening meal and a platter of mixed cheeses from the fridge onto the marble worktop. They should come to the exact room temperature just before serving.

A glance around the area confirmed that the worktops were clean and uncluttered, the glass and stainless-steel surfaces smear free. Another quick look, this time to the far end of the room at the large kitchen table, positioned where it benefited from the riverside views she loved, and already laid for dinner. With all the items mentally crossed off her checklist, she headed upstairs.

In the bedroom, she kicked off her jeans and sweater and stuffed them into the back of the wardrobe. Once showered, with her hair washed and dried into a dark bob, she sat at the dressing table and expertly applied her make-up.

In front of the full-length mirror, she slipped on dark slacks and a cream cashmere sweater and eased her feet into a pair of impossibly high-heeled shoes. She smiled. Still slim and fit, she looked good for a thirty-eight-year-old. Of course, the diamonds and the expensive cut of her clothes helped.

A car came down the drive and headed for the garages. She gave herself one final check over, then glided downstairs and walked gracefully along the polished floor to the front door – James's preferred entrance.

She reached to undo the lock, then stopped, her hand in mid-air. The tip of an envelope poked through the letterbox. She grabbed it. Somebody had typed Rosa Trevail and her address in capital letters on the front. Ripping it open, she partly pulled the contents out, then gasped.

James's feet crunched on the gravel outside.

She shoved the item back into the envelope, jammed it into a drawer in the hallway table, ran a hand over her hair and smoothed down her crease-free slacks.

A blast of cold air accompanied her husband into the hallway. 'Hello, darling.' He dropped his briefcase with a thud onto the floor. 'Any post?'

Her heart thumped. 'Not today.'

He leaned forward and kissed her on the cheek. 'You won't believe the day I've had. Can't wait for a glass of my favourite red.'

'It's ready and waiting in the kitchen.'

'Thank goodness. I can't tell you the hours of tedious discussions I've had about volatile shares and falling interest rates.' He moved down the hallway, then turned around. 'What about your day? Been out and about?'

'Only Newquay.' She smoothed down his coat with quick strokes. 'The Atlantic Hotel. A committee meeting regarding the Treloar School Gala Ball. I mentioned it at breakfast.'

'So,' he bobbed his head a couple of times, 'you had a boring afternoon as well.'

She watched his back until he disappeared into the kitchen, then she bent down, picked up the briefcase and headed for his study.

James was sipping from a generous glass of wine when she returned and headed towards the oven.

'I thought we'd eat in here this evening. It's more comfortable and less formal than the dining room.' She smiled and gestured to the table laid out for dinner. 'The meal is almost ready.'

'What are we having?'

'Boeuf Bourguignon with crushed new potatoes and wilted spinach.' She picked up the serving dishes. 'And chocolate frangipane tart with pears. Your favourites. Oh … what's the matter?'

'I'm so sorry, darling.' He wrinkled his nose. 'It sounds wonderful but I'm not sure I've enough appetite for it.

You know what these business meetings are like, long lunches and everybody pushing food at you, the richer the better. I don't suppose I could have a light snack instead?'

Her shoulders sagged and unwelcome tears sprang into her eyes. She'd worked flat out to get it all prepared before she'd left at 11:30 a.m.

'You could've said, James.'

He came up behind her and put his arms around her waist. 'You're right. My fault. Of course I'll eat it.'

She leaned back against his muscled chest, and he nuzzled the back of her neck. A warm glow of love for him flowed through her body. She turned to face him.

He straightened and reached for his glass again. 'But maybe in future you ought to check the dinner menu against my work diary?'

Rosa opened the oven door, took a deep breath and reached inside.

'Call me when dinner's served. I'll be in my study.' James topped up his wine glass and moved away. 'I'm happy to eat in here tonight but, you know me, darling, I'm a stickler for tradition and ...' his voice took on a childlike whine, 'well, I feel quite strongly that we should always eat in the dining room in the evenings.'

Rosa stared at him as he left the kitchen and then at the already laid table. James could be a right numpty at times. She shook her head. But then he was her numpty, and she loved him.

3

Shannon sneezed for the third time. Rats, all she needed now was a cold. Who knew greenhouses could get so dirty and so icy in winter? In the past week, she'd brushed out three of the glass monsters and wiped the panes and metal surrounds with a strong disinfectant. Now, she was up to her elbows in soapy water, cleaning a bottomless pile of empty plant pots and trays.

Not that she would openly complain. She was down to her last few tins of tomatoes and a packet of dried pasta, and the work at Mrs Martin's was a godsend. Old Jack, Mrs Martin's employed gardener, had broken his leg a few months back and she was keen to get the basics done before he returned.

'Well done, Miss Reid.'

'Shannon.'

'Oh, yes, Shannon.' Mrs Martin stepped inside. 'You've done a wonderful job. Jack will be pleased.'

Despite being wrapped in an old sheepskin coat and trilby hat, Mrs Martin, who had to be in her seventies, still managed to look glamorous. For a moment, Shannon was acutely aware that the extra-large scarf wrapped around her neck several times, her wool hat and ragged puffer coat made her appear like an over-stuffed elephant. A bit ironic, considering she was only five-foot-three and a stiff wind would likely lift her off her feet. But her body was tough and wiry through years of hard, manual work, and she was confident she could stand her ground in most situations if she had to.

'Will you finish today?' Mrs Martin scrutinised the rows of newly scrubbed pots and the ones yet to be cleaned.

'That's the plan.' Shannon took a deep breath and rushed on. 'The gutters around the tool sheds are full of leaves and moss, and there's a lot of algae in the water butts.' She crossed her fingers behind her back. 'I could clean those for you as well, if you like.'

Mrs Martin surveyed the large walled garden before she turned to face Shannon.

'I think that's a good suggestion. In fact, my dear, there's probably enough work around here for another week.'

Shannon's heart leapt. A week's worth of work meant she could give her so-called landlord the rent money she owed him, get in a supply of food and a new gas bottle to heat the caravan and water. With luck and a following wind, Mrs Martin might even need her for more work. Not that she wished further ill-health on Jack.

'Thank you,' she spluttered.

'No need to thank me. You'll do an excellent job, I'm sure. I want the place to be ship-shape for Jack. He won't be up to heavy work for a while.' Mrs Martin straightened her trilby hat and looked again at Shannon. 'I can give you a cheque today if you'd like, or would you rather wait until the job is finished?'

'A cheque? I … I was hoping for cash.'

'I don't offer cash for casual labour. I know it's traditional around here with the farmers and others, but not me. I believe everyone should pay their share of income tax. Being a member of the parish council, I need to be beyond reproach.'

Shannon gritted her teeth. She wasn't against the idea of paying tax, but her meagre earnings didn't even warrant her opening a bank account. How the hell could she sort this out? She crossed her fingers behind her back again. 'Would it be possible to make the cheque out to Trevor Harris? See, I owe him rent and ...' Shit, once again she was at the mercy of others and could only hope that Mrs Martin would agree, and that Trevor wouldn't tell her to shove off.

'That's not something I'd normally do.' Mrs Martin frowned, then smiled. 'However, seeing that it's Trevor, I'm sure that will be alright.' She stepped away. 'I'll go and write the cheque immediately.'

Shannon let out a long breath and smiled in return. 'I thought I would take a quick tea break, Mrs Martin. If that's okay with you?'

'Of course, my dear. I'll be back in ten minutes or so with the cheque.'

After Mrs Martin left, Shannon sat outside on Jack's faded canvas chair and poured tea from her battered flask. She took a sip. Birds flitted in and out of the nearby shrubs and bushes surrounding the vegetable plots. Two palm trees, erect and proud, took centre stage in the flower garden. After a while, she opened her sketch pad and began to draw.

Later that afternoon, Shannon parked in the yard at Carnmarth Farm and scanned the scene in front of her. Trevor was a hard man to fathom. The bits of rusted machinery dotted around the place, the enormous muck heap in one corner, and the overall neglected state of the main house and out-buildings was at odds with the fact that his animals were always a picture of health. The flock of sheep in the fields and the mixed herd of Aberdeen Angus and Hereford beef cows about to give calf all seemed content and very well-cared for.

Flo, Fern and Kim rushed out of the main farmhouse door and jumped up at her car in a flurry of black and white. In the middle of the barking collies, Whisky – a Jack Russell terrier – yapped the loudest. His head bobbed up to the driver's window in a flash of pink tongue and white teeth, before he dropped to the ground and repeated the whole exercise again.

Trevor stepped from the house. 'Ger away, you stupid buggers.'

The dogs immediately fell silent, dropped back a few paces, and sat with eyes fixed on him.

She got out of the car.

'Before you start, I haven't got any work yet. Too early in the season.' Before she could answer, Trevor put his hand up. 'And don't complain about the caravan. You pay shit rent, and you owe me two months.'

She cricked her neck to look up at him. Not that he was much above average height for a man, but he seemed to tower over her.

'I've got a cheque from Mrs Martin. Sorry, it's in your name.' She dug the toe of her boot into the ground. 'I don't have a bank account and ...' She rushed on. 'Well, I'm hoping you'd take what I owe you and give me the balance in cash.'

'Bloody Ada,' he growled. 'You'd think she worked for the flipping tax office.' Black clouds rolled overhead, and large raindrops peppered the ground and their clothes as Trevor nodded toward the farmhouse. He glared at her for a heartbeat. 'Better come in then.'

She stood just inside the entrance and peered into the kitchen. Holy cow, it was even more dishevelled and cluttered than she remembered. Stuff everywhere. Old newspapers and farming magazines sat piled on the worktops, bags of dog food stood in the corner, and various sauce bottles and other bits covered the large wooden table. The place, like him, exuded the impression that it simply couldn't be bothered. Still, what business was it of hers how Trevor wanted to live?

He rummaged inside one of the cupboard drawers, hopefully for money.

'I was wondering if you'd seen any strangers in the lane recently?' she called out, keeping her gaze firmly on her earth-covered work boots. 'Like … someone on the way to my place, for example.'

'Why? You got trouble? That photo thing Zach mentioned?'

'That? No, that was nothing,' she lied. Her stomach did a flip-flop. 'Saw a few footprints in the mud outside the caravan, that's all.'

A gust of wind rattled the windows.

'For God's sake, shut that door. Don't want the roof to blow off.'

The dogs shot past her into the warmth just before she clicked it shut.

She could see into the living room from where she now stood. More clutter, more stuff, although the sofas surrounding the granite fireplace looked well-used and comfortable. In the nearly five years she'd lived at Carnmarth Farm, this was the furthest she'd ever come into the house. Usually, she posted the rent through the door or handed it to Trevor in passing.

'You certainly like your stuff,' she said.

'My house, my business.'

She held up her hands and smiled to herself. Gruff as he was, she understood where he was coming from. Her rule in life was never to volunteer any information about herself, and he never asked for any. Fair enough that the same principle should apply the other way around. Precisely the way she liked it.

'You know, I could help with the cleaning if you–'

He slammed the drawer shut, a faded leather wallet gripped in his hand. 'Don't want some woman mucking up my place,' he said.

Trudie, an old collie who hadn't bothered to come outside to greet her, rose to her feet from her position in front of the Aga and ambled over to Shannon. The animal pushed a wet nose into her hand. She bent down, whispered sweet nothings to the dog and stroked her silky ears.

'Don't go fussing the animals. These are working dogs; they don't do well with fussing.'

Laughter burst from her mouth and the unfamiliar sound echoed around the room. She nodded towards the three younger collies and Whisky, stretched out in a heap in front on the Aga.

'Aren't working dogs supposed to live outdoors?'

He grunted, removed several notes from his wallet, showed them to her, then took two away and handed over the remainder.

'Thanks.' She reached for the door handle. 'So, you haven't seen any odd people wandering around here?'

'Only Zach and Vic.' He seemed to attempt a smile. 'But they've no reason to go traipsing around your place.'

She nodded. 'Don't forget, I'm available for any work.'

'Don't you ever shut up?' He yanked a chair out from under the table. 'Give it a week or two.'

She had reached the car when he called out to her. 'Hey.'

'What?'

'If you've got trouble, I can't have the police snooping around here, sticking their noses in. You know that, don't you?'

'I know,' she said.

The pub was rammed, mostly with college students and young people on the pull, jostling and elbowing in all directions. Shannon held her ground in a spot by the bar. At the end of the room, a live band blasted away.

She lifted her pint glass and raised it towards her lips. Cider sloshed over her hand. Damn, she'd drunk far too much. She'd have to sleep in the car.

An arm wrapped around her waist and squeezed her closer. 'Hey, sweetie, you want another one?'

She shook her head. 'Need to go.' Even to her own ears, her words sounded slurred.

A pair of bloodshot but beautiful blue eyes peered at her. A nose almost touched hers. Warm, beer-laden breath blasted into her face. 'You're very beautiful, Sharon.'

'Shannon,' she said.

'What's that?'

'Never mind,' she shouted. 'Sharon will do.'

What did it matter? She wouldn't see him again. She couldn't remember his name either. Matt? Mark? Mark sounded familiar.

Mark planted kisses along her neck and twisted his fingers around her plait of fair hair. 'Nice,' he murmured. 'Don't see many of those things on women your age.'

She slipped underneath his arm. 'Got to go.'

The combination of pounding music, sweaty bodies and strong perfume made her queasy, and she stumbled as she pushed her way through the crowd. Why had she come to Falmouth? Now and again, she guessed, even the most isolated people craved warmth and company.

Mark followed her outside and put his arm around her shoulders. He bent towards her and kissed her hard on the mouth. They stopped and leaned against the granite wall of a shop. A stone jabbed into her back. The cold night air pierced her thin sweater. She didn't want this. Sometimes she did, but not tonight. Too much rattled around in her head, too many images: the ripped photograph, her mum's eyes, that last day with Rosa and her mum.

She pushed Mark away and tottered down the main street to the car park. Mark followed, grabbed her hand, and walked with her. 'I'll see you safely to your car. Don't want anything to happen to you.'

Shit. She was old enough to have known better.

Down over the slope they swayed. In the car park, she had no idea where her vehicle was. Waves slapped against the sea wall below. Yellow lights glowed over the pay machine. Pools of darkness pockmarked the edges.

Mark and Shannon staggered towards one of the corners. Did she walk there, or did Mark steer her? She giggled. She was beyond thinking. Mark burrowed his face into the crook of her neck. His hand slipped under her sweater and massaged her breast, a bit like the kittens did to the cats at Carnmarth. She snorted.

Mark tightened his grip.

Such strong hands. Nice, strong hands. She shook her head. She wanted to lie down. She tried to push him away. Where was her car? Had she parked it at the other end of town?

Mark's kisses were more urgent, his hand had moved to the top of her jeans, and fingers slipped inside her pants.

Her head flopped onto his chest. She let out an animal-like groan.

Mark lifted her chin. 'What's up, babe? You okay? I thought you wanted it?'

His soft words and gentle voice hit a spot. Stupid tears of gratitude pricked the back of her eyes. She kissed him and willingly submitted to the comfort of his caresses.

Against the wall of the car park, she allowed Mark to do what he'd wanted to do ever since they'd met earlier in the evening; ever since he'd plied her with several pints of cider and a couple of bags of salt and vinegar crisps.

Legs hoisted around his waist, she went with the flow. What the hell did it matter anyway? Nobody in the world cared what she did.

4

Rosa finished her run with a sprint across the beach. She stopped halfway, bent over, and placed her hands on her knees. Clouds of condensation puffed from her mouth. After a few breaths, she dropped her running belt onto the sand and ran into the sea.

The freezing water made her gasp, but she ploughed back and forth until her limbs ached, then she returned to the beach.

With her belt clipped on again, she pulled out a plastic bottle and took a big swig of water. She glanced at her mobile phone and frowned. James had called several times. She shoved the phone into the belt pocket and zipped it up. She'd ring him when she got back to the house.

For a while, she jogged on the spot and watched the yachts tack across the Helford River. She'd never felt physically better. Lean and toned, she had the body of someone years younger. Running and swimming not only allowed her to escape the house but temporarily drove out the demons that filled her head.

At Curlew House, she stood under the power shower and let the hot water blast her skin back to life. Hands placed on opposite walls, she hung her head in exhaustion. Perhaps she would give the resistance training in their basement gym a miss today. Maybe an hour of yoga or meditation would help?

At the sound of her mobile phone, she stepped quickly out of the shower and picked it up.

'Darling. Thank goodness you're okay.' James's voice pulsated in her ear. 'I thought something had happened to you. I tried your phone several times, but you didn't answer.'

Rosa's heart lifted at his words of concern. 'Oh, I'm so sorry. I–'

'Where were you?'

'I went for my usual run and swim. You know how it helps my migraines.'

'Is that all? Do me a favour, darling, and push the ringtone up. I've been really worried about you. Sorry, got to go.'

The screen went blank. Charming.

When she'd first met James in what now felt like another lifetime ago – what *was* another lifetime? – his love and affection for her had been blinding. He'd showered her with gifts and wonderful words. She wasn't an idiot; men had said those words before and she'd seen through them. With James, it had been different. She'd felt sure the words were real. The way his beautiful blue eyes lit up when she entered a room confirmed it.

Her dad had looked at her mum like that.

Those were the childhood memories that Rosa held onto. She couldn't believe her luck to have found the same thing.

But – and when it came to the men in her life there was always a but – since moving to Cornwall six months ago, James had become … well, less attentive, more whiney. Maybe the stress of getting his own business off the ground was taking its toll. Or maybe this was just marriage. Men changed. Was he turning into her father? The father who'd become a different man overnight when her mother had died. It seemed that the love Rosa's dad possessed for his wife had been too painful to hold onto,

19

and when she'd died, it had withered and perished. Rosa's eyes brimmed with tears because, at the same time, he'd also stopped loving his daughter.

She shook that memory away and dabbed her eyes with the corner of a towel. What did she have to cry about? She had everything she'd ever dreamed of. She would do whatever it took to make James happy. His job enabled her to enjoy this lifestyle, and her job was to make his life outside of work as comfortable and stress-free as possible.

In her craft room, clothed in an oversized dressing gown and with her hair wrapped in a towel, she ran her fingers along the shelves of puzzle books, crosswords, and various travel tomes. All of them eased the boredom that swamped her some days. As did her personal computer with its access to the outside world at the touch of a few keystrokes. In the corner, the partly completed cross-stitch illustration of a tall ship – a gift from James – did not.

Craft room? James had come up with the name. What did that matter? She was so lucky; most women would die for a hobby room, a personal space to call their own.

She glanced at her watch. He wouldn't be home for a couple of hours.

Opening one of the cupboards, she slid several containers to one side, lifted the corner of the carpet and removed one of the floorboards. She reached inside the space below and withdrew a vintage red vanity case.

Inside, the envelope with her name and address in capital letters sat on the top. No need to open it; the contents were etched in her memory. She touched a faded photo album. No need to open that either; she knew all the faces off by heart. Next came a photograph of a boy and girl of about four or five playing on a swing, huge smiles on their faces. She pressed the image to her lips and kissed each of them in turn.

'Darling, I'm home.'

Rosa's head jerked back.

'Where are you?' James called again.

She rammed the documents into the vanity case, shoved it back beneath the floor in the cupboard and yanked the containers into their original place. After closing the cupboard door, she rushed to the cross-stitch, sat down, and picked up the needle in her trembling hand.

'I'm in the craft room,' she replied.

'Ah, there you are.' He bent to kiss her but stepped back a pace and frowned. 'You're not dressed.' He tutted. 'It's nearly noon.'

She feigned a look of surprise. 'Oh, really? I must've got carried away with the cross-stitching after my shower.'

'Imagine if one of my friends, or an important client, had called at the house and found you half dressed? Good job it was only me.'

She bit back her irritation, took a deep breath, and smiled. 'It's such a lovely surprise that you're home at this time of day.' She placed a hand on his cheek.

He pulled her close and undid the belt of her dressing gown. She reached for the towel, tugged it free from her hair and let it fall to the floor. His beautiful eyes searched her face before his lips gently touched hers. She leaned into his arms and eagerly kissed him back.

Freshly showered for a second time, and dressed in slacks and a white blouse, she placed a bowl of salad and a platter of sliced meats and cheese onto the table.

'Sorry, there are only cold offerings to eat, although the baguette is fresh this morning. If I'd known earlier that you'd be home for lunch, I–'

'My work is unpredictable, you know that.' He broke off a large piece of bread. 'You're not married to the nine-to-five type, Rosa. We both need to be flexible.'

Rosa moved tomato wedges and salad leaves around her plate. 'Sorry.'

James smiled. 'Don't worry about it, darling. Maybe in future, you should have something more substantial on standby, just in case. Having said that, these meats are surprisingly tasty. Try some.'

He chatted non-stop during lunch, his cheeks flushed with alcohol.

'Sweetheart,' Rosa said when he'd finished eating, 'Marcus rang earlier about a nature project he's involved in at school, and I was rather hoping that you could take him to Halwyn Woods on Saturday morning.'

'Got a golf match with business associates, I'm afraid.'

'What about the afternoon, or Sunday?'

'I'm pretty sure I'm busy all weekend, but I'll double-check my diary.'

'But … I think he needs something for Monday.'

'Well, we can't always get what we want, can we? It'll be a good discipline for him to learn.'

'Discipline? He's only ten years old and he's looking to you for help. I'm not sure he'll understand why you can't find time for him.'

James tossed his napkin onto the table and stood up. 'I must get back to the office. This place doesn't pay for itself, you know.'

She should have played it differently. Work was obviously getting to him and the last thing he needed was to come home to a nagging wife.

'I'm sorry, I …' Damn it. Why was she apologising? Was it because she always felt the need to put James first rather than the children? She shoved the unwelcome thought away and got to her feet.

He walked over to her for a goodbye kiss, then reached up and released her hair from behind her ears. A smile flitted across his face. 'Okay, I'll *try* and see if I can find a slot for Marcus on Sunday,' he said.

'Thank you,' she replied, kissing him back.

5

Shannon's head throbbed in sync with the raindrops battering the caravan roof. Eyes scrunched tight, she rolled slowly onto her side and slid her legs off the bed. Her mouth tasted like the bottom of a sewer. Christ, thirty-eight years old, and still a good night out for her was to get pissed on cheap cider and have a quickie with a man whose name she couldn't remember.

Images from the previous evening flitted in and out of her mind, but large parts were a black void.

How the hell had she got home?

She stood on shaky legs and peered through the window. Her car stood parked at a weird angle, its back end stuck out into the lane. Tufts of grass and earth framed yet another dent in the vehicle's wing.

Shit.

She slapped her forehead. If she'd killed someone, she would've been no better than her mother.

The milk she'd bought two days ago tasted sour. She spat it out and pushed the bottle to one side. Her stomach rolled. It wasn't worth wasting the last of her cornflakes on breakfast.

As she was pulling off the stained and creased clothes she'd worn the previous evening, she suddenly saw the time. Damn. It wouldn't do to be late for Mrs Martin. Grabbing a clean pair of jeans and a sweater, she shoved a piece of chewing gum into her mouth.

Fresh air and rain blasted her face, and in her hurry, she nearly missed it.

Another note, this time tucked under the windscreen wiper. Probably from Matt? Mark? Whatever.

The note was in a plastic bag; what a pillock.

Except it wasn't a pithy thank you or his phone details. It was a newspaper cutting.

Shannon sat inside the car and laid the article flat on the steering wheel. Her hands shook so much that the old, yellowed paper punctured under her touch. It was a piece from the *West Briton* newspaper. The headline – *Local Woman Responsible for Deaths* – scorched the backs of her eyes. Her chest tightened as the words and images battered her senses and released memories that she'd kept locked in some deep, dark hole for over twenty-three years.

There were the wonderful memories of the celebration they'd enjoyed to mark her and Rosa's fifteenth birthdays. And then there were the hideous memories of the nightmare ending to that day – when her mum had killed Rosa's mother.

The pain in Shannon's chest grew physical and she unconsciously clawed at the collar of her sweater. Momentarily, she thought she was going to die, but she knew it was a panic attack and it would pass. They had before.

Breathe in. One. Two. Three. Breathe out. One. Two. Three. She repeated the routine until her head cleared.

Who was doing this to her? For a nano-second, Shannon wondered about going to the police. A shiver ran over her. No point. What help had they ever been?

A hand slapped on the driver's window. She jerked upright. In her haste to push the newspaper out of sight, she ripped it in two.

Zach grinned at her, his lips distorted by the rain running down the glass.

'What do you want?' She thrust the door open and got out.

'I came to check if you're okay. Your car looks a bit worse for wear and–'

'Leave me alone.' She turned away from him. Her gaze rested on the scrunched-up newspaper. She swung back to face Zach. 'Did you leave this on my windscreen?'

She glanced at his face, then to the newspaper, and back.

'Look, Shannon, I don't know what your problem is. We live in the same place, got the same crappy landlord.' He pulled the collar of his coat up around his ears. 'I only want to help. I thought we could get to know each other a bit more. Like, be friends.'

'I've got enough friends.' She pressed a forefinger against her temple.

'That's not what I hear.'

'Piss off.'

Zach raised his hands in mock surrender. 'Okay, okay,' he shouted over his shoulder as he strolled back down the track.

Shannon ran across the walled garden, chewing on her third piece of minty gum. Thankfully she was on time because Mrs Martin stood in the open doorway of the biggest greenhouse, leaning on a rather large golf umbrella.

'Hi, Mrs Martin. Phew, what a journey. Rainwater is gushing off all the fields and the road's flooded outside of Cribba Village.'

'My late husband used to say that a day like this is only good for ducks.' Mrs Martin let out a little giggle, then straightened her trilby hat. 'I must say the pots and greenhouses are looking in top shape. Jack will be pleased when he returns next week.'

'Next week?'

'Yes, Shannon, that's what I came out to tell you. The doctor has deemed Jack hale and hearty enough to return to work.'

'Oh.' Shannon's shoulders slumped.

'I'm sorry, my dear, but after this week, I won't be needing you anymore. We're all up to date with the finances, I believe, with the cheque I gave you last time you were here.'

'Yes, yes, that's fine. Thank you.'

'Please take these as a little token of my appreciation for all your hard work.'

Mrs Martin picked up a plastic bag by her feet and handed it to Shannon. Inside was a tin of Marks and Spencer's biscuits; as it happened, Shannon's favourites on the rare occasions she could afford them. But a tenner in cash dropped in her palm would have been more welcome.

'Thank you, Mrs Martin, I will certainly enjoy these.'

'Excellent, well that's that. Have a good day.'

'Mrs Martin?'

'Yes.'

'If you need any additional help in the gardens or the house, please would you consider me.'

'I'm rather hoping neither Jack nor Maisie, my darling household assistant, will fall ill any time in the future.' Mrs Martin looked up at the rain thudding onto the glass roof. 'But you'll be the first I'll call should the need arise.'

'Thank you.'

With that, Mrs Martin pulled her sheepskin coat tight across her chest, flipped the multi-coloured umbrella open and headed at a rapid pace towards the main house.

Damn it. Another week or two of work at Mrs Martin's would have meant the difference between paying her rent and not being able to pay it. The difference between scraping by and not.

Shannon parked outside the neat, terraced house in Falmouth. She reached for the door handle, then hesitated. It had been such a hideous day, maybe she should go home and not dump her troubles onto others. She sat for a few minutes, then got out of the car, walked up the path and pushed the backdoor open.

Laughter and happy voices filled the air, and the sweet smell of home cooking and warmth enveloped her in a welcome hug.

'Hi, it's only me,' she yelled.

'Come in, my lovely. I'm in the kitchen feeding the five thousand.'

Mia and Archie scrambled from their chairs and rushed to hug Shannon. She knelt to kiss them and to take in the fragrant scent of their clean skin and freshly shampooed hair. An older boy, Harley, remained slouched at the table. He mumbled a greeting that she couldn't make out. God, how she loved these kids.

Nina stood beside the table spooning Spaghetti Bolognese onto three plates. 'I'm eating with Jake later, but you go get yourself a plate and sit your bum down. There's more than enough here for you as well.'

For a few seconds, Shannon stared at her friend's smiling face, big brown eyes and the mass of curly hair that tumbled down her back, as if seeing her for the first time all those years ago. Nina was the only person in the world, apart from Rosa, who knew all there was to know about Shannon Reid. They'd met at the age of fifteen when they were both in the care of the local authority. Whereas Shannon had never shaken off those awful times, Nina had made good.

Shannon walked over and embraced her friend.

Immediately, Nina squeezed her into a big bear hug. 'Hey, what's up?'

'Shit day.'

'Hmm, that calls for a couple of lagers, I think.' She leaned into the fridge. 'Tell you what, I'll put a few more on ice.'

For the first time in days, Shannon's shoulders relaxed. The rich Bolognese sauce hit the spot as the children chatted over the events of their day at school. When the last mouthful was gone, Nina wasted no time piling up the plates.

'Right, kiddos, off you go and watch the TV. Me and your Auntie Shannon have grown-up things to talk about.'

As soon as the kids were gone, Nina pushed the dirty dishes aside and poured another lager. 'So, spill. What's up?'

Shannon reached for her rucksack, pulled out the two halves of the *West Briton* article and the torn photograph and handed them to Nina. 'I found the photo nailed to the caravan door last week and the newspaper piece was on my windscreen this morning.'

'Whoa. Do you know who they're from?'

Shannon shrugged.

'It's certainly a funny old way of trolling you. If you were on Facebook, you would've had a million comments by now.'

'I think it might be Rosa,' Shannon whispered.

'Rosa? No way.'

'She's the only one who would know all this stuff and who might still want to cause me grief after all this time.' Shannon took a gulp of lager. She shouldn't drink anymore. The cider from last night was probably still lurking in her system. 'But she wouldn't have a clue where I live, so it's probably not her if I think about it logically.'

'You told me Rosa scarpered up-country years ago. Is she back then?'

'I nipped into Falmouth Library after I got the photo. Did a bit ... Well, a *lot,* of googling and stuff on the computer. She's married and living in a posh house on the Helford. Been back six months.'

Nina chewed her lip. 'What are you going to do?'

Shannon shrugged again. 'I expect I've got it all wrong. It's probably some jerk who found out one or two bits of information about me and thinks it's a bit of fun to mess with my head.'

She couldn't bring herself to tell Nina that she'd more or less run out of work, or that this weirdo called Zach was always hanging around her caravan. Her friend had enough on her plate without taking on all of Shannon's problems.

'I'll leave it. I'm sure it'll lead to nothing.'

'These sorts of things always have the habit of coming back and biting you on the butt.' Nina's brown eyes bored into her. 'If you want my advice, you need to see Rosa and get it out in the open.'

'Maybe.'

'Well, my lovely,' Nina clinked Shannon's glass, 'you know I'll always be here for you if you need me. Okay, I know I'm not going to be *here* for the next six months, but I'm not flying off to another universe. They do have phones in California.'

'When do you leave?'

'Next week.' Nina reached for Shannon's hand. 'It's only for six months. Jake couldn't miss the opportunity of working in California, and it will be good for me and the children.'

Shannon forced a big smile onto her face and hugged Nina again. Yep, the girl had made good.

Darkness had fallen by the time Shannon pulled up outside the house on the Helford. Her heart raced as she fought the urge to turn and run. Instead, she forced herself to get out of the car and walk to the enormous door.

Chimes rang inside the house. Shannon looked down at her dirty work boots and scruffy jeans. The door swung open, and the sight of the immaculate woman in front of Shannon rendered her speechless.

Rosa stared wide-eyed at Shannon, then glanced fleetingly up the driveway towards the nearby houses before returning to stare at her again.

'Well, nice to see you too, Rosa,' Shannon finally said, as stepped closer and rapidly waved the newspaper article and photo in her face. 'What I want to know is, what the hell do you think you're playing at?'

In the ensuing silence, blood pounded in Shannon's ears. Was Rosa going to let her in, or what?

6

Rosa's heart thudded against her rib cage. How was it possible that Shannon was on her doorstep? She pressed her palm against her chest. Thank goodness James wasn't home and wouldn't be back for an hour or so. She glanced up the driveway again, checking for nosey neighbours, then back at Shannon. What did this unwelcome visitor from her past want?

It had to be money. What else could it be? The envelope and its contents that she'd recently received from Shannon had clearly been a taster of what Rosa was to expect.

She sighed. In her heart, she'd always known this day would come. Things had been too good to be true for too long.

'Damn it, Rosa, I'm here now, so whatever you've got to say to me, say it to my face.' Shannon stopped waving whatever she'd been brandishing and stood, hands on hips, waiting for a reply.

Rosa had plenty to say but there was a more pressing need. While a well-dressed person on her doorstep might not warrant a second look from neighbours, this shabby-looking individual would. Above all else, she had to think, think hard. Think about how to handle the situation. Keep her head.

She pushed the door wide open and motioned for Shannon to come inside. At a pace that seemed extraordinarily slow, Shannon stepped over the threshold.

Rosa slammed the door shut and took a deep breath. She stood in the centre of the hallway, blocking her intruder from pushing further into the house. 'Well, Shannon, you're an unexpected surprise. How can I help you?' She forced a smile. Even she was impressed by how calm she sounded on the surface.

'Damn you, Rosa, you've got some front.'

'*I've* got some front?' Rosa blinked. 'Look, whatever it is you want, we should at least try and be civil.'

'Civil? You want me to be civil?' Shannon thrust the items she was holding at her. 'Why did you send me these?'

Rosa gasped at the sight of the ripped photo and newspaper article. Her head spun. What was going on? Whatever it was, this wasn't as simple as Shannon wanting money. She could handle that. But if somebody was targeting both of them? Reluctantly, she stepped to one side. Whatever it was, it needed to be sorted, and the quicker the better.

Shannon started to stomp down the hallway.

'Oi.' Rosa shouted, nodding in the direction of Shannon's boots. 'Take those dreadful things off first.'

Shannon hesitated, then retraced her steps and slowly untied the laces.

Rosa's nose wrinkled. Such awful boots. And those dreadful socks weren't much better: heavy-duty men's socks with a hole in the big toe. Flipping hell, what was that? She stared at the raggedly cut, unvarnished nail. Everything about Shannon seemed more than a bit rough: her hair tied into a long pigtail that hung down her back, her cheap jeans and jacket, and her face naked of make-up. Coarse was the word Rosa was searching for. She briefly studied her newly varnished fingernails, then directed Shannon towards one of the doors. Thank goodness she had netted James, who provided her with the security and money to pamper herself to the standard she'd always dreamt of.

33

'Wait in the kitchen. I need to get something from upstairs.'

Rosa took the stairs two steps at a time. Several minutes later, she returned with a plastic wallet in her hand. She pulled out a couple of items and shoved them across the work surface towards Shannon. 'I got these too.'

Shannon's face paled as she looked at the ripped photo: the half that showed the smiling faces of Rosa and her mum.

'Oh, my God,' Shannon whispered as she fingered the faces on the print, then reached for the piece of newspaper yellowed with age. 'It's the same article that someone sent to me. What the …?'

'Indeed,' Rosa said.

'I came here because I was so sure it was you.' Shannon looked daggers at her. 'As far as I'm concerned, it can't be anybody else.'

Rosa glared back. None of this was making any sense. 'Why would I send the photo and newspaper cutting to myself?'

'Well, if it's not you, and it's not me, then who?' Shannon looked at the two halves again, then put the pieces together. A perfect fit. 'This photo was taken on the day of the accident; we both know that. I've never seen it before. Have you?'

Rosa shook her head.

'Your mum had a camera that day,' Shannon said. 'Remember? She grabbed that woman with the kid in the buggy and got her to take the snap of us four.' She smoothed her hand over the roughly joined photo. 'If neither of us has seen the original photograph until now, then presumably your dad must've had the camera and printed it off at some point. I'm assuming the police would've given him your mum's belongings after the accident.'

A bolt of hurt shot through Rosa's body at the mention of her dad. 'I wouldn't know on either account,' she said. 'I never saw the camera again after that day.'

'You could ask him though.'

Was Shannon mad? Just like that, go and ask him. 'We lost touch when I left home.' She swallowed hard. 'I'm in no rush to get back into contact.' She took a deep breath and moved towards the coffee machine on the worktop. 'Subject closed. End of conversation.'

Her large kitchen suddenly felt very claustrophobic, almost like she was back in her mum and dad's old two-up, two-down. Memories threatened to overwhelm her. She pushed them away. She didn't need to remember the crap that was her childhood home after her mum died, or her friendship with Shannon all those years ago. She glanced at her once friend, who was still scrutinising the photo.

'Coffee? Flat white okay?'

Shannon glanced up. 'Fine,' she said. She returned her attention to the photo and newspaper clipping. 'So, who could be doing this? And what could've triggered some shite to send these things to both of us?'

Rosa filled two mugs with coffee. 'Maybe the articles can tell us something?'

She placed one of the steaming mugs in front of Shannon, then picked up the faded newspaper articles. Thank goodness they were identical – less to read. Time was beating on, and she needed Shannon to be gone.

Scrutinising the grainy black and white pictures from the *West Briton*, Rosa's eyes unexpectedly stung with tears.

'Dear Mum, she was the life and soul of the party,' she whispered. Then in a louder voice, 'I still can't believe she died in front of me.'

'I know that feeling. I *was* there. My mum died as well, remember?'

Rosa refused to let the images of the accident push their way any further into her mind. She fiddled with the edge of the fragile paper and flattened it against the marble top. 'Let's see if there's anything in the article that can help us. The names of the others involved might trigger something.'

'William and Megan Whittaker,' Shannon spoke softly. 'And Paul, their seventeen-year-old son.'

'Oh, was that what they were called?' Rosa straightened up. 'I try not to think about them.'

'I can't forget.' Shannon stood with her back rigid, her lips in a tight line.

Rosa carried on reading.

'Perhaps it's some sicko who knows us?' Shannon tugged the end of her pigtail. 'Or a classmate we went to school with? Or a little shit who's come across old information about the accident and is playing a silly prank on both of us.'

'Or hoping to get a shedload of money from us.'

'Well, they won't have any luck with me,' Shannon said.

Rosa flinched. She didn't want any undesirables from anywhere popping out of the woodwork and tapping her for money. James's face flitted into Rosa's mind; her stomach churned.

'If not for money, then what?' she said.

'Revenge, maybe? I'd want payback, and justice, if somebody had done what my mum did ... what we did.'

'That's nonsense.'

'Is it? You and I were messing about in the back of the car that day. We're at least partially to blame.'

Rosa picked up her half of the photo and newspaper article and returned the items to the plastic wallet. 'Okay then, who would want revenge?'

They both looked down at the sellotaped *West Briton* article in Shannon's hand and stared at the blurred faces of Mr and Mrs Whittaker laughing in a pub garden somewhere, and a separate image of Paul in what appeared to be a school photograph. 'No ... not ...' Rosa glanced at Shannon.

Shannon, now wide-eyed, nodded. 'We're thinking the same thing. If it wasn't you, and it wasn't me, then it's most probably a relative or friend of the couple killed in the other car.'

'The Whittakers,' Rosa sighed.

Shannon stared at the grainy newspaper photos again. 'Did you know that Paul was injured in the crash?'

'What, like broken legs or something?'

'I don't know. Whatever, I still feel bad about it.'

'Least he got out alive.' Rosa flicked her hair. 'Point is, where is he now?'

'I guess he went back up-country after being discharged from hospital.' Shannon frowned. 'But it makes no sense for him to come after us now when he could've screwed us years ago.'

'How did whoever the person is who is doing this *find* us? That's what I want to know.'

'I found you.'

'So you did.' Rosa swallowed. 'And how in the world did you manage that?'

Shannon went on at an annoying length to tell her that she'd explored Google and various social media accounts with no luck but, apparently, a check with one of the 'research your family history' sites – using the free trial option, of course – came up with Rosa's married name. Another search, this time using James's name, turned up his business details in Cornwall, and, hey presto, apparently it was pretty easy to find their home address after that.

'I couldn't find *you*. I tried when I received the photo,' Rosa said.

'Guess I'm better at covering my tracks.'

Rosa ground her teeth. 'So, what now, smarty pants?'

'Nothing much, by my way of reckoning. Guess we wait for the next lot of crap to arrive.' Shannon stared at Rosa. 'Unless you've got any better ideas. You're the one with the money and the resources.'

'Shove off.' Rosa turned away quickly.

Blast, she was angry with herself for reacting so defensively. Yes, her old school pal was sarkier than she recalled, but she needed to remember that she was the one who had everything, whereas it appeared Shannon had barely dragged herself up an inch from the gloom of the life they'd shared on the Pengollan Estate.

Shannon suddenly started to turn in a circle, her eyes wide. Rosa couldn't help smiling to herself. *Out on stalks,* her mum used to say about Shannon's eyes.

'Wow, Rosa, you've done alright for yourself,' Shannon said. 'I need sunglasses with all these shiny surfaces.'

Rosa felt a glow of pride. 'Not bad for a girl from the Pengollan Estate, eh?'

'Blimey, how did you manage to escape that place and end up having all this?'

'Oh, you know me, I always have several plans up my sleeve. If one doesn't work, another one will.' A high-pitched laugh that she didn't recognise as hers, accompanied the words.

Shannon ran her hand over the polished surface of the ceramic oven top. Rosa flinched. For crying out loud, she would have to wipe it down again before James got home. She glanced at the clock on the wall: still enough time.

'I couldn't get that any cleaner myself even if I was paid twice as much.'

'You clean for a living?' Rosa couldn't keep the astonishment out of her voice. Shannon had been the bright one when they were at school.

'Among other things.' Shannon stepped up to a montage of photographs on the wall next to the kitchen table. 'These your kids?'

'Twins. Marcus and Freya. They're ten years old.' Pride edged into Rosa's voice. There were many things in her life she'd got wrong but having Marcus and Freya had not been one of them.

'The place doesn't look like kids live here. Blimey, Rosa, when did you get so tidy and anal about cleanliness?'

'And what would you know about me?' she snapped. 'You haven't seen me for more than twenty-three years.'

Shannon shrugged. 'So, where are Marcus and Freya? School's already out for the day.'

Rosa busied herself with collecting up the empty mugs. A few drops of coffee dregs dripped onto the surface. She cursed under her breath and wiped them away with her fingertips.

'They're at school. The Treloar School in Truro.'

'Boarding school?' Shannon grunted. 'Huh, the posh people's equivalent to children being in-care.'

'Don't be ridiculous, it's a brilliant school. They come home on Friday evenings for the weekend. They love it there.'

'You've asked them if they like it?'

'James thinks it's character building for them.'

Rosa could've bitten her tongue out. Why the heck was she defending her and James's actions to this has-been from her school days?

Shannon stared at James and Rosa's wedding photograph for several moments, then pointed towards another picture on the wall: a large headshot of James; big smile, perfect white teeth, and blue eyes.

'Your husband's a handsome-looking guy. Shame he doesn't want his kids around all the time. It's no fun being separated from your family. I should know.'

Rosa placed the mugs into the sink with a thud. Shannon didn't need to know any more about her current life. 'Right, is there anything else we need to discuss? James will be home soon, and I don't want to explain your presence to him.' Rosa looked at her watch again. She moved to the oven and switched it on.

'Why? Am I too shabby to meet the husband?'

'He doesn't know about my background.'

'What?'

'I didn't think he needed to know where I came from or what happened to my family. It was all so long ago.' Rosa rubbed her forehead. 'How the heck was I supposed to know that he would up sticks and move us all to Cornwall?'

'He knows absolutely nothing about you and Cornwall, or the accident?'

'Nothing. And I want to keep it that way.'

Shannon picked up her photo and newspaper article. 'Well, that's that then. One big, fat dead end. No need to keep in touch, I guess.'

'You know where I live.' Rosa glanced at Shannon. 'What about your address, in case the sicko should send us any more … material?'

'Give me your mobile. I'll put my number into your contacts.' Shannon held out her hand.

Rosa passed her phone over. No address then? Untrusting as well as sarky.

She watched Shannon drive away, then tapped at her phone and edited Shannon's name in the list of contacts to a less identifiable one should someone else happen to read it. Not that she would need the number; she had no intention of keeping in contact with Shannon. The woman was a lame duck. Goodness, she was a cleaner and a poor one at that if the way she dressed was anything to go by. Just because they were friends at school, and they shared a horrible history, didn't mean she owed Shannon anything. The relationship they had as kids would've died away anyway, like these things do.

Her phone pinged a reminder that James would be home in about thirty minutes. She quickly shut the door and rushed into the kitchen to tidy up, wipe the surfaces and put food in the oven.

Upstairs, she shoved the wallet back into its secret hidey-hole in the craft room cupboard before rushing into her bedroom and into the en suite bathroom, where she stripped, draped her clothes over the chair and stepped into the shower. The hot water cascaded over her face and body. Images from the newspaper article, along with the photo of herself and her mum, filled her head. And then Shannon's fifteen-year-old face suddenly swept into her mind.

No. Enough.

She flicked the shower to icy cold.

She had no time to help such a dismal loser. Neither did she want to remember anything about the past. She had to put all her energies into keeping James happy ... and her children.

She reached for the fluffy bath towel and wrapped it around her body. She had a wonderful life; she didn't need anything or anyone else.

Besides, there was no need to worry about the photo and the newspaper article, no need to think about what had happened twenty-three years ago. As Shannon said, it was probably a blooming weirdo behind it all.

She was right. Wasn't she?

7

Shannon's hand moved deftly over the paper, her pencil only stopping momentarily while she glanced up at the dog fox before continuing with the sketch. The fox sat upright, his amber eyes fixed onto her other hand, the one filled with tantalising cubes of cooked sausage. She stopped, placed the pencil on her pad, and studied the wonderful creature. His bright eyes stared back at her. The black ends of his ears stood out against the brilliant red fur and white chest. The huge fluffy tail, tipped with white, curled around his front legs.

Whenever she got up early, the fox, a regular visitor to the caravan, would appear from over the hedge and sit several feet away with an expectant look on its face.

A dog barked in the Carnmarth yard. The fox stood and moved his weight from one foot to the other. She tossed the last bits of sausage towards him. He snaffled the pieces, then leapt gracefully over the hedge and disappeared.

The day promised to be a beautiful, sunny one. The sky was already a rich blue with only a few wispy clouds propelled gently overhead by the breeze. The early beginnings of spring caught Shannon's eyes wherever she looked: yellow flowers had emerged on the gorse bushes, primroses bloomed in the hedges, and the buds were bursting forth on the sycamore trees in the lane. Peace, quiet, and solitude, with nobody to judge her looks, how she dressed, or what she did. Exactly how she liked it.

Sketching the fox had been a temporary break from all the thoughts and images that still rattled around in her head from yesterday's visit to Curlew House.

Rosa had changed so much. Nobody would guess that she was the kid born on the wrong side of town. With her posh voice, immaculate hair and clothes, and flashy, expensive jewellery, Shannon could see how Rosa passed for one of the toffs who lived in the wealthy coastal areas of Cornwall.

The life her old friend had forged for herself seemed to suit her. And yet, she was so jittery? Defensive? She might look like she had it all, with those fabulous looking kids and handsome husband, but Shannon couldn't shake off the feeling that all was not right in the world of Rosa Trevail.

Not that it mattered to Shannon. Their paths would never cross again. She was too much of a reminder of the old times. Besides, Rosa seemed to have shrugged off all the tragedies of their joint past. Shannon sighed. Perhaps she would've had a family and kids if she'd been as hard-hearted as Rosa.

What did it matter? Her brief encounter with Rosa was exactly that – a brief encounter.

She picked up her sketch, wrote a short note and date in the corner, and placed the pad and pencils back into her rucksack. She glanced at her watch. Rats, she had only five minutes to get to work.

'Hi Peggy, sorry I'm late. I met the milk tanker coming into the village and had to back up for ages.' Just a harmless lie.

Peggy, bent over her Zimmer frame, stirred teabags around in a huge teapot. 'Don't you worry, my dear. Come, sit down and have a nice cup of tea and a piece of this delicious Victoria Sponge my Tracey made.'

Whipped cream and strawberry jam oozed from the middle of the sponge. A wave of nausea rolled over Shannon. The cake looked delicious, but the milk she'd had for breakfast had been slightly off, and the thought of whipped cream being added to the mix didn't bear thinking about. She sat at the table and took a welcome sip of the dark brown tea.

Peggy reached for the knife.

'Not for me, Peggy. I'll drink this and then get on with the cleaning. I'll do the usual, but do you want me to dust and hoover the spare room, or can it wait until next week?'

Peggy suddenly grabbed her hand. The papery, dry skin and knobbly fingers felt weird against Shannon's own roughened flesh.

'Shannon, my dear, I won't need you next week.' She coughed. 'Or the following week.' She removed her hand and shoved an envelope across the table. 'Here, please take this.'

A throbbing started up in Shannon's temple. She opened the envelope and frowned. There was at least one hundred pounds in cash inside.

'What's this for?'

'My dear, that's a thank you for all you've done for me. I …'

With a knot of fear in her stomach, Shannon scanned Peggy's face. Tears tracked down the wrinkled cheeks.

'I don't understand. I …' Shannon mumbled.

Peggy blew her nose on a lace handkerchief. 'Our Tracey said I must use a person from a registered agency and pay by direct debit, not cash. She thinks an agency carer would be more trustworthy.'

'Trustworthy? I've been cleaning and shopping for you for over two years.' Shannon ran the back of her hand across her eyes. 'I thought you were happy with my work.'

The knobbly hand grabbed hers again. 'I am, I am. If I had my way I wouldn't change, but someone told my daughter that it was illegal to pay you with cash.'

'Rubbish. Who told her that?' Shannon could hear the panic in her own voice.

'Tracey wouldn't say. But she did seem very upset, and our Tracey rarely gets upset. I think the person frightened her.' Peggy patted Shannon's hand. 'I hope you understand.'

Shannon didn't understand at all.

Peggy pushed a large slice of Victoria Sponge towards her. 'Take this home with you. You might fancy a piece later.'

A few hundred yards from Peggy's house, Shannon pulled into a layby, switched off the engine and leaned back against the seat. What was she to do now? She'd lost two jobs in the space of forty-eight hours. A coincidence? Mrs Martin's work was only ever going to be short-term, so that didn't count, but her weekly cleaning at Peggy's was regular. The cash kept her afloat during the winter months when most of the seasonal work had dried up. Bottom line? No money, no food. She fingered the hundred pounds in her pocket. That had to be kept safe to pay for essentials like the rent, petrol, and another gas bottle. Food tonight – and most nights – would be baked beans and sausages in a tin, or whatever was very cheap or on offer when she next stepped into a shop.

Shannon whacked the steering wheel. And there was Rosa, lording it up in her mansion. The bracelet her old friend had worn yesterday would pay Shannon's rent and food for a year, she was sure of it. It wasn't fair.

An image of the car crash all those years ago flashed into her mind.

She bowed her head. No, it was perfectly fair. Shannon had the life she deserved for what her mum had done, and for what she herself had done. It was crude justice, but she accepted it, like always.

With a sigh, she started the car and headed back to Carnmarth.

As she roared up the lane, Trevor waved for her to stop. He leaned against the gate into the yard. Three collies, tongues lolling, stood close to his side, watching his every move. Whisky, the terrier, was frantically digging a hole at the bottom of the hedge.

'Bloody hell, Shannon, you trying to rip the guts out of that car of yours?'

He was right. If she wrecked this car she would have no transport on top of all her other money worries. No transport and rural Cornwall didn't go well together.

He grinned. 'I guess you could call that thing a car ... at a stretch.'

Shannon glared at him. 'What did you want me for?'

'I've been seeing more foxes about recently. Sniffing around the hen coops at night, they are. I can smell them in the morning.' He spat on the ground. 'I hope you haven't been feeding the beggars.'

'Not me.' Another lie. 'I can hardly feed myself.'

He squinted at her from under his beanie hat, and she quickly changed the subject.

'Looks like you and the dogs have been busy.'

'Brought a few of the ewes into the yard. They'll be lambing soon. I want to check them over.'

'No work for me, I suppose?'

'You suppose right,' he grunted.

She sighed as she reached for the ignition key.

'What's up?' Trevor rubbed the stubble on his chin.

'Peggy's given me the old heave-ho.'

'Not Peggy, surely?'

'Seems her daughter has found somebody, or some stupid agency, who she thinks will do a better job. And it'll be all legal like.'

'That Tracey was a stuck-up cow when we were at school together. Why is she sticking her nose in now?'

Shannon shrugged. Trevor didn't need to know the ins and outs of everything. Besides, Shannon didn't think Tracey had much choice in the matter from what Peggy had said.

'You got other work to replace Peggy's?'

'Oh, yeah, more than enough.' Her voice had a slight tremor in it. 'Don't worry, you'll get your rent.' More lies.

Trevor stared at her, then shook his head. 'Well, I gotta get on. Sheep will be getting teasy.'

She released the handbrake.

'Whoa, wait a minute, I've got something for you.' Trevor walked across the yard into the farmhouse, then quickly came out again. 'Here, have these.'

Shannon looked inside the old, cracked pudding bowl at six brown eggs.

'The hens are laying more than I can eat.' Trevor said as he strode away, the dogs keeping pace with him. 'I'll have the bowl back. No rush.'

Tears sprang into Shannon's eyes. She would eat well tonight. Omelette with baked beans and sausages on the side followed by an extra-large piece of Victoria Sponge.

See, everything would be okay. Of course it would.

8

Rosa's hand jerked at the sound of James's voice. Hot coffee splashed over her fingers. She placed the mug back on the table and shot to her feet.

'Rosa, where are you?' he shouted again.

'I'm coming.' She forced a light note into her tone and rushed from the kitchen to his study.

James was pacing the room. The printer was churning out a sheet, and the second it hit the print tray, he snatched it up. A deep line formed between his eyes as he stared at it.

'I've been checking the household accounts and I'm confused.'

'Is there a problem?'

He flashed the printout in front of her, then whisked it away before she could read the detail.

'Our joint household account shows two payments to the Atlantic Hotel, and I haven't been there in the last few weeks.'

Rosa bent over and peered at the open computer screen. 'Ah, that was the day I met with the Treloar School Committee Members regarding the Gala Ball. I did tell you. Remember?'

'Huh,' he grunted. 'I can see an amount that could represent lunch and refreshments for one person, but the other ...' he waved the printout again, 'the other amount is huge.'

Rosa touched her cheek. It felt hot. Damn James, at times like this, why did he have to make her feel like a naughty child. What was he even doing at home on a weekday? If he intended to annoy her, he was succeeding.

She lifted her chin in the air. 'I paid for coffee and cakes for everyone.'

His eyes widened. 'Whatever possessed you to do such a thing?'

Heavens above, why was he being such a prat?

'Oh, come on, sweetheart, it was a good PR exercise for Trevail Financial Services. Most of the members are wives of your clients, including Laura Saville and Ruth Glover, whose husbands' firm, I believe, is your single biggest account.'

James glared at her from under his eyebrows.

Rosa met his stare. For heaven's sake, she'd done a good thing. As far as she was concerned, she was an asset to him and his company. He should be praising her, not ridiculing her like this.

She took a deep breath. 'James, those ladies all appreciated the kind gesture, and I made a point of telling them you were behind the generous treat.'

'Mmm, well.' He reached over and closed the computer screen. 'It might work in my favour when I next meet Alan Glover, but you should always check with me first before spending such an amount. I don't want people taking advantage of you, darling.'

She smiled, touched that he wanted to protect her and amused that he felt he needed to. 'I was on my own a long time before we met and I'm quite savvy, you know.' She brushed a piece of fluff from his sweater. 'I fully support your work and I wouldn't do anything I thought would hurt you, or your business's reputation. Kind gestures will always be remembered. They help your career.'

'That may well be, but it does leave me somewhat concerned about your money management.'

Was he kidding? She would've given any other man in her life a mouthful by now. But this was James, and he was obviously worried about something – money? – so she counted to ten. 'For goodness' sake, I didn't go as far as buying lunch for everyone. It was just coffee and cakes.'

'This is how these things start. Careless financial controls and suchlike. We don't have the money to spend willy-nilly. It would be best if you sought my agreement for such spending in future.'

'Oh, James, whatever's the matter with you?'

'Well, one of us has to take care of the family's finances.' James turned his back on her and stomped out of the room.

Rosa glared at his retreating frame. Were they in some kind of financial trouble? She prayed not. And, if they were, she prayed James wouldn't make the situation worse by turning into a sulker.

The following morning, she sipped prosecco from an ice-cold glass as she scanned the expansive lawns and gardens of the Budock Vean Hotel. Her body tingled from the afterglow of her recent back, neck and shoulder massage.

On arriving earlier for one of her frequent spa treatment sessions, she'd started the day with a swim in the pool and a stint in the sauna. The massage afterwards was much needed. It had removed the tension that had settled in her neck following James's tedious lecture about money the previous afternoon.

'Such a beautiful place, don't you think?' Ruth said.

Rosa smiled at her and Laura, who both sat alongside her sipping from long glasses.

'One of my favourites,' Rosa replied. 'I feel so relaxed, I think I might lie here forever.'

'You can't do that.' Laura laughed. 'We've got lunch shortly and maybe a stroll afterwards through the grounds and down to the water's edge.'

'Talking of lunch, we need another meeting to finalise the Gala Ball.' Ruth raised her glass to Rosa. 'Coffees and cakes on me next time.'

Rosa let out a silent sigh of relief. At least James wouldn't be able to have a dig at her again.

It was an unusually warm and sunny day for March and Rosa was happy to lean back against her chair and join in the amiable chatter with Ruth and Laura. It was what friends did. Rosa smiled to herself as she took another sip of her drink. But, listening to Laura and Ruth talk between themselves for a few minutes, she knew in her heart that they weren't real friends, not ones she could confide in about the recent events that had rocked her world. Yes, the women sitting next to her were good company and made her laugh, but they would drop her like hot coals if they ever discovered that she'd been brought up on the Pengollan Estate, or that she'd done the things she'd done. In her past life, she wouldn't have cared what their opinion of her was. Did she now? Before she had time to answer herself, she pushed that unwelcome thought away.

She closed her eyes and let the sun caress her face. This was it; she was living the dream. While other people worked their socks off, she, Rosa Trevail, enjoyed this luxurious life; the lifestyle she had craved while growing up. James may well foot the bill for it all, but she was worth it. She gave him what he wanted: a beautiful woman to grace his arm, intelligent conversation, and terrific sex.

From the minute they met, they'd clicked. That first evening, his eyes had fixed on hers over the backgammon table at one of London's most prestigious casinos, and they'd got talking. They'd quickly established that they had tons in common, despite their very different backgrounds: same taste in music, films and food. She'd been on cloud nine for days.

The fact that he was one of the wealthier clients who frequented the establishment where she worked, and that she was merely a croupier, never seemed to bother him. She loved him for that. Whether he would love her so much if he knew what she'd had to do to survive in London when she'd first pitched up in the city as a naïve sixteen-year-old was altogether another thing. She was too canny and too much of a fighter to put it to the test by telling him. And look at her now, lying here, sipping prosecco.

An image of Shannon in her awful boots and cheap clothes flitted into her mind. An involuntary tremor coursed her body. Damn and blast. Shannon's recent intrusion into her perfect life made Rosa realise how fragile her new existence might be.

'Rosa? Rosa, it's time for lunch.'

She sat up abruptly and blinked.

'My goodness, I think you nodded off in the sun.' Laura smiled at her. 'Oh, if only I could sleep like that. It must be wonderful.'

A waiter stood by the door and held it open as they made their way into the hotel.

James had filled a lonely spot when he'd come into her life. His very presence had allowed her to banish all traces of her old ways and existence. She decided to let her irritation over his behaviour yesterday go. He loved her and gave her every opportunity to enjoy the standard of living she deserved. That was what mattered.

Nothing and no one would take this lifestyle away from her.

9

The men's rich tenor and baritone voices filled the public bar as they reached the finale of the popular Cornish song *'Going up Camborne Hill, Coming Down.'* The regulars burst into cheers and applause.

Shannon grinned to herself as she looked at the punters from over the beer pumps. She loved working at The Wheatsheaf in Cribba Village, her second shift of a two-night stint. The place was one of her favourite gigs, with its welcoming log fire and homely smell of warm beer and cooked food. Most of the people in the pub were locals she'd known for ages. She smiled at one of the regulars and placed a pint of Tribute on the counter alongside a gin and tonic with ice and a slice. For the first time in a long time, she felt comfortable and happy, and why wouldn't she be? She got to spend two evenings in the warmth, and Bill, the landlord, always made sure she had a hearty meal and a pudding before each shift. On the house. What more could she want?

Well, some work would be good for starters.

While chatting with the customers, she'd put out feelers for any jobs. No luck. Too early in the season. So, unfortunately, life in general was still crap. The caravan was cold; even though she'd bought a new gas cylinder with a part of Peggy's pay-off monies, she was using it sparingly. And she desperately missed Nina. There was so much she wanted to share with her friend, but she couldn't afford to ring her. Even if she could, it would be wrong to dump her problems onto Nina when she was enjoying life in California and couldn't do anything to help anyway.

'You're looking happy tonight, girl.' Old Vic, her fellow caravaner at Carnmarth Farm, smiled, sending his weather-beaten face into a mass of wrinkles and deep lines. 'I'm ready for a top-up. Lager for his nibs over there.' He nodded toward Zach in the far corner by the dartboard, who raised his near-empty glass in her direction and winked. She forced a tight smile, then looked away.

'The silly devil could do with a decent drink. Doom Bar, like me. Would put hairs on his chest.'

Shannon laughed and reached for clean glasses.

'Indoor work suits you,' Vic said. 'All rosy-cheeked and bright-eyed.'

Shannon laughed. 'An offer of work would suit me, Vic.'

'Don't worry, girl. Trevor will be wanting help with them new-born lambs soon. So will others round here.'

'Not sure I can wait that long.' She pushed two pints towards him and took his money.

'Well, if you want a bit of company some evenings, you know where my door is.'

'Thanks, Vic.' She handed him his change, kissing him on the cheek at the same time. 'You're a star.'

Several of the dart players cheered as a red-faced Vic made his way back to his seat. One shouted, 'Looks like Vic has found himself a young bit of stuff.'

'Bugger off you lot.' Vic picked up his darts. 'Who's up for a challenge? Time this 'ere old man showed you youngsters a thing or two.'

Bill, the landlord, came up beside Shannon and handed her some cash. 'Thanks for helping out at such short notice. Much appreciated.'

'I can work a few more evenings if you like?'

Bill screwed his face up. 'Sorry, but Kate rang earlier. She's feeling better and said she'll be back in tomorrow evening for her shift.'

Shannon forced herself to smile. 'Thanks so much for the money. You're a good boss.'

He laughed. 'Guess that's why the regular staff stick around for so long.' He patted her shoulder. 'I've got your number should I have any temporary work again.'

When Bill rang the bell for last orders, Shannon's feet were aching, but she'd enjoyed the banter and it felt good to be part of the local community. They were people she knew, and they included her.

Zach and Vic had already left by the time the last customer departed, and she began the task of putting all the glasses in the dishwasher and wiping the surfaces down. She took one final look around the room and headed for the door. 'Bye, Bill.'

'Cheerio, love,' Bill called through the kitchen serving hatch. 'Thanks for everything. See you anon.'

In the car, Shannon pushed the accelerator down hard and the ancient engine moaned as she urged it up the hill out of Cribba towards Carnmarth Farm. The words of *'Trelawny'* beat a tattoo in her head. She drummed her fingers on the steering wheel as the lyrics from the Cornish anthem eventually spilt from her mouth. Views of a clear sky with tons of stars filled the front windscreen. Cold though; her breath condensed before her. She reached over to the controls and zapped the heater on, which resulted in a lot of noise and bangs but not much else.

Driving through the country lanes, she flexed her fingers and continued singing two or three of the sea shanties and other songs the locals had belted out earlier. She braked sharply as a fox crossed the road, then took a deep breath before she turned the next corner.

An orange-red glow lit up the horizon.

Her heart thumped.

A fire? It was way too early for gorse fires; the foliage was still too damp following the recent winter storms.

She urged the vehicle onwards. Where was the fire coming from? Everything was distorted by the orange-red light that seemed to take up so much of the horizon. Then a tremor ran down her body. The fire was at Carnmarth Farm. Dear God, if it *was* Carnmarth, please let it be one of the barns, not the farmhouse. Her lips moved in prayer. Please let Trevor be okay. And the animals in their houses. Please. Please. Her hands trembled as she neared the farm. Her breath came in gasps. Only one more corner and she would be home.

A fire engine blocked the entrance, its lights filling the night with intermittent flashes of blue. An ambulance was parked further up. No. No. Please let everybody be okay. She braked hard, jumped out, ran up the lane, and then stopped abruptly. Another fire engine was parked at the end of the track, near the gateway to her field.

Her legs nearly gave way as she realised that the firefighters were putting the final flames out on what remained of her caravan.

Sharp pains jabbed in Shannon's chest. Most of the severance money Peggy had given her had been stashed in the bottom drawer. She forced herself to breathe in. One. Two. Three. Then out. One. Two. Three. Then she let out a guttural laugh. Well, at least now she really did have nothing else to lose. All she had left in the world was her nearly clapped-out car, her rucksack, and the bit of money that Bill had given her earlier. Thank God, the treasured and irreplaceable half-photo of her and her mum was inside her sketchbook in the rucksack.

Zach came running up to her. 'Trevor. Vic. Shannon's here. She's okay.' He touched her arm. She flinched. 'You're okay, aren't you?'

Her gaze remained fixed on the ruins that had been her sanctuary for nearly five years.

A firefighter clad in protective gear, like a character out of a film, moved in front of her. 'Miss Reid? Shannon Reid?'

'Yes.' She finally turned her gaze onto him.

'So sorry, but as you can see there's nothing left of the van.' He removed one of his heavy gloves, pushed his visor up, and scratched his nose. 'It looks like it might be deliberate. We found a petrol can nearby. Any ideas who might've done it?'

She shook her head.

'We'll catch up with you tomorrow with our findings and for a chat. I'll take your mobile number so I can contact you to sort out a suitable venue and time.'

She nodded and gave him her number.

'Take care in the meantime, Miss Reid.'

She watched him go. Maybe she deserved most of what came her way ... but this? Did she really deserve to lose *everything* for what her mum had done? She wiped her nose and eyes with the sleeve of her well-worn puffer coat, turned, and walked back down the lane.

Vic, breathless and pale-faced, caught up with her. She thought for a split second he was going to hug her. Instead, he bobbed his head several times in her direction. 'You're a sight for sore eyes, girl.' He dipped his head again, this time in the direction of his caravan, the windows full of light.

Trevor stood a few feet away. He nodded at her, his face smeared in bits of ash and his eyes appearing bloodshot in the flickering blue lights.

'You look worse than me,' she said.

'Bloody smoke and fumes. For a minute, I thought you were in ...' He rubbed his eyes. 'You trying to get me killed or what?'

She looked down and noticed she had her decent pair of trainers on. At least they'd been saved. Her work boots and heavy coat were in the back of the car. Saved as well. Bloody hell, she was rich.

A police car pulled up at the end of the lane.

Trevor stepped closer to Shannon. 'You got trouble?'

A sob threatened to burst from her mouth. She swallowed it down and shook her head.

Two police officers got out of the vehicle – a man and a woman – and strode up the lane towards them, adjusting their hats as they walked.

'I told you before that I can't have the police snooping around here,' Trevor said.

Shannon reached for Trevor's arm but stopped halfway. 'Please, Trevor, I need to stay here. I feel …' She wanted to say safe, but she knew it would sound naff and wouldn't cut it with Trevor anyway. Still, she pushed on. 'I'll stay in the car. I'll still pay you the usual rent. Please.'

How she would pay the rent she didn't know. She swallowed again. Harder this time. Damn it, why didn't she leave Cornwall? Where was her courage? Why did she still act like the scared fifteen-year-old orphan who'd been taken into local authority care?

Trevor shifted from one foot to another as the police officers drew closer. 'You can stay in the car for a few nights, but you'll need to be gone by the end of the week.' He turned and walked briskly across the yard to the farmhouse.

The police officers looked at one another and followed him.

Vic tipped his head at Shannon. 'You're staying with me tonight, me girl. No arguments.'

Tears welled in her eyes as he took her by the elbow. Out of the corner of her eye, she could see Zach standing to one side, watching. Lurking? Why was he still hanging around? Her caravan was gone. The excitement was over. Nothing else to see here, folks.

An involuntary shiver rolled over her body. Zach always seemed to be around when significant things happened to her. He was in her face when she found the ripped photo, and he was there again when she discovered the *West Briton* article under her windscreen. And her caravan? Her heart raced. He'd left The Wheatsheaf with Vic some while before she did. More than enough time for him to set the fire in her caravan and be on the scene to help when she'd arrived back at Carnmarth.

'You ought to get your car and get it parked up next to Vic's. Don't want another nasty fire tonight, do we?' Zach gazed at her through half-closed eyes.

A loud howl filled the air. Startled, she realised it had come from her. Oh, my God, it was him. She clamped a hand over her open mouth. Had she said that out loud? No. Just as well; there was nobody here she could confide in, nobody here who could help her.

A sob wracked her body.

Vic took her into his surprisingly strong arms. 'There. There. Everything will seem better in the morning.'

When she finally stopped crying, she stepped away from him. Zach had gone.

'What about Trevor?' she said. 'He won't like me staying with you. He might throw you off Carnmarth as well.'

Vic let out a chuckle. 'You leave Trevor to me. I came to work for his pappy when I was fifteen. I've known that lad since he was in nappies.' Vic tapped his nose with his forefinger. 'Old Vic knows too much to be given the old heave-ho from this place.' He chuckled again. 'Trevor acts like a hard nut, but he's a real softie once you pierce that outer shell.'

59

Shannon's eyes widened. Some chance of that.

She glanced back at the farmhouse as she and Vic walked down the lane to the car. The police officers were still talking to Trevor. He wouldn't like that.

As they reached her vehicle, the last fire engine pulled onto the road to Falmouth in a hiss of brakes.

She knew Trevor wouldn't let her stay for long, not if the police were sniffing around, which they would be if the fire service deemed that somebody had started the fire deliberately. They might, of course, conclude that she'd left the gas cylinder switched on or some such thing. But, if it *had* been started on purpose, then the question was, by whom? Now she had a bit of time to think, she realised she was being foolish – hysterical even – to believe it was Zach; he was just some clown that she didn't like, nothing more. But then what did she know? She had no idea who'd burnt her caravan to the ground.

Damn it, she wouldn't be driven out. She loved Cornwall; it was her home. Why should she leave? Involuntary tremors ran up and down her legs, and she stumbled. What she really wanted to do was lie on the ground and scream like a toddler. Fuck, she had lost everything: her sad little home, her surplus money, her usual work sources.

She couldn't tell the police what was happening; they'd never been on her side and her only dealings with them all those years ago had left her wary and scared of people in authority. And Rosa? Well, Rosa didn't want to know, didn't want her neat and tidy world disrupted. Shannon swiped tears from her eyes again and leaned against her car as she waited for Vic to ease himself into the passenger seat. Breathe in. One. Two. Three. Breathe out. One. Two. Three.

She looked around. The quiet of the night had returned and the stars twinkled brightly overhead, as if nothing of importance had happened.

10

Rosa picked up the freshly laundered bedding and made her way upstairs. In Freya's room, she shook out a pink pillowcase and duvet cover patterned with unicorns and rainbows and made her daughter's bed. In Marcus's room, she did the same, except his bedding was blue, with planets and rockets.

Today was Friday and the children would be home for the weekend: two whole days and three nights of cuddles and fun.

Rosa danced to the music that poured from the central sound system as she worked: Dolly Parton and other country and western singers, not James's taste at all.

A quick vacuum and dust of both rooms, then she fetched fluffy white towels and new bars of soap for their en suites. She was being ridiculous really, making such a fuss – the bedrooms were good enough for any boutique hotel – but she couldn't help spoiling them. Washing the bedding after each weekend visit was probably unnecessary, but somehow it filled the need she had to mother them.

She took one last look around the ultra-tidy accommodation. For a moment, the pride she felt in being able to provide her children with such beautiful rooms was assailed by sadness. The spaces were so impersonal: no posters on the walls, and all their clothes and toys were stored out of sight. James liked it that way. And, well, what James … She shrugged the rest of the thought away and went downstairs.

It looked like James would be busy working tomorrow, and Rosa was full of plans on how to spend Saturday with

Freya and Marcus. Maybe they would go to Newquay Zoo, Flambards Theme Park or the Indoor Play Area at Roche? She would do whatever they wanted. If the weather was good, perhaps they would even don wetsuits, pull out the kayaks and head for the beach. Plans swirled inside her head as she baked chocolate chip cookies, chocolate brownies and vanilla cupcakes.

In the middle of mixing the icing for the topping, she heard the front door open. Footsteps echoed down the hallway and James strolled into the kitchen.

Rosa wiped her hands on her cotton apron and rushed over to kiss him on the cheek. 'What a lovely surprise, sweetheart. I didn't expect you until this evening.'

'I was passing so I dropped in to see my beautiful wife.' James wrapped his arms around Rosa's waist. 'I'm allowed to do that, aren't I?'

'Of course you are. It's just that I wasn't expecting you and the place is in such a mess.' She stepped away from him. 'I'm baking for the weekend.'

'That's fairly obvious. What a tip.'

She blinked. For a fleeting moment she remembered how, when they were first together, he'd loved to help her to cook and bake. He hadn't cared a hoot about the clutter back then.

'All Freya and Marcus's favourites, I see.'

'I've made a Victoria Sponge with fresh cream and strawberries, especially for you.' Rosa glanced at him, then picked up the metal spoon and resumed mixing the icing. 'Would you like a piece now, with a cup of tea or coffee?'

'I think I'll try one of these biscuit things for a change.' He picked up a warm chocolate chip cookie and took a bite. 'Not bad. Bit too sweet maybe.'

Rosa felt heat rise in her cheeks. 'That's because they're for the kids.' It wasn't like he didn't know that.

James ambled over to the floor-to-ceiling windows and drummed his fingers on the kitchen table as he looked out over the Helford River.

Rosa's hand wobbled. Blast it, she'd made a mess of the icing on the first cupcake. She sighed, scraped it off and abandoned the task. Why was James home in the middle of the morning on a working day anyway? She reached to switch on the kettle, then hesitated. 'Tea? Coffee?' she asked as she looked from the tea container to the coffee machine.

'Tea.'

'Are you staying or going back to the office? Do you want something to eat? An early lunch perhaps?'

'What are we having this evening?'

'Cottage Pie with mushy peas.'

'Freya and Marcus's favourites … again.'

'You like my Cottage Pie too.'

'True.' He turned from the window, moved over to the worktop, and picked up his tea. He patted her bottom as he passed her. 'What a grump I'm being. Cottage Pie will be wonderful, darling.'

A happy glow flowed through her body. It was going to be a good weekend.

'Seeing you're so busy,' he said, 'how about I pick up the children from school this afternoon?'

The backs of her eyes prickled. Seeing her children's faces as they flew out of Treloar School into her arms was one of the best bits of her week.

'I … I thought you were busy today … and this weekend. There's no need to upset your schedule.'

'A client cancelled this morning so I'm more than happy to help you out. Besides, that school needs to see my face now and then, if only to remind them who pays the bills.'

Tears sprang to Rosa's eyes. She quickly blinked them away. Arguing about who would pick up Freya and Marcus would be pointless. If she insisted, it might put James in a bad mood for the weekend.

'Does this mean you'll be free to join us tomorrow?' she asked.

Being out and about as a family would be good on one level but, to be honest, she loved it when it was only her and the kids and she could give them her whole attention.

'Not sure yet. We'll discuss it at breakfast tomorrow.'

Damn.

'Have you decided about lunch? I can make you something?'

'I won't have time. Not if I have to pick up the children. My schedule for the rest of the day is now very tight. I'll pick up a sandwich at the garage when I get petrol for the trip to Truro, then I'll work through lunch to catch up.' He made for the hallway, then turned. 'Anyway, you'll need all that time to clean this place up, won't you?' He strode down the hallway and out of the front door, which closed behind him with a slam.

Rosa stared at the empty space where James had been. What was wrong with him? With everything else going on, she really could do without this aggro. 'Damn you,' she shouted as she flung the icing bag into the sink.

An hour and a half later, she scanned the kitchen. Everything was perfect; the cooking and baking were all done, and the surfaces were wiped and shiny. She sat at the table and watched the yachts bob at anchor along the river while she ate crispbreads, cottage cheese and sliced tomatoes for lunch. Her pudding sat in a glass dish beside her: six fresh strawberries.

Another two hours and Freya and Marcus would be home. How would she pass the time? Maybe a run along the clifftop or a session in the gym?

The doorbell rang as she placed her plate and bowl into the dishwasher. A courier stood on the step with an unmarked, beige cardboard box in his hand. 'Parcel for Mrs Rosa Trevail?' the courier said in a jolly but brusque voice before jogging back to his van.

She balanced the box in her arms. Quite heavy. She hadn't ordered anything since James had his strop about her so-called overspending at the Atlantic Hotel. She took the parcel into the hall, placed it on the floor, and closed the door behind her. The name and address on the label stood out in bold black print. There was nothing to indicate who the sender or supplier was. She leapt to the assumption it was James, making amends for his moodiness recently. In the early days of their relationship, he'd constantly bombarded her with gifts. Excitement ran through her as she wondered what it could be.

Her hands reached for a letter opener in the drawer of the hallway cabinet, and she got down on her knees and pierced the beige masking tape that the sender had used to thoroughly seal the parcel. A rank smell stung her nostrils. Instinctively, she leaned back onto her heels and turned her head away. Jesus, what could it be? Gone off food? Dead plants?

Only one way to find out. She grabbed the letter opener again and ripped the top open. The smell was so bad that she leapt to her feet and opened the front door before turning back to the parcel. She flipped the lid fully open with the toe of her shoe.

Fucking hell. No. No.

Dead magpies. Seven. Lifeless, unseeing eyes. Their normally iridescent black and white plumage dulled in death and flecked with blood.

She covered her mouth with her hand. Then she saw it taped to the inside of the lid - a note. She read the words. Her stomach heaved. She ran through the door and vomited onto the gravel. Then retched again.

A few minutes later, she dragged herself back to the hallway, picked up the box and took it outside. Gulping fresh air, she read the note once more.

Seven for a secret never to be told.

The words of the nursery rhyme rang through her head as she stared at the dead magpies. Then the next line of text hit her.

I know your secret.

Her legs crumbled and she dropped to her knees. Panic rolled over her. Think, Rosa, think. With a jolt, she realised that James, Freya and Marcus would arrive in two hours or so. The hallway and house reeked of rotting flesh. For crying out loud, she'd thrown up all over the drive.

Her breath came in short gasps as she rose abruptly to her feet.

She needed to think and act like a girl from the Pengollan Estate, not some pathetic wuss from a posh house where the inhabitants had only to worry about what luxury they would indulge in next. Come on, Rosa, get a grip.

She ran inside and flung open all the windows and doors to draw the air through. At the same time, she squirted a mix of polish and perfume lightly throughout the rooms. In the kitchen, she pulled out a box of rubber gloves and a roll of black plastic bags from one of the drawers, then rushed back outside. She ripped the label and note off the cardboard box and stuck them into the pocket of her jeans. Then, with her nostrils and mouth pinched tight, she tipped the contents of the parcel into one of the plastic bags. Beads of sweat ran down her face as she crushed the cardboard box with her feet and stuffed it into another bag. She double-wrapped each bag for extra strength.

Next, she ran into one of the outbuildings and snatched up a gardening spade. She heaped the vomit-covered gravel into yet another bag, then moved across the driveway to a spot under the shrubs where she scooped up fresh gravel and refilled the patch so it looked like it hadn't been disturbed. Finally, she got out the hosepipe and washed the area down. At the same time, she watered the shrubs so as not to give James any reason to ask any unwanted questions.

She glanced at her watch. One and a half hours before he got back. Time enough to dispose of the bags in different waste bins or skips.

Rosa suddenly sat down on the doorstep and stared at the black rubbish bags. Sobs wracked her body. She needed to tell somebody about this. Not her spa mates, Laura and Ruth; they would never understand. Nor James. He wouldn't understand either, especially as most of her life was a secret to him. The police? She let out a grunt.

For a brief second, she wondered what would happen if she told James everything.

Her heart sank. It was all too late for that. She placed her head into her hands, then stood, pushed her shoulders back, and pressed a contact on her mobile. It rang and rang as she paced the garden. Finally, her call was answered.

'Hello,' Shannon said.

'I need to see you. Now. It's urgent.'

'I can't. I don't have much petrol left and–' Shannon's voice sounded quiet and flat.

'Trust me, Shannon, this is urgent. Urgent, I tell you. I'll meet you at the Chapel Cove Beach Café in thirty minutes. Hurry.'

Rosa cut off the call before Shannon could reply.

Back in the house, she shut most of the windows and doors. Thankfully, the air smelt normal. She exceeded the speed limit all the way to Chapel Cove, except when she stopped at three different locations to dispose of the rubbish bags with their hideous contents.

Shannon was already seated at a corner table on the outside terrace when Rosa arrived. Her old friend's head was bowed, the table bare.

Rosa rushed over. 'Do you want coffee or tea?'

'Coffee.'

No offer to pay she noticed, but Rosa didn't care. She needed to get this chat out of the way, get home, showered, and suitably dressed in time for James and the children's arrival. She slammed the tray with two cups of coffee onto the table.

Shannon lifted one of the cups and wrapped her hands around it. Flipping hell, the woman looked even more neglected and tatty than the time she'd turned up on Rosa's doorstep.

'I've had another parcel,' she said, and the relief of being able to discuss it led to the words pouring out of her: the magpies, the vomit, the dumping of the bags, the drive here.

'Shannon? Shannon, are you listening to me?'

'Yes, you've had seven dead magpies sent to you in a parcel. So?'

'What the hell's wrong with you? Don't you realise how serious this thing with the stalker is becoming?'

Shannon shrugged again. 'I've got nothing to lose.'

'You might not have, but I have everything.'

Shannon glared at her so hard that Rosa turned away and looked down at her untouched coffee.

'What about your *life* then, Shannon? This person means business. I think that he or she, or they, might go as far as injuring or even killing us.' She shoved her cup roughly to one side. 'Any ideas on how we get ourselves out of this mess?'

Shannon picked up a sugar lump and sucked on it. Her eyes were dull and flat.

'Shannon? Shannon, for God's sake, will you listen to me. Dead magpies, that dreadful note and so on. You've got to understand how serious this is.'

'What, as serious as having your caravan burnt down? As serious as having most of what you own destroyed?'

Rosa stared wide-eyed at Shannon. 'Oh, my God, what happened?'

In a still flat voice, Shannon told her about the fire three days ago and how her landlord now wanted her as far away from his place as possible.

'Where are you staying?'

'With Vic, the old bloke I told you about who lives in one of the other caravans.'

Rosa breathed a silent sigh of relief. There was no way she could offer Shannon any help with accommodation. 'Are you okay being with this Vic? Can you stay until you get back onto your feet?' She was asking out of curiosity rather than compassion.

Shannon shook her head. 'The landlord wants me gone.'

'You're okay for work though? That cleaning job you talked about must bring in a bit. You could always rent another van somewhere, couldn't you?' James's finger on all the finances meant Rosa couldn't offer Shannon any money even if she wanted to, so she rushed on. 'Look, I've only got limited time. This isn't good. Your caravan, then this creepy note with the magpies.' She rummaged in the pocket of her jeans for the label and note and dropped them in front of Shannon.

Shannon read the note and sat up straighter. 'Shit.'

'Quite.'

'This really is serious, isn't it?'

'You don't say.' Rosa nodded at the note and label. 'Could you keep those for me? I don't want James or the kids finding that stuff.

Shannon reached for her rucksack and placed the pieces of paper in one of the side pockets.

Rosa took a glug of her coffee. 'What the hell are we going to do, Shannon?'

Shannon clenched her jaw. 'I guess we have to stop sticking our heads in the sand about what's happening and find a way to fight back.'

'Like, how? There was nothing on the packaging to indicate who sent the parcel. Nothing on any of the other stuff we both received either.'

Shannon rubbed her eyes and pulled her coat around her body, which looked even thinner than the last time they'd met. 'Well, you could start by checking out the courier company. You and I know in our hearts that this is linked to the accident when we were fifteen. We need to research the names in that article, find out, whatever … I don't know.' Shannon rubbed her eyes again. 'I suppose I could check out Zach.'

'Zach?'

'He's a new fella renting one of the other caravans. He freaks me out. Always seems to be in my face, and always around when something bad happens to me.'

'Do you think he's responsible for sending the photos and the *West Briton* articles?' Rosa's heart thumped against her ribs. 'And the magpies?'

'Not really. Possibly. Yes. Christ, I don't know.' Shannon moaned. 'I don't feel I know anything anymore.'

Rosa fought the urge to shake Shannon and to tell her to get a grip. Instead, a twinge of sympathy ran through her at the sight of the dark patches under Shannon's eyes, but she pushed it away. She had to look after herself and the children.

'You're right. We need to jointly track down where this stuff's coming from, and you definitely need to follow up on this Zach fella. He sounds very suspicious to me.' Rosa stood up. 'Do you hear me?'

'Okay, okay. I'll do it.'

'Good. I have to go now. I suggest we meet here regularly to catch up and decide what we need to do next.' She glanced around. It was a good spot. The café was okay, but best of all, the terrace was hidden from the road. Better still, so was the car park. 'I'll ring you tomorrow,' she called over her shoulder as she ran to her vehicle, 'to finalise a plan.'

Hurtling along the country roads back towards Curlew House, Rosa thumped the steering wheel. Damn. She'd let Shannon back into her life. Only a bit, but possibly enough to bring Rosa's world crumbling down around her ears. Damn. Damn. Damn. She thumped the wheel again.

11

Shannon watched, arms folded across her chest, until the brake lights of the police car flickered off as it accelerated from the lane at Carnmarth onto the road towards Falmouth.

Vic strolled onto the small, decked area outside his caravan, placed two mugs of coffee onto a weather-beaten bistro table and flopped down into a wooden chair. 'Any joy?'

She walked from the lane to join him in the only other chair. 'Diddly-squat. The police officer only called by to confirm what I already knew from the fire service.' She took a sip of coffee and nodded at Vic in thanks. 'Arson. But no evidence as to who did it.' She mimicked the police officer's voice: 'The police won't be taking their investigations any further unless something else comes up at a later date to help them with their enquiries.'

'Thought as much.' Vic leaned back into his chair. 'And you've no idea who did this?'

Shannon shrugged. As much as she wanted to offload onto somebody, there was no point in telling Vic about the half photo or the newspaper article. What could he do?

'Well, me girl, you're more than welcome to stay with me for as long as you like.' Vic chuckled. 'My standing in The Wheatsheaf has gone up tenfold now I've got a young lady living with me.'

'Thanks, Vic. You're a star.'

'Still, you've got your own life and won't want to stay in with an old man, like me, night after night. I know you'll want to move on soon but, seriously, there's no rush on my part.'

'That's good to know. For now, I'm still thinking through my options,' she said.

What options? She'd already contacted Bill at The Wheatsheaf for any possible work. One evening shift last week, but nothing else. She was also doing the rounds visiting local farmers. A few promises of work in the next month or so when the holiday season started, or they needed extra help on the farms, but nothing for now.

'You alright for money?' Vic asked. 'I can lend you a quid or two to tide you over if you want.'

'If only everyone were like you, Vic.' Shannon plastered a smile onto her face. 'Honestly, I'm okay. Things will improve soon.'

'You've not wanted to stay with that lass you know in Penryn?'

Tears sprang into Shannon's eyes. If only she *could* go and stay with Nina, or even talk to her for that matter, she knew everything would feel so much better.

'I didn't know you knew about Nina.'

'You mentioned her once.' He tapped the side of his head with his forefinger. 'Old Vic never forgets.'

'She's in California for six months and her house is rented out to some university professor. I don't half miss her.'

'That's the way it is with real friends.'

Vic got to his feet. 'Better gobble down a sandwich before Trevor starts on about me being late back from lunch. You want one? Got plenty of ham and cheese.'

Shannon stood and reached for her rucksack and car keys. 'No thanks. I've got a few places I want to visit this afternoon.'

She didn't want to be too much of a burden on Vic. He didn't look like he had that much dosh to spare, and she didn't want to outstay her welcome. She'd been there for two weeks already. Time to move on.

She'd barely opened the car door when a voice startled her and she jerked around.

'Off out somewhere nice?' Zach stood much too close to her, with a big smile showing off his perfect teeth.

She pushed the door wider, forcing him to step further back and putting a wall of metal and glass between them.

'You know me, life is full of parties and fun.' She got into the car. The sooner she was away from here, the better. There was something about this man that made her spine tingle. She tried to tug the door shut, but he put his hand on the top and pulled it back.

'Hey, what?'

'You still looking for employment?' he asked, stopping her in her tracks. She badly needed work. She released her hold on the door.

'Do you know where I can find some?' she replied.

Zach shook his head. 'Sorry, only wondering what you were up to, that's all.' He let go of the door and stepped a couple of paces to one side. 'Now that you're living a life of leisure at Vic's and all.'

'Right.' She yanked the door shut. Dickhead. She switched on the ignition and pushed the vehicle into reverse.

Zach jumped out of the way. She could still see his white teeth in her rear-view mirror as she accelerated down the lane.

Despite what she'd agreed with Rosa, up to now she hadn't put her heart into investigating who Zach was. Bottom line, he was a right plonker and she didn't like him, but deep-down she couldn't believe that he was their stalker. Trevor got on with him. Also, Vic seemed to like him, and Vic was a good judge of character. But, what if ...

She gripped the steering wheel hard. What if, for once, she was right, and Vic was wrong? What if her initial instincts after the fire were right?

She pulled her car into a farm gateway, her heart racing fast enough to kick off a heart attack. Oh, my God, she took three deep breaths, then another three. In. Out. One. Two. Three. She told herself to calm down, be rational. Zach was just a dickhead, but her pulse raced harder. Maybe he *was* a relative of those killed in the car crash after all? Could he even be Paul Whittaker? Did the ages fit? She let out a deep breath. Yes, it was possible. Zach looked to be in his late thirties or early forties and was clearly pretending to be someone he wasn't.

Hands still shaking, she switched the ignition back on and headed towards Cribba Village. She would start checking him out. Fingers crossed, she would have something to report back to Rosa when they met again next week. Since that first meeting at Chapel Cove, they'd seen each other once and spoken on the phone a couple of times, but Shannon hadn't had anything much to contribute. She'd agreed a plan with Rosa to also research what had happened to the Whittakers after the crash, but the truth was, she couldn't afford the petrol to and from the Falmouth Library to use their computers. If only she could get a bit of money together for fuel.

In Cribba Village, Shannon popped into the local shop, then came out a few minutes later empty-handed. As a last resort, she'd tried the new owner to see if there was any shelf-stacking work or general cleaning, but nothing. Shit, how she hated to beg for work.

One more cold call and she would call it a day.

She turned into the tree-lined drive of Ada Martin's place. Sunlight pierced the overhead canopy of trees and dappled the road in front of her. She parked next to the walled garden, got out and walked through the archway.

Mrs Martin and Maisie, her household assistant, were at the bottom of the vegetable garden chatting to Jack, who was measuring out rows with string in readiness to plant seeds when the time was right. He walked with a bit of a limp but otherwise seemed fit and well. Everything looked ship-shape and in order. Rats, no work for her here.

'Hello, Miss Reid,' Mrs Martin called out. 'How nice to see you. What brings you to Cribba House?'

Shannon smiled as Mrs Martin came up to her. She looked very fit and spritely, as did Maisie, who stood beside her with several stalks of rhubarb and a large, savoy cabbage in a wicker basket. Not that Shannon wanted any of Mrs Martin's staff to be sick, but maybe an annoying cough or cold would've allowed her to find a bit of work for a few days.

'Hello, Mrs Martin. I was popping in on the off chance that you might have some work for a few days ... a day even.' She rushed on. 'I can turn my hand to anything ... anything.'

Mrs Martin nodded at Maisie, who swapped the wicker basket from one hand to the other and walked off towards the main house.

'Shannon, my dear, I heard about the fire and the destruction of your home.'

'Oh.'

'I was so sorry to hear the news. I hope the police have been able to find the culprit. Must be an outsider; no local would do that to you, I'm certain.'

'The police haven't a clue.' Shannon blinked, then blinked again. She couldn't cry in front of this woman. 'Thank you for your concern, Mrs Martin. I'm sorry to have troubled you.'

Mrs Martin touched her arm. 'My dear, don't rush off. I might have something for you.'

'Seriously?' Blood pulsed through Shannon's ears.

'Primrose Cottage. I'm not sure if you know where that is?'

'In Cribba Village. Right opposite the shop, isn't it?'

Mrs Martin nodded. 'I own it, and the tenants are leaving in a couple of weeks. I always ensure my rental properties are thoroughly cleaned and redecorated before any new tenants come in. Would you be interested in undertaking the work?'

'Yes. Yes, please.' The words tumbled out of Shannon.

'It would probably be a good week or ten days of work to clean everything, including the kitchen appliances, bring the small garden back into shape, and do a little basic decorating where needed.'

'Fantastic.' Shannon wanted to hug the woman but knew that wouldn't be acceptable. 'Thank you so much.'

'You did a good job with the garden, so I expect the same quality of work as before. Same hourly rate if that's agreeable.'

'Totally. When can I start?'

'I'll give you a ring to confirm. Should be two weeks today.'

An idea flashed into Shannon's mind, and for a second, she wondered whether to say anything or not. She didn't want to jeopardise the job, but the words came out anyway.

'Mrs Martin, would … would it be possible for me to stay in Primrose Cottage while I'm doing the work?' She sucked in a deep breath. 'I … I would be ever so careful and tidy, and you could deduct any costs for electricity and water I use.'

Mrs Martin was shaking her head.

'Oh, not to worry. It was just a thought.'

Mrs Martin shook her head again. 'No, no, that's not what I mean. That would be perfectly fine with me. It sounds like a solid idea, considering your circumstances. I should've thought of it first.'

This time Shannon did hug Mrs Martin. The woman quickly stepped away. She waved a dismissive hand at Shannon before moving off, but there was a smile on her face.

'I'll ring you shortly, my dear.'

As soon as Shannon stepped out of her car at Carnmarth Farm, Trevor appeared at her side.

'Been trying to catch you for days. You avoiding me or what?'

'I've been out looking for work. Have you got any for me?'

'Nope.'

'Then what do you want me for?'

She took a deep breath. She needed to play it a bit carefully; there was no point in aggravating Trevor, even though she already knew what he wanted.

'I need you gone.'

'Vic's happy that I stay with him until I get myself sorted with some seasonal work. What's the problem?'

'Vic's not in charge here.'

'I don't understand what the issue is?'

'I saw the police car this morning. I said before that I can't have trouble brought to Carnmarth.'

Shannon clenched her fists and then released them. 'I've got ears you know. When I first came to Carnmarth, I heard people passing my van in the middle of the night, sneaking up the lane and onto the path to Carnmarth Quarry. I even followed them once.'

Trevor scowled.

She swallowed. 'I saw things loaded from one vehicle to another. Saw them drive off with their headlights dimmed. Nothing about that was suspicious, eh? Really?'

'I admit, I did stuff in the past I'm not proud of when times were hard, but what you saw was done without my permission. I put a stop to it.' Trevor ran a hand through his hair. 'I've not been involved in any funny business for years now.'

'I wouldn't tell the police anything.' She lifted a hand towards him, then dropped it. 'You must know that. The police have never been a friend of mine.'

Silence fell between them. What else could she say?

'Why do you want to hang around Carnmarth anyway?' Trevor grunted. 'You don't have family hereabouts, as far as I know. Why not leave here and start afresh?'

'What with? Peanuts? Not that I could afford those at the moment.'

'Why do you even stay in Cornwall with its crippling housing costs and low wages?'

'Cos it's my home. It's where I was born. Why should I be shoved out by others? By you?' She glared at him. 'I was hoping that you would find another caravan so I wouldn't have to go. I've been a reasonable tenant to you. Paid my rent and haven't complained.'

'Oh, yeah, that sounds like a great plan, what with the police snooping around?'

She turned away from him and stomped towards Vic's caravan.

'Bloody hell, Shannon, you don't help yourself, do you? You probably know who torched the van, but you won't say, will you?'

She carried on walking, shoulders hunched. Nobody could, or would help her: not Nina, not the police, not Trevor. And Rosa, well, Rosa was in a world of her own, and if she never laid eyes on Shannon again, it would be none too soon.

'I need you gone. By the end of the week, you hear me,' Trevor called out after her.

From Vic's decked area, she watched him walk across the yard and into the farmhouse. The door slammed behind him.

What now? She'd hoped to continue to stay with Vic until Mrs Martin rang with a firm date to start the Primrose Cottage job. But for Vic's sake, she would move on in the morning.

Two weeks, that was all it was until she had a roof over her head again. She could survive two weeks sleeping in the car, in whatever layby or deserted lane she could find. She'd done it before, and she could do it again. No problem.

12

Rosa placed the tray onto the table and looked across Chapel Cove. Waves gently lapped the sand before rolling over a strip of pebbles on their journey back out to sea. Seagulls called out overhead and, on the horizon, a tanker made its slow way to the docks at Falmouth. Marcus and Freya skimmed pebbles on the water's edge. A couple of older children and a little terrier dog had joined them. Their laughter and voices floated in the air. Thank goodness they seemed to be enjoying themselves; it was their Easter holiday break after all.

Rosa turned back to Shannon, who had horrible dark smudges under her eyes and looked even worse for wear than she had at their last meeting.

'Okay, let's quickly catch up.' She took a sip of her coffee. 'I contacted the courier to see if I could find out who sent the dead birds, but either they don't have a record, or they're keeping quiet. What about you? Any joy on the wider Whittaker family?'

Shannon turned bloodshot eyes onto her and shook her head. Uncombed curls blew around her face. 'I've not had the chance to get into Falmouth to check out any of the old newspaper articles. To be honest, I don't even know if the library is the right place to start.' She pushed her empty cup away and picked up a sugar lump to crunch. 'Might have to go to County Hall or wherever the County Records Office is located and see what they have to say.'

'Why haven't you rung them?' Rosa gritted her teeth. 'A phone call would've at least provided us with some info or a steer on where and what to do next.' Blooming hell, why was Shannon being so pathetic? She'd manage to track down Rosa and James to Curlew House quickly enough, using social media and suchlike. Why was she playing the I-can't-do-it card now?

'My phone charge is low. Can't waste it as I'm waiting for a work call.'

'Won't that old bloke let you use his charger?'

'I've moved on from Vic's place.'

Loud dog barks filled the air. Rosa shoved her chair back and rushed to the edge of the patio area. Marcus and Freya stood up to their knees in what had now become quite big waves. The other children were further out. Their terrier ran back and forth along the beach.

'Marcus. Freya. Come in at once.'

The children turned and waved.

'We're having fun,' Freya shouted.

'Just five more minutes,' Marcus begged.

'Now.' Rosa beckoned them towards the café and relief shot through her as they made their way back to the shoreline.

Really, she needed them all to be gone from there. There was no way she wanted any of her new friends or neighbours to see her with Shannon.

Back at the table, she said, 'Before the children get here, so you're in the know, I've told them you and I are fellow committee members, here to discuss the agenda for the next meeting.'

'Oh, and what committee would that be? Flower arranging?'

'Be serious. I need a cover story should James or anybody else we know see us together.'

'Am I so terrible to be seen with?'

'Now you're being thoughtless. I've already told you that James knows nothing about the accident or my background. I want to keep it that way.'

'Sounds like a strange old marriage to me.'

Rosa scowled at Shannon and forced herself to keep the irritation out of her voice. 'Don't you have anything at all to report?'

'I do, as it happens.'

'Oh?'

'Something I found out about Zach, the guy I told you about, who turned up at Carnmarth Farm just before we received the half photos. Rents a caravan from Trevor.'

'Trevor? Carnmarth Farm?'

Shannon reddened but said nothing.

'Is that where you're living?'

'Not anymore.'

'Where are you staying now?'

'Here and there.' Shannon glanced at her phone and sighed. 'Don't worry, you can still contact me on my mobile. I'll get it charged soon.'

Rosa didn't push Shannon for more details on where she was living. She didn't want to know her problems anyway. Keeping the peace between James and the children during the holidays was more than enough for her to handle. Blooming hell, James was getting tetchier every day.

'So, what have you found out about this Zach?'

'I asked Vic for the low down on him, but he couldn't tell me anything much except that his last name is Smith and that he often rabbited on about what fun he'd had during his university days.' She picked up two more sugar lumps and popped them into her mouth. 'Vic is good at pumping people for information. Yet, when I was working at the pub one evening, Zach told me something different. He'd insisted on sitting at the bar and chatting to me. I had no choice but to put on my customer-friendly face and be polite, and he took it as an opportunity to come over all pally-pally with me. He took pride in saying he'd left school at sixteen and immediately got a job in a local factory.'

'A liar then,' Rosa said. 'And if he can lie about whether he went to university or not, then he can lie about other things as well, like whether he's a member of the Whittaker family.'

'That's what I thought. I'll see if I can find anything on Facebook about him when I get the chance.'

Marcus and Freya raced across the beach and arrived breathless and rosy-cheeked at their table.

'Can we have a toasted sandwich, Mum?' Marcus asked.

'Please, Mum. Ham and cheese.' Freya threw her arms around Rosa's neck and kissed her several times. 'Please. And ice cream.'

Rosa smiled and stroked her daughter's hair. It was lunchtime, so maybe it would be easier to agree. 'Okay, you two go and order. Toasted sandwiches first, then maybe ice cream afterwards. I'll have cheese and tomato on brown.' She glanced at Shannon, who didn't look in a hurry to leave. Blast. 'Do you want one?'

Shannon nodded. 'Ham and cheese would be great.'

Rosa handed the children a handful of cash, and they shot off like bullets to order the food while she walked over to the outside self-serve area and picked up four sets of knives, forks, and paper napkins. Salt and pepper and ketchup – an essential part of all meals for Marcus, much to James's annoyance – were already on the table.

'Your kids are lovely,' Shannon said.

Pride shot through Rosa, like it always did when anybody praised her children.

Shannon took the offered cutlery. 'You always were the lucky one.'

'You know me, I make my own luck.' She glanced over at her children inside the café. 'Although, to be honest, I didn't exactly plan to have the twins. When I found out I was pregnant, I hot-footed it to the first abortion clinic.'

Shannon raised her eyebrows.

'Plan B kicked in as they wheeled me into the surgery.' Rosa smiled at the memory. 'They'd all been so nice and matter-of-fact about the abortion: the doctor, the nurses, even the receptionist. But when the surgeon turned her kind face to me, all I could see was Mum.'

'Your mum?'

'Yep. You know how she looked at me when she knew I was about to do something wrong? Well, it was that look. I high-tailed it out of there. My best Plan B ever.'

'What about James? What did he say?'

'I hadn't met him then.'

'Oh, I thought …' Shannon raised her eyebrows again. 'So, what did whoever is the father say?'

'Never told him. Or them. Could've been one of two men, but I didn't care to tell either of them. They were both decent blokes, but they would've stayed with their wives. The women in their marriages held the purse strings, you see.' Rosa picked up one of the paper serviettes. 'Besides, having no father's name on the birth certificates equals no complications and an easier life all around. James is their father now. Full stop.' Rosa folded and unfolded her napkin. 'He loves them. Well, in his own way, he does.'

'Seriously, Rosa, you are more than lucky. Mind you, you were totally spoilt as a child by both your parents. You could wind your father around your little finger. A proper Daddy's girl. It seems to me you've now got your husband doing your bidding as well. Guess you get out of life what you expect.'

'Like you said, lucky me.' Rosa's heart raced. A Daddy's girl. Oh, the irony. If only Shannon knew everything that had happened.

The children ran back to the table and flopped into the vacant chairs.

'The food's coming soon,' Marcus said.

'Good, we need to eat up quickly. I want to get back and start dinner for later.'

Freya put her hand into her jacket pocket and pulled out four shells. She gave two to Rosa.

'Oh, that's so sweet, darling.'

Then, with her head tilted downwards so she looked out from under her dark eyelashes, she pushed two towards Shannon. 'They're for you.'

Shannon reached out, picked up the shells and turned them over in her palm. 'Th ... thank you so much,' she breathed.

Thank goodness the waitress arrived with the toasted sandwiches as Rosa was sure Shannon was about to shed a tear. Instead, she tore into her sandwich like she'd not eaten that day. Freya mimicked her actions, and then Marcus did the same. The three of them were soon laughing as they gobbled their food.

Rosa gritted her teeth. Shannon was not the example she wanted her children to follow. The quicker she got them away from her the better. She stood. 'Time to go.'

'What about our ice creams, Mum?' Freya said.

'You can have some when we get home. There's a huge selection in the freezer.'

They moaned, but with one look from her, they got to their feet and raced to the car, shouting their goodbyes to Shannon as they ran.

Rosa's instinct told her that Shannon had no money to pay for her food, so she picked up the bill. Just as well she'd paid in cash. James couldn't query what he couldn't see in print.

'See you here next week? Same time, same day?'

Shannon nodded.

'In the meantime, let's both keep researching stuff on the Whittakers where we can. I'll ring the Records Office if that would help?'

Shannon nodded again. 'Thanks for the food. I'll pay … next time.'

Huh, Rosa would believe that when she saw it.

She raised her hand in farewell. She got it that Shannon was going through a rough time and presumably had very little money, but it was a real cheek of her to assume that Rosa had no financial restrictions of her own. She shouldn't be expected to pay *every* time.

Marcus and Freya tumbled out of the car as soon as Rosa pulled to a stop outside Curlew House. Several vans blocked her way to the rear of the property. What was going on? Who were these people and who'd let them in?

In the darkened interior of the hall, her eyes took a moment to adjust, then she saw James, clipboard in hand, in a deep conversation with a suited man who appeared to be in charge.

'James?'

He came over to her and kissed her cheek. 'Darling, did you all have a lovely morning?'

'What's going on? What are all these men doing?'

A man in a suit moved past her with a big box in his arms and headed for James's study, where, judging by the noise, another person was hammering and drilling something. A ladder appeared by the entrance door and was placed against the wall.

'Nothing for you to worry about.' James peered around her towards a third person climbing the ladder to reach the wall above the doorway. 'I'm having security cameras installed.'

'But we already have one in the front and one at the back. Why all this extra stuff?'

'It's state-of-the-art technology. I'll be able to see everybody coming and going.'

Rosa swallowed. 'Why?'

'There's been a couple of burglaries around the area recently and I want to catch any idiot who thinks he can take what's mine.'

'Oh.'

'Our cars are fair game for any thief on the lookout for a quick buck or two. They'd think all their Christmases had come at once, what with my classic Jaguar and our two BMWs.'

She waved her arm in the direction of more boxes being unloaded outside. 'It all seems a bit over the top. A bit claustrophobic, don't you think?'

'Surely, this will make you feel safer when I'm away during the day, or overnight on business?' He grabbed her elbow and steered her towards his study. 'Come and look at this.'

She stared at a bank of computer screens. Blank now, but she knew shortly that they would monitor her every move. Were recent thefts in the area the real reason, or was he concerned about her more frequent comings and goings? Her heart crashed against her ribs. Maybe she should come clean about the stalker and her past. Tell him everything. She quickly pushed the thought from her head; he'd never trust her again. No, he couldn't know anything about her problems. This was more likely to do with his business dealings than anything to do with her.

'Oh, Rosa, come and say hello to Mike Spencer, owner of Dunmere Security Systems,' James said. 'He's responsible for all this.'

'Good to meet you, Mrs Trevail.' The suited man held out his hand to her.

She shook it.

'Even if I say so myself, Mr Trevail has picked an excellent system, by far our superior product. It will keep tabs on anyone and everyone that comes to the property.' Mike Spencer grinned, then stared into her face. 'Do I know you from somewhere? Are you local?'

'My goodness, no.' James laughed. 'We only moved to Cornwall six months ago. It was Rosa's first visit to the county.'

Mike Spencer stared at her for a few more moments before he bade them farewell and made his way outside.

A shiver dashed down Rosa's spine.

'Are you alright, darling? You know I've only done this for you.'

Rosa sucked in a lungful of air, then reached over and hugged James. 'That's so thoughtful of you, always putting me first.' She had to keep a grip on herself. James was her everything and she wasn't going to lose him over some stupid stalker.

Sat at the kitchen table, she watched Marcus and Freya through the window playing football on the lawn, her eyes drawn to the stripes of well-manicured grass that flowed to the edge of the Helford River. Even their laughter and the sight of the yachts drifting lazily on their anchors couldn't calm the anxiety that had formed in her stomach. Perhaps James was picking up on her moods, her insomnia, and her less-than-honest answers to his questions about where she'd been and what she'd done on any particular day. Rosa's hand flew to her mouth. Early on in their relationship, James had confided that a previous partner had cheated on him. Dear God, perhaps he thought she was having an affair. Perhaps that was what all the cameras were about.

Oh, how she longed for those early days when they first met and exchanged intimate details about their backgrounds. There was nothing to match that wonderful feeling of closeness, of love, that the sharing of personal information provoked. James, in a sad, quiet voice, had told her about his parents' deaths from cancer and how he was an only child. She'd felt an instant bond at the revelation and told him that she was an only child as well, and an orphan. Okay, a real whopper of a lie, but there was no way she was ever going to introduce James to her father.

James had been quite forthcoming about his background. She'd been less so. What's more, he knew it.

'We're all entitled to our little secrets at our age,' he'd said with a wry grin.

He'd been so handsome and gentlemanly. Everything she'd wanted and dreamed about. He'd freely told her all about the betrayal by his ex-partner, in fact, his ex-wife, Celia, and how much it had scarred him. So much so that he hadn't believed he'd ever marry again – until he met Rosa. When he'd declared his love for her, she'd immediately accepted his proposal and settled quickly into the high life. She'd known then that she had to tread very carefully to win and keep his trust. Was this stalker business and her reunion with Shannon putting that trust at risk?

She rubbed her forehead and took another gulp of coffee. Lately, her dream had taken a bit of a battering. Damn it, what if it really was her? What if her tense behaviour of late, her secret meetings with Shannon – ironically not some man – was the real cause of the changed behaviour in James? If only she could tell him the truth. She took a deep breath.

She had to brave it out. Everything would surely go back to normal when the whole thing with Shannon and the stalker was sorted.

The words she'd said to Shannon earlier, about making her own luck, came into her mind and unexpectedly gave her a sense of renewed strength and self-confidence. She stood and put her mug into the dishwasher. If push came to shove and her marriage went belly up, she *would* survive, like the old version of Rosa with her Plan B's always did. Well, to be honest, she and the children would more than survive on her half-share of Curlew House.

Rosa smiled. She made her own luck. Always had.

13

Shannon pulled into the car park at Chapel Cove. Rosa had beaten her to it and stood leaning against her shiny BMW, tapping her fingers on the bonnet. As soon as she saw Shannon, she stomped over.

'You're late.'

'Only a couple of minutes. What's happened? We only met yesterday.'

'James is installing a ruddy spy system in the house.' Rosa ran her hand through her hair. 'There are video and security cameras everywhere.'

'What's that got to do with me?'

'I'm here to tell you not to call at Curlew House under any circumstances. I can't have him seeing you and asking awkward questions.'

'For your information, I wasn't planning to visit Curlew House any time soon. Is that all that you wanted to say? You could've told me that by text.'

'You …' Rosa dragged a hand through her hair again. 'You don't understand. He'll now know my every move.'

'So? He's your husband. Surely, you'd tell him anyway if he asked.'

Rosa glared at her. 'If he notices that I leave the house at the same time on the same day every week, he'll start asking questions. And there's no way I can come clean about you or our past.'

'Tell him to mind his own business.'

'You don't get it, do you? Then again, you've never been married or lived with anyone, have you?'

'He needs to butt out.'

'Frankly, you have no idea how a marriage works. I'm worried that he thinks I'm having an affair.' Rosa blew out her cheeks.

Shannon shrugged. 'Sounds like you married a clown to me. Changing the subject, are we having coffee?'

'I don't have time.'

Shannon momentarily closed her eyes. She'd hoped for another free toasted sandwich, or at least a hot drink. 'What's the urgency? What have you found out?'

'I haven't found out anything. I just told you I'm dealing with workers tramping all over the house and garden. Not only that, but the owner of the company also thought he knew me from somewhere?'

'Did you recognise him?'

'No, but it's unsettled me. I can tell you that for free.' Rosa paced back and forth. 'What have you found out about the Whittakers?'

'Nothing, but I did drop into the Falmouth Library this morning and did a search for Zach Smith. Dead end. Nothing that matched the guy who's been following me around like a pain in the arse.' Shannon rubbed her hands together. 'I'll try again next time I'm in town.'

'You could use your phone.'

'So could you,' Shannon snapped back. 'Besides, my phone's not up to it. Old style, not that you would know anything about that.'

'I hope you got it charged since I saw you last?'

'Some, at the library, but it's low again and …'

Rosa stopped pacing and stood with her hands on her hips. 'You're waiting for a business call. Yes, you said last time. So, you've got nothing?'

'It's only been twenty-four hours.' Shannon pulled the half photo of her and her mum from her back pocket.

'But I do have this.' She shoved the photo into Rosa's face. 'You remember Mum's necklace, don't you? She wore it all the time. Her grandmother gave it to her.'

'What? Why should I remember it?'

Shannon tapped the photo. 'Because there it is. See.'

She pointed to the necklace, with its little circle of tiny gold leaves, a light green stone in the middle, and a couple of pendant stones in the same colour that hung down from the bottom of the circle.

'Not valuable, but a precious family gift. My great grandmother's engagement present from her fiancé.'

Rosa shrugged. 'So?'

'It got lost in the accident,' Shannon said. 'Never came up as part of Mum's belongings, and it should have. Would you ask your dad if he's got it?'

'You've got to be joking.'

'You need to see him about the photo anyway. You could ask him about the necklace at the same time.'

'Are you stupid?' Rosa shouted. 'I'm not in contact with my father and I'm not going to see him.'

A couple of people in the café looked in their direction and Rosa quickly turned her back to them. Shannon stared at her. The woman was coming unhinged. What did she have to be falling apart about, her with her great big house, gorgeous kids and handsome husband?

'Rosa,' she said, slowly, clearly, 'you have to see him. This photo could only have come from him. He holds the key to how the half photos got from him to us. You must see that?'

'I won't do it.'

Shannon clenched her jaw. 'At least *you* have a dad you *can* visit.'

'Not that old chestnut again. What a shame your mother never told you who your dad was. If she did, you could go and ask him for help.' She looked Shannon up and down. 'You clearly need it.'

'Piss off.' Shannon turned and hurried towards her car.

Damn Rosa with her perfect life. Shannon knew she looked scruffy compared to Rosa's expensive jeans and top, but she was clean, and her hair was less dishevelled than Rosa's. She was more than thankful that she'd managed to sneak, unseen by Trevor, into the small shower block at Carnmarth Farm late at night on a few occasions since she'd left the farm ten days ago. Vic had seen her once and winked, but she was sure Trevor hadn't twigged, otherwise, he would've put a lock and bolt on the door.

'Wait,' Rosa came up to her. 'I'm sorry.'

Shannon sighed. She'd given up long ago wondering if the butcher or the local shopkeeper was her dad, or some married man she passed every day when she travelled to and from school. Or was he a tourist who'd left behind a baby along with the discarded flip-flops that he wouldn't need in his nice up-country home?

'What more do you want me to say?' Rosa dug the toe of her shoe into the sandy surface of the car park. 'The past is the past.'

Shannon's stomach rumbled in the silence. Rosa was right. She should accept it was simply another secret she had to live with.

Rosa straightened up. 'As I said, I'm in a hurry. Let's meet a week on Monday at 3:00 p.m. We both should have more to report back by then.'

Hurt pulsed through Shannon. 'Your dad broke his promise to my mum and your mum after the car crash,' she said. As the words fell out of her mouth, she wondered why she was doing this. Why was she picking at old scabs?

'What are you on about now?'

'Our families promised to look after each other if anything happened, and then he just abandoned me.'

'He abandoned *you*?' Rosa's face reddened. 'He abandoned *you*,' she shouted. 'Fucking hell, you don't see it, do you? It was *me* he abandoned. Me, his own daughter, when he took up with that dreadful woman. That's why I won't see him ever again.'

Rosa pressed her key fob, opened the door, and jumped into her car. Before Shannon could answer, the vehicle pulled away in a shower of sand and pebbles.

Shannon watched the car speed along the road towards the Helford River. She rubbed her temple. Her head throbbed. Why couldn't Rosa see that having one parent had to be better than having none?

Slumped into the driver's seat of her car, she looked at the happy snap of her and her mum again and sighed. Until the accident, she'd thought her father's name was the only secret her mum had kept from her. And then the police had told her that they'd found traces of drugs in her mum's system that day. A jolt of almost physical pain shot through Shannon. Breathe in. One. Two. Three. Breathe out. One. Two. Three. Even now, after twenty-three years, she couldn't believe the betrayal. She and her mum had shared everything. Or so she'd thought.

What a screwed-up pair she and Rosa were. Shannon's mother had lied to her, and Rosa believed her dad had abandoned her. No wonder they were such a mess.

That night, Shannon pulled into an isolated lay-by a couple of miles outside of Cribba Village; she rarely parked in the same spot for more than two nights. She blew on her fingers and pulled her old puffer jacket over the top of the clothes she wore. How she longed for her sleeping bag, but that had been lost in the fire along with all her bedding.

How the hell didn't Rosa realise how lucky she was with a roof over her head and a family who loved her? Mind you, that husband of hers sounded like a bit of a screwball with all that security stuff. This was Cornwall, for heaven's sake. And, blimey, why was Rosa going on about an affair? Maybe all was not quite so picture-perfect at Curlew House after all.

Her head still throbbed, and a tremor tore through her body. She reached for her old work socks, pulled them over her hands and tucked them under her arms.

After Rosa had left Chapel Cove, Shannon had eventually gone inside and bought a cup of tea and a packet of crisps with her last few coins and sat at a table near an electric socket. Thankfully, she'd managed to top up most of the charge on her phone before she had to leave.

It was only six days until she could move into Primrose Cottage for a couple of weeks. Heaven. She stared at her phone and willed Mrs Martin to call and confirm that, then she leaned her head back against the seat, closed her eyes, and fell into a dreamless sleep.

A loud noise woke her. Her phone. Mrs Martin? She ripped the sock off her hand and scrambled to answer the call.

'Hello.'

'Hi, my lovely. How's tricks in Cornwall?'

Shannon's heart sank and leapt at the same time. It was not Mrs Martin calling to confirm the date to move into Primrose Cottage but dear Nina calling from California.

'Oh, Nina. It's so great to hear your voice.'

'You okay? You sound a bit hoarse.'

'A cold, that's all.'

'Everything honky-dory at Carnmarth Farm?'

'Yep. Nothing exciting going on here.' What else could she say? There was no point in upsetting Nina. There was nothing she could do. 'Trevor's his usual grumpy self. I'm busy with the new lambs, and …'

'Well, you'll never believe what we've been up to.'

Shannon flopped back against the seat and immersed herself in the happiness of her friend's upbeat voice as she flooded Shannon with news of her children, their schools and Jake's new job. Shannon's body relaxed as she listened to the faraway voice. Only now and then did she look at the charge on her phone as it slowly dropped away.

'Well, my lovely, I must go. You take care. Love you loads.'

'Love you too.'

'Bye.'

'Bye,' Shannon whispered into the cold night air.

She sighed and took a deep breath. If only … A long coughing fit interrupted her thoughts. Shit, she definitely was going down with a cold. She couldn't wait to get into Primrose Cottage. She'd passed it that morning and seen the removal van outside. Maybe she would leave it until after the weekend and then ask Mrs Martin if she could move in a few days early. What harm would it do?

14

Rosa's cheeks flushed with warmth and her body tingled with happiness as she sped along the country roads in James's classic Jaguar E-Type convertible. Her hair lifted in the breeze as she turned to look at her husband at the wheel. A smile played on his lips, and she knew why; he was driving his 'baby,' the piece of metal on which he bestowed an enviable kind of love. Securely locked in the second double garage for the majority of the time, James checked the machine every evening, often merely sitting in the leather seat listening to music, or he took it outside to polish and preen the already glossy red paintwork.

'Oh, James, that was such a wonderful treat. Thank you.'

James grinned. 'I knew you'd like The Cove.'

'And it was so nice that you took time off work as well.'

He rested his hand on her thigh and gave it a loving squeeze. 'I got to the office and suddenly felt the urge to take my wife out for lunch. You deserve it for everything you do for me and the children.'

She placed her hand over his. 'Thank you.'

James turned the car towards Falmouth rather than making his way directly back to Curlew House. Rosa smiled to herself. It was show-off time. Out of the corner of her eye, she could see James's chin tipped upwards as he drove around Pendennis Point, along the seafront and then past Swanpool Beach. He travelled at a leisurely speed, revving the engine now and then to attract admiring glances from walkers and other drivers.

Rosa loved taking this dog-leg route home. The scenery was breathtaking on what she called a Mediterranean day. There wasn't a cloud in the bright blue sky, and the sea sparkled as if decorated with a coat of diamonds.

'Are you returning to work when we get back?'

'I think I'll take the rest of the day off. The Jag will need a clean and polish before I put her away. Why? Will I wreck your plans by staying home?'

'Of course not. I'll be busy getting things ready for Freya and Marcus. I can't wait to see them. If it's sunny like this again tomorrow, I think a trip with the paddleboards to the beach will be on the list.'

James touched her arm. 'The children are lucky to have such a wonderful mother.'

They passed the entrance to the road that led towards Chapel Cove, and an image of Shannon flicked into Rosa's mind. She tried to push it away. She didn't want anything or anyone to spoil what was a perfect day. However, for a few moments, she let the fact that Shannon had re-entered her life roll over her; it made her more determined to ensure that nothing would wreck what she and the children had with James.

As he pulled the Jag to a stop outside of Curlew House, she turned and kissed him, long and passionately.

'Well, that was very welcome, thank you.' James kept his eyes on her as he got out of the car and came around to her side of the vehicle to help her out. 'I think I'd like several more like that.'

Hand in hand they went inside.

A while later, she handed him a mug of fresh coffee and then sat opposite him at the kitchen table.

'I was wondering what you might like for your meal this evening?'

'We won't want much, surely, after such a marvellous lunch?'

'Maybe not, but Freya and Marcus will still need a proper meal after I've picked them up from school. I'd planned to cook fillet steaks for all of us and, well, my plans have been thrown out today,' she reached for his hand, 'in all sorts of delightful ways.'

He grinned at her. 'Darling, I think fillet steaks would be just the job. Only a small one for me though, with a side salad.'

'And for me. I'll add chips and other bits for the children.'

James stood and placed his mug in the sink. 'Must go. The Jag awaits.'

Rosa remained at the table and watched James leave the room. A rush of love for him overwhelmed her and she wiped her eyes. Goodness, she was being so pathetic, welling up. Was it because she'd had such a fantastic day or because she could be so close to losing it all if James found out about her lies, her background, and her contact with Shannon? And what would happen if another dreadful box of dead magpies or similar arrived on her doorstep? She shivered.

Picking up her mug, she placed it in the sink next to James's. On top of everything else, she couldn't shake off the suggestion from Shannon that she should visit her father and ask him about the photograph. Jesus, one person from her past coming out of the woodwork was bad enough. At least Shannon hadn't tapped her for money, other than for the odd cup of coffee and a toasted sandwich. Her father was another kettle of fish. He, or more to the point, his second wife – she could never bring herself to call that dreadful woman her stepmother – would milk Rosa for everything they could get once they knew where she lived and who she was married to.

She turned on the tap, washed the mugs and put them on the drainer.

Yes, it probably made sense to check out her dad, but, other than money, he'd no reason to be involved in any of the recent incidents. In her heart, she couldn't believe he would deliberately hurt her, even after all these years.

At least the stalker hadn't sent any more photos or stuff recently. Maybe it was simply some sad schmuck or kid playing with their minds.

She and Shannon were due to meet on Monday. She hoped Shannon had found out more than last time. Rosa's own searches for old newspaper articles online had, after several numbingly boring hours, proved fruitful; she'd discovered that, at the time of the accident, the Whittakers had been travelling from their home in Surrey to West Cornwall for a family wedding. What's more, it looked like they'd been loaded, with a big house in the country and a very successful business. Surely, this meant that it was unlikely that any member of their family or relative would be hounding them for money.

Rosa picked up a mug and wiped it before placing it in the cupboard with its handle facing to one side.

Everything about the scene in front of Rosa filled her with joy as she cooked the fillet steaks and chips. James and the children sat around the kitchen table for once, and the chatter between the three of them was easy and lively. Freya and Marcus talked non-stop about their school week; a good one for Marcus and his maths test, and Freya had got a gold star for her spelling and reading aloud. James was in excellent form as he told them about the boat trip he'd booked for the next day as a special treat. The trip would take the four of them out into Carrick Roads, at the mouth of the Fal River, where James hoped they would see basking sharks and dolphins or, at the very least, a couple of seals. Rain began to beat against the window, but James didn't seem to notice or be worried, presumably he'd checked that the weather forecast was good for the boat trip tomorrow. Not that it mattered, the wildlife cruise would still go ahead unless there was exceptionally bad weather; they would have to wear waterproofs, that's all.

James was being the father figure that Rosa had so hoped he'd be, and the children were relaxed in his company, asking all sorts of questions about what sharks and dolphins ate and what noises they made. Her husband's laughter grew louder as the questions grew sillier and sillier. Love for the handsome, amiable man at the table flowed through her again. She hummed to herself as she laid four plates in a row on the worktop and placed a piece of steak on each. She then added salad – more for her and James and less for the children – before putting triple-cooked chips, mushrooms and peas onto Freya and Marcus's dishes. She laid the meals in front of each of them and sat down.

The children immediately picked up their forks and knives and tucked into the chips. James pulled the cruet set towards him, added extra olive oil to his already dressed salad, then reached over and picked up the white ceramic mustard container. He lifted the lid and stared at the contents.

Rosa joined in the carefree chatter with Freya and Marcus, each of them in turn making noises that they thought dolphins and grey seals made. Laughter and giggles filled the room, then Rosa's happiness faded away as she realised that James was still staring at the mustard container.

She glanced over his hand. The pot was nearly empty.

'Would you like me to refill that for you?'

'What? Oh, yes please.'

She got to her feet and took the pot from his hand. 'It'll only take me a minute.'

Rosa reached into the larder cupboard for a new jar of English Mustard. Her hand hung in mid-air as she realised there wasn't one. She was sure she'd purchased another jar.

'It looks like I haven't got any,' she called over her shoulder. 'Drat. Never mind, I've got plenty of French Mustard or various other relishes. Can I get you one of those?'

'I only eat English Mustard with steak, Rosa. You know that.'

Was that true? She was sure she'd seen him take French Mustard before. 'But ...'

James pushed his plate into the centre of the table. 'Forget it. I'm not hungry anyway.'

Marcus and Freya stopped talking and turned to look at him.

Rosa removed more condiment pots and bottles from the cupboard in the vain hope that she would find at least some powdered mustard she could quickly mix up, but there was nothing. Blooming hell, why was James being so awkward when everyone was having so much fun?

She picked up the French Mustard jar and returned to her seat.

A sudden gust of wind and rain buffeted the window.

James snatched the jar from her hand and slammed it onto the table. 'Is it too much to ask for English Mustard when I want it?'

'Mummy?' Freya wailed.

Rosa flinched and attempted to get to her feet, but James gripped her elbow. She turned and waved her free arm at the children. 'Go to your rooms, darlings. I'll be up shortly.'

'But, Mummy, I haven't finished my meal,' Marcus said.

'Please do as I ask. Go now.'

The children scrambled from their chairs and ran to the door.

When she heard their feet trample overhead, she snatched her arm from James's grasp and stood up.

'What the hell was all that about? You've upset the children over a dollop of stupid mustard.'

'I've upset them?' he shouted. '*I've* upset them? You're the one who failed to keep the larder fully stocked.'

'James, it's a pot of mustard. I thought I had plenty. I'm sorry. What else can I say or do?'

'You can do the job you're supposed to do, and that's looking after me.'

Rosa blinked. She knew that was the deal, but he'd never put it so crudely before.

He pulled his plate towards him and poked at the meat. 'I was looking forward to my steak and you couldn't even sort that out for me.'

She stared at him, words failing to come.

'Do I really need to remind you that I'm the one who puts food on the table around here? How many children in Cornwall do you think are eating fillet steak for their dinner tonight?' His face was flushed but his voice had grown quiet. 'Just what is it you've been so busy doing, Rosa, that it's causing you to neglect your primary role in this household?'

So that was it. He was looking for signs of an affair and finding them in an empty pot of mustard.

'Oh, James, please don't,' she whispered.

James got to his feet. As he did so, his hand knocked the offending ceramic mustard pot. The lid slipped off the table and broke into two pieces on the floor. He gave it a fleeting glance, then strode towards the door.

A bead of sweat ran down the side of Rosa's face. What had happened to the amazing husband and father of only a few minutes ago?

'Where are you going?' she called.

'Out.'

The door slammed behind him.

Rosa placed her head in her hands and let out a moan. How could she have forgotten such a basic ingredient in her larder? A spare pot of English Mustard should've been a standard item for her to put her hand on. Had Shannon and recent events been distracting her from her household duties? The security system, and the creepy Mike Spencer, had also knocked her off her guard. This whole episode was down to her. James had become upset because of her actions. Admittedly, he had his issues, but she was triggering them by going around acting in a way that was making him suspicious and defensive. Yes, it was her fault. She'd forgotten that treating James as her number one priority was the deal she'd signed up for. She couldn't afford to be distracted; everything she held dear depended on it.

At the sound of the Jaguar roaring up the drive, Rosa lifted her head. Ashen-faced, she walked across the kitchen, out into the hallway, and went upstairs to placate her children.

She needed to sort this stalker mess out, and fast, if she wasn't going to put her marriage and her whole future in jeopardy.

15

Rain hammered on the roof of Shannon's car. She tugged her woolly hat further down over her ears and pulled her coat tighter around her body. A flash of lightning lit up the encroaching darkness and, right on cue, a clap of thunder rumbled overhead. What an evening it had turned out to be after the wall-to-wall sunshine of the last two days. Two glorious days, which had thankfully enabled her to dry her clothes and had taken away the damp smell from the car's interior. She'd hoped for another rain-free night to ease her cough and give her a few hours of uninterrupted sleep. 'No bloody chance of that,' she shouted to the sky and was immediately struck with another coughing fit.

She blew her nose. Primrose Cottage nagged at her thoughts; warm, cosy, and soon to be her home for a week or so. What she wouldn't give to be there right now, in a hot bath with soap suds up to her chin.

Normally, she wouldn't be so rude as to bother Mrs Martin in an evening, but – she coughed again – she'd driven through Cribba Village an hour ago and was certain the cottage was empty; the curtains had been open, and the place was in darkness. Her phone charge had all been used up, so she couldn't ring. She had to visit. Mrs Martin had only ever shown kindness to her before; she would surely understand Shannon's predicament, understand her desperation for a roof over her head.

She turned the ignition key and released the handbrake.

Having parked her car in the usual spot by Mrs Martin's walled garden, Shannon glanced through the archway. What was a beautiful garden during the day now gave her the creeps. New Zealand Flax leaves twisted and flapped in the wind like dark tentacles from the deep, and a shrill whistling sound emanated from the palm trees. She shivered. Rain bounced off the ground and splashed the legs of her jeans. She walked to the front door and knocked.

Maisie answered, waved her quickly into the large hallway and rushed off.

'My dear Shannon, what brings you out so late and on such an atrocious night?' Mrs Martin called from one of the doors. 'Take off that wet coat and those boots and come in here by the fire. Hurry, before all the warmth seeps out into the hallway.'

Mrs Martin turned to Maisie with a smile. 'A large pot of tea, please. And a couple of slices of that delicious cake you baked this morning. Sit down, Shannon. Here, next to the fire. You look frozen and rather under the weather, if I may say so.'

Shannon's vision dimmed momentarily, and she wobbled. A reaction, she supposed, to the sudden difference between the cold outside and the warm atmosphere inside.

'Thank you so much.' She managed to whisper to Mrs Martin.

'My goodness, what a day. Fine one minute and dreadful the next.' Mrs Martin rattled on. 'It's what my husband used to call a typical Cornish day.' She let out a high-pitched laugh, then coughed. 'You know, four seasons in one day.'

Shannon nodded politely until Maisie returned with a tray.

'Oh, that's wonderful, Maisie.' Mrs Martin took the tray, lifted the teapot lid, and stirred before she handed Shannon a plate containing a large piece of fruit cake. 'Oh, my dear, I know what you're calling about. I'm sorry I haven't been in contact.' She cleared her throat. 'I'm afraid I was being a coward and putting off the bad news.'

'Bad news.' The cake in her mouth, dry and tasteless with her cold, caused Shannon to splutter and cough. She caught the crumbs in her hand and dropped them onto the plate. 'Mrs Martin, please don't tell me I can't live in Primrose Cottage while I clean and redecorate. You won't know I'm living there. I promise.'

Mrs Martin shifted in her seat. 'I'm so sorry, but the offer of work at Primrose Cottage is no longer available.'

'What?' Shannon blurted out. 'Why?'

Mrs Martin hesitated, then leaned forward. 'I've been approached by somebody. A very unsavoury man who I've never seen before. He made it very clear that I shouldn't employ you.'

'I don't understand.'

'Frankly, neither do I if I'm honest. But the truth is, I'm too old to be threatened by such a nasty individual. Too old to be involved in any sort of shenanigans.'

'I don't understand,' Shannon repeated. 'I ...' A chesty wheeze echoed in her ears.

'My dear, whatever you are involved in, all I can say is, you've made a very powerful enemy.'

Shannon opened her mouth to speak but stopped. What was the point? The stalker had struck again. She couldn't blame Mrs Martin; she was an old woman who didn't need the hassle of being associated with the likes of Shannon Reid.

She got to her feet. 'I need to go. Thank you for the tea and cake.'

'Shannon, wait. I want to give you a little something.'

Shannon waved the money away. She may have nothing else left, but she still had her pride.

Under the cover of darkness, she drove down the windy lane to Carnmarth Quarry on dimmed lights and parked in the far corner. Hidden by a hedge of gorse bushes, she was invisible from the occasional hiker who might use the path above the quarry. She would stay there for a few days until she worked out another plan.

Rain battered the roof, and the car rocked in the squally winds. What had her life come to? Tears flowed down her cheeks. She blew her nose and became consumed by yet another coughing fit. The stalker would be the death of her if she didn't find out who he or she was soon.

She coughed again. This time, the harsh noise went on and on and on.

16

Rosa paced to and fro in the kitchen, then stopped and punched in James's mobile number for the umpteenth time. Still no answer. For crying out loud, it was 4:00 a.m. on Saturday and he'd still not returned home after the mustard incident the previous evening. Where was he? Why was he being so awful, so childish?

She rubbed her eyes; there was no way she would sleep tonight. Her mind was full of questions. Had she made a mistake marrying James? But how could she have when he was such an amazing person most of the time? On the other hand, he'd been keen, insistent even, that they married quickly, so maybe she'd put the children's financial security ahead of really knowing what he was like.

As she paced the floor, it occurred to her that James's mood swings might be about something other than his paranoia around her having an affair. Now that she thought about it, he was more likely to be feeling stressed because he was in trouble moneywise. Maybe the move to Cornwall, and the setting up of a new business, had been harder than he'd anticipated. Was that why he was so uppity about her buying cakes and coffees at the Atlantic Hotel? If only he'd talk to her more about that side of his life. She'd be an asset to his business ventures if he'd only let her in.

She pulled a chair out from under the table. Not only had James punished *her* with his behaviour last night, but he'd also upset the children and that wasn't on. She closed her eyes at the memory.

After he'd stormed off, the children had eventually returned to the kitchen to finish their meal. Then the questions had begun.

'Why was James so grumpy?' Freya asked.

'When will he be back, and will he still be angry?' Marcus added.

'Sweethearts, James didn't mean to upset you. He was very tired from working so hard all week.'

'But he shouted at you when there was no mustard.' Freya's bottom lip trembled. 'Why?'

Rosa blinked back the tears that threatened to spill from her eyes. 'Darling, don't upset yourself. I was a bit silly and forgot the mustard when I last shopped.'

'We could hear him shouting from upstairs.' Freya's cheeks reddened. 'He frightened me.'

Rosa swallowed. 'Don't fret, darling. You know James can be a bit gruff at times but this was a one-off. He'll apologise when he returns, and tomorrow, we'll all have a wonderful day out in the boat.' She quickly got to her feet. 'How about I put a nice film on for us all to watch,' she'd said, and that was how they'd spent the rest of the evening.

A branch tapped against the patio door. Rosa shivered and looked around the kitchen. Bloody hell, she *hoped* this strop of James's was a one-off.

She rubbed her eyes again. What was she to do about the boat trip? Would James be back in time to join them? And, if so, what if his mood was so awful that it spoiled the outing for them and the other passengers? If they waited for him to show up and he didn't, then the booking and the money would be wasted. Rosa looked at the montage of photos on the wall. James's twinkling blue eyes seemed to challenge her. She glared back at his smiling image. Damn it, they *would* go. With or without him.

It was the right decision. The trip was wonderful. Another Mediterranean day, and Marcus and Freya took great delight in spotting a harbour porpoise and several seals. To finish off a perfect day, Rosa treated them all to a fish and chip supper, which they took home and ate at the kitchen table.

During the meal, James returned. He acted as if nothing had happened. 'Well, that food smells marvellous. Did you get any for me?'

Rosa glared at him. 'I didn't know when you'd be home. There's food in the freezer if you want me to cook something.'

He turned his back to her. She got to her feet and moved to the sink.

'Did you have a wonderful time out in the boat?' he asked the children. 'Tell me what you saw.'

Marcus and Freya burst into excited chatter as they vied to tell him about the harbour porpoise and the seals they'd seen.

Rosa turned the tap on and squirted detergent into the bowl, not that there was really any washing-up to do.

James eventually came over to her, put his arms around her waist and kissed the nape of her neck. 'I'm sorry,' he said.

Rosa reached into one of the shopping bags, removed two jars of English Mustard and placed one in the deep recess of the larder cupboard. The other one she put on the worktop, along with a new white, ceramic mustard pot she'd purchased from the supermarket. She quickly washed the container and filled it with mustard. She chewed her bottom lip. Monday morning wasn't her normal shopping day, but she'd felt the need earlier to stock up on essentials. After unpacking the rest of the shopping, she left the kitchen spotless and tidied up the living area before she walked into James's study with a duster in her hand. The cleaner came every Wednesday, but Rosa ensured the main pieces of furniture and James's study were dust-free every day.

As usual, James's cupboards and desk drawers were locked. She wiped over a green metal cabinet secured to the wall in the corner. The gun cabinet. Oh, how she hated that thing. It held a handgun, a revolver of some sort. James made her hold it once. An awful, heavy piece of cold metal, and the thought that it could kill a person caused a shiver to run down her spine. Why did James feel the need to own such a thing and install all this unnecessary security? Not for his job, surely? His clients were ordinary everyday citizens, weren't they?

As she continued to dust his study, the CCTV central console flicked onto the screen. Rosa watched Samuel, the postman, get out of his van and push the mail through the letter flap in the door. Thank goodness she'd warned Shannon never to come to Curlew House again. Her scalp tingled as she watched the post van pull away.

Finally, Rosa made herself a mug of coffee and sat outside on the terrace to drink it with a chocolate brownie that she'd treated herself to for once. James liked her to keep a trim figure, so she would be sure to bury the packing deep in the bin when she finished. Over cautious? Maybe.

Several seagulls swooped in the air above her head. She covered the brownie with her hand. Lots of people called them sky rats because they snatched food from unsuspecting hands when the chance arose, but she rather liked them. They were survivors, like her.

Rubbing the last crumbs from her fingers, she sat back, pulled out her mobile and flicked onto the half photo of her and her mum. It was now on her phone, along with a picture of the four of them; she'd snapped the image when Shannon had brought the other half of the photo to Curlew House and they'd put the two pieces together.

She studied her mum's face. A young person then, no older than Rosa was now. Her dad would've been young as well at the time. He'd remarried quickly after losing her mum, and Rosa had never forgiven him for how fast he'd moved on with his life, and the speed at which he'd no longer needed or wanted her.

She closed her phone, but the memory of her dad wouldn't leave her mind. Shannon was right; she ought to visit him and find out what he knew about the photograph. Damn it, he did hold the key to tracking down the information they wanted to know.

With a sigh, she picked up her mug and plate and went inside.

In the bedroom, she took off all her expensive pieces of jewellery and dropped them on the bedside table. Removing her normal clothes, she pulled on faded jeans and a checked shirt she used when she occasionally helped the gardener. She finished the down-beat image with scuffed trainers, a hoodie and her hair pulled back into a ponytail. She was as ready as she would ever be to pay her father a long overdue visit.

She parked in the multi-storey car park and walked, with her hoodie pulled over her face, half a mile to the Pengollan Estate and her old house. The outside paintwork and garden of her childhood home looked as if they'd seen better days. It was painful to see. Her mum had loved their tiny house and handkerchief-sized garden, spending many hours pottering around planting bulbs and other seasonal plants. Not that any of the neighbours much cared, but their cats loved the freshly turned soil. Clearly, the replacement wife had no interest in the house or the garden, and neither did her father. Rosa swallowed hard, shoved her hands into her pockets and walked up to the front door.

After she'd knocked a second time, she heard someone fiddle with the lock on the inside. Her stomach flip-flopped. The door opened. Then he stood before her.

Her dad.

Complete with a thickened waist, grey hair and receding hairline. Blooming hell, he was old. What did she expect? He would be in his sixties if her calculations were right. No doubt she looked different if his open mouth was anything to go by.

'Hello, Dad.' She was surprised by the weakness in her voice. She couldn't be getting emotional; she was here on business, not for a family reunion.

'Rosa! Bloody hell, Rosa, what ….' Her dad's voice was husky as if he smoked twenty a day. But he'd never smoked? Maybe he did now. How would she know?

'It's starting to rain. Can I come in for a few minutes?'

He opened the door wide and gestured for her to step inside. Mercifully, he didn't attempt to kiss or hug her. She kept her hands firmly in her pockets.

The first thing that struck her was that the house no longer smelt like it belonged to her mum and dad. But then, why would it? She'd loved the aroma of her childhood home: a mix of baked cakes, polish, and flowers. Now, all she could detect was fish and chips, her dad's aftershave, and dust.

With her hands still deep in her pockets, she waited while he made her a cup of tea. Awful builder's tea, but she couldn't be bothered to explain to him that she'd never taken it that way, or to ask why he hadn't remembered that. Thankfully, it looked like he was the only person at home. A meeting with the hated second wife was something she hoped to avoid at all costs.

He pushed the tea in front of her, along with a pack of biscuits. 'So, what brings you home after all these years? Not trouble, I hope.'

An involuntary bristle ran down her back. She so wanted to show him her house, her husband and children, how well she'd done for herself. But no good would come of it. Instead, she took a deep breath and counted to ten.

'I had the chance to come to Cornwall for a flying visit and thought I'd pop in to see how you are.' She took a sip of tea. Dreadful, but she took another sip to collect her thoughts. 'So, how's things?'

'Ticking on. You?'

'Same.'

A terrible silence fell between them. What happened to those days when she and her dad had chatted forever about nothing and everything? She had to get him talking to make her visit worthwhile, so she asked the question she didn't want to ask.

'How's Sue? And the baby?' She said the words without thinking before realising that 'the baby' would be at least twenty-two years old by now.

'Lily, your sister, is travelling at the moment. In Thailand for a few months, then onto Australia.' A smile lit up his eyes as he looked in the direction of a photograph on the wall of a pretty young woman in jeans and a white shirt. A pang of hurt shot through her. He used to look at her like that.

'That's good. What about Sue?'

He bent his head and stared into his empty tea-stained mug. 'We split up ages ago. A few years after you left.'

'Oh.'

'Thought that bit of news would please you. Your old man made a mistake like you often said I had. Thankfully, Sue stayed living nearby and I saw little Lily regularly.'

'A new daughter to replace me, eh?'

Her dad looked at her and shook his head. She looked away first, and it was several minutes before she said anything further.

'Do you ever think of the old times ... when Mum was alive?'

'Of course I do. What a stupid question.'

'Just wondered, that's all.'

He coughed and got up to pour himself another mug of tea. 'And what about your life now? You married? Got kids? Am I a grandfather and never knew about it?' His voice grew huskier as he spoke.

A spike of guilt ran through her, but she pushed it out of her thoughts. He was the one who'd betrayed her, the one who'd abandoned her.

'Nope. Neither.'

'Thought you would've had the sense to have found yourself a rich husband.'

Rosa's cheeks flushed with warmth. She hurriedly pulled out a tissue and pretended to blow her nose. 'Nope, as I said, I'm a free agent. Always was, always will be.'

'So, what's the real reason for your visit? You haven't bothered to see your old man for well over twenty years, so I guess it's more than a quick hello.' He looked at her scruffy jeans and faded hoodie. 'I'm not flushed, if it's money you want.'

'Nothing like that.' She cleared her throat. 'Dad, I've been thinking about Mum a lot recently, especially the day of the accident.'

'Oh yeah.'

'It was such a wonderful day with Shannon and her mum. We even got a stranger to take a photograph of us four on the beach at Marazion. It had St Michael's Mount in the background.'

'I remember it.'

'You remember it? How? It was taken with Mum's camera. I thought it had been lost in the accident.'

He shook his head. 'Three or four months after you left, and all the rigmarole around the post-mortems and other such stuff were concluded, the police returned your mother's handbag, camera and other bits that were in the car.'

Rosa's throat tightened and she had to take another sip of the awful, now cold, tea before she could answer. Her mother's personal bits and pieces. What she wouldn't give to touch and smell them again. Her eyes welled with tears that she quickly blinked away.

'Can I have the photograph, Dad? I want something of Mum, and that day was perfect.'

'You can't.'

'Can't I see it, even if you don't want to give it to me? Please. I could take a photo with my mobile. That would be enough.'

'I gave it away.'

'You gave it away?' She was shocked, even though she knew, logically, that had to have been the case.

'When? Who to?'

'Several months ago now. A journalist from one of the tabloids knocked on my door. He was writing an article on how families recovered from terrible tragedies. Wanted to hear my story.'

Rosa bit her lower lip. She wanted to shout: it happened to me as well.

'Which newspaper? What was the journalist's name?'

'Think he was called John. Not sure what paper it was.' Her dad stood, opened one of the kitchen unit drawers and pulled out a card.

'It says here his name is John Smith and he works as a freelance journalist. No newspaper name, I'm afraid.'

Rosa took the card. It was clearly a fake, one of those printed off in supermarkets or other outlets for a few quid. She began to tap the number on the card into her phone.

'Don't bother. I tried. The line's dead.'

Of course it was.

'What did he pay you?'

Her father looked at her from under his bushy grey eyebrows. 'He gave me fifty quid upfront but promised me a cheque for five hundred smackers in the post.'

'Oh, let me guess. It never arrived.'

Flipping hell, when did her dad turn into such a deadbeat who'd sell his crown jewels if someone paid him enough? She got up to go.

'Off already?'

'Sorry, we're heading back tonight, and I don't want to miss my lift.'

'Let me have your address, love.'

For a few seconds, the term of endearment he used for her and her mum when Rosa was growing up almost caused her to sob, but she checked herself and reeled off an obscure address in Clapham. He would never check it.

'If the journalist contacts you again, would you ring me?'

'I need your number,' he grunted.

She hesitated, then took the pen and piece of paper he handed her and wrote down her number. Next, she took his number and punched it into her mobile. Not so much to keep in contact with him, but in case the stalker's actions forced her to speak to him again. For now, he was yet another name to hide in her contacts list.

On the doorstep, her father touched her arm. 'I've missed you, love. Don't leave it so long next time.'

A lump formed in Rosa's throat. She nodded, then moved away from him with a final wave of her hand.

She walked down the street, shoulders hunched and head bowed in her hoodie. In her pocket, she gripped her dad's cheap biro pen between her fingers. When she turned the corner, she straightened up and walked quickly towards the car park. That was that. Probably the last time she would see her father. It had to be that way if she wanted to keep James and the life she treasured. But an uneasy sadness settled over her as she travelled along the country lanes towards Chapel Cove and her meeting with Shannon.

She waited for over half an hour, but Shannon never appeared. Rosa rang her mobile number several times, but it was dead. No service. Damn Shannon, she must have run out of battery charge. What was she playing at? Hopefully, she would contact her at some point. There was nothing else Rosa could do that day.

Back at Curlew House, Rosa read her emails and saw a message from her bank. She glanced at her watch; she had about enough time to go online to check the full missive in her personal account before she needed to prepare James's evening meal. She tapped in the password and security numbers. Her account sprang into life.

She stared at the computer screen in disbelief. The account was empty.

That wasn't possible. There had been money in the account a few days ago, and she hadn't used her card since then. Looking closer, the evidence in front of her indicated she had transferred the balance into one of James's accounts. She shook her head. It had to be a mistake. Either that or her account had been hacked. By whom? Not the stalker, surely?

She gasped.

She'd given James her bank password and security information when she'd been bedridden with the flu and he'd offered to make a couple of urgent payments on her behalf. But that was over six months ago, and he hadn't touched her account since. She put her head into her hands. Wives often shared passwords and stuff with their spouses, didn't they? But that didn't mean they could go in and move the money when they felt like it.

She groaned as she realised that James had never shared his own details with her. The only money she could access now was the household expenses account she shared with James. He would see every drop of money spent on her debit card, and even cash withdrawals – like coffee with Shannon – would be visible. She would speak to the bank but knew it wouldn't change anything.

Had James done this because he needed the money for his business? No, the amount in her account wasn't enough to bail out any company in financial trouble. Was this all about James going nuts over her spending? Yes, she'd overspent at the Atlantic Hotel that time, but hadn't she been punished enough for that? This was unfair; she was entitled to her own money. Or was it her fault again for being so stupid and running about exactly like a cheating wife would, sneaking off to secret meetings and the like? Did he think that if she had no money, she couldn't afford to have an affair? What kind of screwed-up thinking was that?

Rosa rushed out of the room, grabbed her swimming gear, and ran to the beach. Involuntary tremors scurried over her body. She plunged into the cold water and swam up and down the Helford River with fierce strokes.

Her heart hammered against her rib cage. Stupid, stupid, and stupid. The words beat a tattoo inside her head as she swam. Eventually, she flopped onto the beach. Exhaustion had finally pushed the demons away.

After a while, she got to her feet and trudged back to Curlew House. James would be home soon, and she hadn't even started to prepare the evening meal yet.

17

Shannon no longer had any sense of time. The heavy rain and the thick gorse bushes surrounding the car had turned days into nights, and the previous night had been lit up by flashes of lightning again. Her wheezy chest and cough caused her to drift in and out of sleep. How long had she been here, hidden in the Carnmarth Quarry? She didn't know. The phone had died ages ago so she couldn't check the date or time. She needed to get help, but how? Who would she ask?

A strangulated cough caused her to suck hard for breath. Nausea sat like a rock in the pit of her stomach. She coughed again and blackness filled her vision. Was it nighttime already?

She woke with a jolt. Rain splashed onto her face. Rough hands grabbed her. She fought the attacker away with what strength she had left. Her fist hit flesh.

'God dammit, Shannon.' A gruff male voice bounced around the interior of the car. 'We're only trying to help you.'

Shannon fought harder. 'Leave me alone.' Flu-like pains shot through her head.

'Shannon. Stop. It's Trevor. You're sick. I'm here to help you.' He gripped her arms and peered at her so close his nose nearly touched hers. 'Trevor. And Vic.'

Trevor and Vic. They'd come to help her.

Black spots flecked her vision and darkness returned. This time she knew it wasn't night.

Did she float, or did someone lift her out of the car? Then she was sprawled against the back seat of another car with strong arms holding her upright as the vehicle bumped over ruts and dips. Later, more sounds and scenes. A female voice asked her ... what? That image drifted into another one. A strange male voice. Hands stripping away her wet clothes. She struggled but to no avail. What did these visions mean? Sometimes, when she'd had awful nightmares in the past and she'd gone round and round in circles trying to solve a problem or escape from an unknown danger, she'd known that it wasn't real and would wake herself. Why couldn't she do that now?

Darkness took over once again.

Pins and needles in her arm woke her. Her head thumped like she was suffering from the worst hangover ever. She forced her eyelids to open over gritty eyeballs. Soft brown eyes stared straight at her. She opened her mouth to scream but nothing came out. Her throat felt like sandpaper, her lips cracked and dry. The brown eyes blinked. A black head with a white strip down the centre tilted to the left, then to the right before it rested once more on her numb arm.

Shannon moved her head a little to get a closer look. Trudie, Trevor's old sheepdog, blinked again.

On a sofa opposite, two cats were curled into one big fluffy ball. A fire blasted heat into the room. She was in Trevor's living room, with all his clutter and his granite fireplace. But how?

She lifted her hand to stroke Trudie and a spasm in her chest caused her to cough. A moan spilt from her lips.

'Good to see you awake, sleepy head.' Trevor walked across the room. In his hand, he held a glass of water and a metallic strip of pills.

Trevor,' she croaked.

'Don't bother to speak for now. Swallow this and take it easy. You need to rest.' He punched out a large red and yellow capsule and handed it to her. 'Antibiotics. Four times a day. You've got a bad chest infection.'

'But ...'

He thrust the medication at her again, along with the water. She took both items and swallowed, then winced when one of the blankets heaped on top of her slipped down and she realised that she was clothed in someone else's pyjamas. Dear God, had Trevor undressed her?

'Before you say anything, my cousin, Sheila from Trebarvah Farm, came over and helped.' He waved his hand aimlessly. 'You know, with all the personal stuff.'

Shannon shook her head in an effort to clear her confusion.

'Bloody hell, Shannon, you were in a right state when Vic and I found you. We didn't know what to do, so I called Sheila. She's a community nurse at the surgery that covers Cribba Village.'

'I know her. Done ... done occasional decorating work for her ...' Shannon paused to draw in a breath.

'Sheila called one of the doctors. He suggested we request an ambulance, but I knew you wouldn't want that if it could be avoided.'

She nodded.

'After some persuasion, and probably a great deal of bribery on Sheila's part, the doctor came out to Carnmarth and prescribed you a course of antibiotics; injections to start, followed by tablets now you're awake. Vic shot off like a madman to get them for you.'

Trevor threw two more logs onto the already roaring fire and sat on the edge of the other sofa. The cats immediately uncurled, stretched, and moved onto his lap. He leaned back and closed his eyes for a few seconds, his hand stroking one of the cat's ears.

'How long have ... I been here?' She swallowed.

'It's Wednesday afternoon. We found you on Monday.'

'Wednesday?'

'Why didn't you tell me you had nowhere to go when you left Vic's?' He shuffled further back into his seat and the cats clung to his legs until he was settled. 'If only you'd told me on the day of the fire what trouble you were in, I'd never have turned you away. Bloody hell, I had to wait for Ada to tell me something was wrong and that you were in danger.'

'Ada?'

'Ada Martin.'

Shannon's heart raced. What had Mrs Martin told Trevor? She couldn't talk to Trevor about her visit to Mrs Martin's or any of the other stuff that had happened to her. Besides, she had a more pressing concern: she needed a pee. Weakness and embarrassment rolled over her. How? Where?

'Trevor. I … I need the loo.'

He nodded, lifted the cats back onto the sofa and got to his feet.

'I'll help you.' He gripped her arm and she rose to her feet. Her legs shook like jelly and her knees buckled. He wrapped his arm around her waist. 'Lean on me, unless you want me to carry you?'

She shook her head as hard as she dared.

He grinned. 'There's an old shower room through here.'

He helped her from the living room down a short corridor. Various wax jackets and other coats hung on hooks along the wall. Wellington boots and old footwear lay in heaps underneath. The corridor led to the backyard and garden. Thankfully, Trevor stopped before he got to the outside door.

'Here it is. Nothing fancy so don't expect too much. Give me a shout when you're ready to come out.' He turned to walk back to the living room. 'Don't go locking the door. I don't want to smash it down if you faint or whatever.'

She leaned against the closed door and looked around while she gained the energy to walk across the room to the toilet. Trevor was right, the shower room and toilet were far from fancy. The place looked like municipal toilets did in the sixties, with old chipped white tiles from floor to ceiling. But while the chunky white washbasin and toilet were old-fashioned, everything was at least clean, and the shower was modern enough. Shannon smiled. As far as she was concerned, this was what luxury looked like.

Back on the sofa, wrapped in her blanket, she let Trevor place a tray on her lap. A bowl of Heinz tomato and basil soup steamed from a bowl. A warm roll with butter sat on a side plate.

'Eat. Please.' He put a soup spoon into her hand. 'Sheila will call in soon and she'll tear a strip into me if you haven't eaten anything. She's been coming several times a day to check your vitals or whatever.'

Tears welled and threatened to roll down her face. She blinked and took a sip of soup. Her stomach spasmed. For a moment, she thought she would be sick, but then it settled, and she took another sip.

How did …. how did you find me?'

'Ada. She rang me early on Monday morning. She was worried about you after your visit. She'd been trying your phone, but you'd obviously run out of charge.' He rubbed the stubble on his chin. 'I said I thought you were okay and that you would've found someone to stay with. But she insisted that something was wrong. Then she told me she'd withdrawn an offer of work at Primrose Cottage because she'd been threatened.'

'Oh.'

'Oh? Is that all you can say? Bloody hell, Shannon, I was worried sick and so was Vic. We looked everywhere for you. Laybys and farm lanes. I even walked the footpath route to Carnmarth Quarry but couldn't see you.' Trevor poked the fire with fierce strokes. Sparks and flames flared up the chimney. 'It was Vic who insisted we drove over there and searched all the corners.' He poked the fire again. 'You could've died in that hellhole if Ada hadn't rung.'

A sob escaped from Shannon's mouth and, finally, tears rolled down her face.

Trevor got to his feet quickly, took the tray and placed it on a side table. Trudie sat up and eyed the bread roll. 'Ger off,' Trevor growled at the dog, who lay down and stretched out in front of the fire again. 'Hey, come on, Shannon, there's no need to cry and go all girly on me. You know I don't know how to cope with that sort of stuff.' He let out a wobbly laugh.

She tried to force a smile, but the tears kept flowing, and then she started to hiccup. 'You said you couldn't have trouble.'

'I know. I know.' He ran his hand through his hair. 'It's just that I don't like not knowing what problems might come my way. I can handle it when I know what I'm dealing with, and you wouldn't tell me.'

More tears flowed and she wiped her nose on the back of her hand.

Trevor left the room and returned with a roll of toilet paper. 'Here, use this.'

She tore off several sheets and blew her nose. 'Thanks.'

'Talk to me now. Tell me what's been happening.'

She bowed her head and blew her nose again. She couldn't, she simply couldn't.

'Ada's told me what she knows. Is it to do with the ripped photograph that Zach said he saw? And the caravan fire? Did that have something to do with it as well?'

129

A knot formed in Shannon's stomach. She wanted to get up and leave, but she didn't have the strength to stand. She leaned her head back against the sofa. What had she got to lose if she told Trevor everything? She'd got nothing anyway, and if he told her to go, so what? She expected nothing else.

She turned her gaze onto him. 'You don't want to know who I am.'

'You're Shannon Reid. So what?'

'A terrible thing happened in my past. I'm the Shannon–'

'You're the Shannon Reid who was involved in a terrible car crash years ago. I believe your mother and others were killed at the time.'

Shannon gasped. 'But ...'

'But what? You thought I didn't know. I'm not a total country bumpkin. I generally check out who wants to live at Carnmarth. A quick look at the computer tends to give me what I want. Failing that, Vic knows most things that's ever happened in Cornwall.'

Another sob spluttered from Shannon. She wiped her eyes with yet more toilet paper. 'How come you never said anything?'

'Why would I? It didn't affect your living here and you paid your rent on time ... well, mostly.' A grin flashed across his face.

'I caused the accident,' she whispered.

'Really? Were you driving?'

'No.'

'Thought not. So, tell me, why would you think you were at fault when two other adults were in the car and you were no more than a child?'

His words floored her. Had Trevor really said it wasn't her fault?

He nodded at her. 'Come on, tell me all of it.'

She took a deep breath and told Trevor everything that had happened in recent weeks.

'This Rosa, why didn't she help you?'

'It's complicated. She's got her own problems.'

'Doesn't sound like much of a friend to me.' He stood. 'You're exhausted. Let's talk more when you're stronger. In the meantime, Sheila will be here soon, so start getting that soup down your throat or she'll skin me alive. I'll warm it again if you want?'

'It's fine.' She took another spoonful and a bite of the bread roll. 'Thanks. You and Sheila ... Vic ... have been so kind to me.'

'You know a lot of people care about you and have been asking after you. Vic and Zach, to name a few.'

'What did Zach want to know?' A muscle twitched under her eye.

'Just how you were doing. Like I said, people care about you. My ear has been ringing every day with Ada on the phone.'

She didn't want the tears to spill again, so she changed the subject. On the sideboard stood a framed photo of a young Trevor with two small children. They all smiled broadly for the camera.

'You all look very happy. Who are they?'

For a second or two, he hesitated. 'They're my children.'

'What?' she blurted out. 'You never said.'

'Guess we both have our secrets.' He got to his feet. Trudie did the same.

'Trevor?'

'Yes?'

'What happens now?'

'You stay on the sofa until you're better. After that, well, we'll take it from there.'

She fought to stop the threatened tears from spilling over again. 'Thanks,' she said.

Trevor reached the door leading to the hallway and the kitchen.

'Trevor?'

'What now?'

'Did you check Zach's background when he arrived at Carnmarth?'

He frowned. 'Couldn't find anything on him, but he seemed a decent enough bloke, so I let him stay. He pays his rent and keeps to himself around me, which is all I want.'

'Would you mind if I used your computer?' She nodded towards the office desk and computer set up in the corner of the living room.

'When you're better.' Trevor pointed at the cats that had now settled on the sofa next to Shannon's thigh. 'The black one is Sooty, and the tortoiseshell is Tootsie. If they're a nuisance, push them off. They should be outside catching rats anyway.'

She smiled. Trevor acted like a hard man when really, he was nothing but an old softy.

He left the room and quietly closed the door. She yawned. Her eyelids felt heavy. Yes, she needed to rest, but as soon as she was well enough, she would continue her research into Zach. She ought to ring Rosa, who would've turned up for their meeting on Monday and wondered where she was, but she didn't have the energy. Besides, she had no idea what had happened to her phone. It was probably a goner in the rain.

Her eyes flickered and she snuggled down under the blanket to sleep. Was Trevor right when he said that the accident wasn't her fault? After their talk, it seemed absurd that she'd not told him the truth when she first arrived nearly five years ago. But then, was he the right person to advise her, considering he'd got his own secrets in the shape of two children that no one had ever mentioned?

Warm, and with food in her belly, she drifted into a dreamless sleep. But not before she realised that everything in her life had suddenly got a whole lot better.

18

Rosa barely got out of third gear as she drove along the twisty lanes. She'd left Cribba Village fifteen minutes ago and had expected to reach her destination by now. Just as she was about to pull over and reset the Satnav, it broke into life: *You have reached your destination.* She pulled the vehicle to a stop at the entrance to a long, rutted lane, and hesitated. The last thing she needed was a dent or scratch to the BMW's bodywork, followed by a long inquisition from James. Was it worth the risk of driving up this dreadful track or would it be best to park the car and walk? She glanced down at her feet, clad in a pair of expensive shoes; high-heeled and in pristine condition. She sighed, released the handbrake, and steered the vehicle slowly up the lane.

In the farmyard, she got out and looked around at the dismal buildings. So, this was Carnmarth Farm. What a dump. It no doubt suited Shannon, but it left Rosa cold. How lucky was she to live at Curlew House with its bright riverside views.

An ugly terrier dog rushed up to her and snapped at the air around her ankles. A man walking across the yard stopped and turned in her direction.

'Hello,' Rosa called out as she stepped tentatively through whatever the hell it was that dotted the ground.

The man, ill-kempt and rough compared to James, now stood with his hand shading his eyes.

'Hello,' she called again.

'Yes,' he grunted.

'I need to find Shannon Reid. I believe she used to live here.'

'Might have.'

Rosa searched her brain for his name. Shannon had let slip the names of Carnmarth Farm and the landlord at one of their Chapel Cove meetings, but she couldn't remember his name. Travis? Trevor? Yes, Trevor sounded more like it.

'Are you Trevor?'

'Might be.'

She gritted her teeth and took a deep breath. 'Can't you tell me where she moved to? Or at least, how I can contact her? Her phone seems to have died.'

'She'll contact you if she wants to.'

She tried another approach. 'I'm Rosa.' She glared down at the scruffy terrier that still yapped at her feet. 'I'm an old friend of Shannon's.'

'A friend? Like someone she ought to have been able to call on when she was in trouble?'

Her stomach cramped. 'Has she been hurt? Please tell me she's okay.'

'Damn it, Whisky, leave the woman alone.' Trevor turned his back on her. 'Best follow me, if you can keep up on them things you're wearing.'

A few minutes later, Trevor opened the door into a cluttered living room. A fire burned at the far end and, on one of the sofas, a small pale figure lay huddled asleep under a blanket. Rosa gasped at the sight.

Trevor touched Shannon's shoulder. 'You've got a visitor.'

Shannon's eyes opened, then blinked. She sat up quickly. 'Rosa! What are you doing here? How did you find me?'

'Good God, Shannon, you look awful.'

'She's been very poorly. Still recovering, so don't go tiring her out.' Trevor's gruff voice filled the air, then he waved his hand at Rosa. 'Help yourself to a seat. Coffee?'

'Oh … Yes, please, that would be lovely.'

'It's only instant. Best I can do, I'm afraid. Same for you, Shannon?'

'Thanks.'

Rosa stared at the now closed door. 'Not exactly friendly, is he?'

'Don't be fooled by his exterior. He's an old softy, through and through. Been really kind to me.'

'What the hell happened? I've been trying to call you since Monday when you didn't turn up for our meeting.'

'Like Trevor said, I've been sick.' Shannon then went on to tell her about living in the car, not getting the promised job with Mrs Martin, and how Trevor and Vic had found her.

Rosa bowed her head. What an awful person she was. She'd known Shannon was in trouble and had done nothing to help her. 'I'm sorry,' she whispered.

The silence was broken when the door banged open. Trevor came in with a tray overflowing with mugs of black coffee, a kilo bag of sugar, an open bottle of milk, and a packet of chocolate digestive biscuits. He placed the tray on a side table and handed Shannon a glass of water and a pill.

'Help yourselves. Some of us have got work to do.' He turned to Shannon. 'Don't you go over doing it now, or you'll have me and Sheila to answer to.'

He left, and the room fell quiet once again.

'How come you're here on a Saturday? I thought you had the children at the weekends.'

'Marcus and Freya are on a playdate and James is away on business today, something he does once or twice a month.'

Shannon leaned over and put another log on the fire. Sparks danced up the chimney. Rosa took the chance to look around the living room. Blooming hell, what was with the clutter? And everything was so well-worn and old. She leaned back into the sofa, which was surprisingly comfortable, and let the warmth of the fire seep into her body. She had to admit the place did have a homely feel. Fleetingly, a jolt of envy threatened to burst the bubble of pride she'd always felt about living in Curlew House.

'What's so urgent that you needed to track me down?' Shannon asked.

'I was worried. Besides, we had planned to catch up and exchange information.' She ran her hand through her hair. 'I feel as if I'm waiting on a knife edge for the next awful thing to happen. Don't you feel the same?'

Shannon shrugged.

'Now that this Mrs Martin has been threatened, it's clear that whoever is doing this hasn't stopped.' Rosa added milk and sugar to her coffee and stirred. 'Did you find anything out about that bloke you were concerned about? The one that was bothering you.'

'His name's Zach Smith. I spent yesterday on Trevor's computer searching Google, Facebook, DuckDuckGo, and heaven knows what for him. Found sweet F.A. So, I've started to search under different names like Zackery Smyth and Smithson, but no luck so far.

'Blast it,' Rosa said. 'I'd hoped we could've solved this problem quickly.'

She picked up a couple of chocolate biscuits. James would disapprove but she was desperate for a sugar fix.

A black cat slunk into the room and jumped onto Rosa's lap. She ran her fingers through the soft, shiny fur. Suddenly, she was blasted with memories of Titch, the family cat she'd had when she was a child. She lifted the animal from her lap to the other side of the sofa.

'Have you found out anything more about Paul Whittaker?' Shannon asked.

'I checked loads of online sites for old newspaper articles and Paul Whittaker was admitted to Treliske Hospital first and then quickly transferred to Derriford Hospital in Plymouth. From what I can tell, he stayed there for a few months before he was discharged.' Rosa licked a smear of chocolate from her fingertips. 'Presumably to his home address, although I couldn't find anything to confirm that.'

'Likely he's married and living elsewhere by now.' Shannon rubbed her neck. 'I've got a friend who might be able to help with the discharge address. Any address, even if it is old, might be useful.'

'I do have some other interesting news. I've found out that there was an older Whittaker brother called Stephen.'

'What? There was no mention of another brother or son in the *West Briton* articles we were sent.'

'Doesn't look like much was said about him at the time. I nearly missed the little bit that was published when I was digging around for info on Paul. Apparently, this Stephen travelled separately to Cornwall by train. From Nottingham. He was at university there.'

'Shit.' Shannon's eyes widened. 'Does that mean we should consider the possibility that Stephen could be the stalker, along with Paul?'

'Looks like it. The way I see it, either one of them, or both of them together, could be gunning for us.' Rosa shuddered. Jesus, the two Whittaker brothers and that Zach fella were all contenders for the 'stalker-of- the-year' title. She rushed on. 'I also gleaned from the same article that all the Whittakers were travelling to Cornwall to attend a family wedding the following day.'

'I remember that. I have nightmares, thinking about what happened to that family on what should've been a happy weekend.' Shannon chewed her fingernail. 'Don't you ever think about what we did?'

Rosa sucked her breath in. 'What *we* did? It was *your* mother who was driving.'

Shannon glared at Rosa. 'You know as well as I do that we were acting pretty silly in the back of that car. Fooling around and giggling. You pushed me and I knocked the back of my mum's head. She wobbled and then … well, the car crashed.'

Rosa got to her feet, walked to the window, and stood with her back to the room. 'You're being *pretty silly* right now. Your mum was driving way too fast. Simple as that.'

Shannon grabbed a toilet roll from the side table, yanked several sheets off and wiped her eyes. 'I still don't understand how I never twigged that Mum took drugs. You were always more attuned at spotting a drug taker than I ever was. Did you suspect anything?'

Rosa's head throbbed. She returned to the sofa and pinched the bridge of her nose. 'For God's sake, how would I know? It was over two decades ago. Frankly, I haven't the time or energy to get into a deep, meaningful conversation with you about why your mother took drugs.' She brushed crumbs from her trousers. 'What's the point? We can't change what happened. As far as I'm concerned, the past is the past. And, if you want my opinion, you should leave it there as well.'

'That's what Trevor said.'

'The man talks some sense then. Take it from me, it's far better to get on with life. People have secrets. We kept secrets from our mums, and your mum kept her drug-taking a secret from you.' Rosa blinked several times as she spoke. All this talk about the crash and drugs was making her jumpy.

'Talking of the past,' she said. 'I paid Dad a visit.'

'At Pengollan?'

Rosa nodded and then gave Shannon the low-down on her visit and the so-called journalist who'd called on her dad and taken the photograph away with him.

'I tried to trace the journalist but couldn't find him. The whole thing was clearly a ruse to get a photo or whatever to stalk us with.'

'Did you ask him about my necklace?'

'I didn't go there to grill him about a stupid, cheap necklace.'

'Well, you should've,' Shannon snapped. 'Honestly, Rosa, you are so cruel and insensitive at times. I would've asked if the shoe was on the other foot.'

'I'm sure you would've.' Rosa got to her feet. 'I need to go. Marcus and Freya will be home soon. And James.' She pulled her phone from her pocket. 'How can I contact you? Does this place have a number?'

'Vic found my mobile and dried it out. He's charging it as we speak.'

'Good, the same number as before then.' She moved to the door.

A cow bellowed in the yard.

Rosa flinched, hesitated, and looked at Shannon, who adjusted her blanket and then rested her hand on the cat's back. Through the window, Rosa could see cows ambling past her car. There was no way she could go outside.

'Are you staying at Carnmarth now?' she said, playing for time.

'While I recover.'

'And then?'

'I'm not sure after that.'

'Right.' She struggled to think of something else to say, but they'd pretty much covered it all and Shannon seemed content to stroke the cat and soak up the silence.

140

At last, the herd moved away from her BMW, leaving her a clear exit.

'Must go,' she said. 'We'll keep in touch.'

Rosa turned out of Carnmarth and headed toward the Helford River and Curlew House. Thoughts rattled around her head. Shannon might be frail physically, but she was certainly feistier than usual. Was it Trevor's influence that had made her more confident and challenging? Or maybe it was the antibiotics?

She drove into Curlew House, and as she soaked up the waterside view, she released the breath she hadn't realised she was holding. This was her home, the place where she could forget about the starkness of Carnmarth Farm.

She pulled on the handbrake and reached for the door handle. Her hand shook. A wave of fear and anxiety that had threatened to erupt for days consumed her. Her head dropped into her hands. Loud sobs wracked her body. She couldn't shake off Shannon's words that she should accept some responsibility for the accident that had killed both their mums.

Finally, she sat up and rested her head back against the seat. She had buried what had happened that day, along with her part in it. Maybe she did need to acknowledge that. Maybe she should even tell Shannon.

Her mobile rang, abruptly interrupting her thoughts.

James.

She got out of the car as she answered his call and hurried into the house. He was on his way home, and she had to prepare a meal, shower, and change her clothes before he, and the children, arrived.

Damn Shannon and her talk of the past. James was all that mattered. She loved him. He was the future.

19

Shannon pushed the blankets to one side, got to her feet and stretched. A couple of tremors ran through her body, but she could breathe in and out for the first time in many days without the accompanying wheezy cough. She reached for her mobile phone. A few more scratches than a week ago, but it worked again, thanks to Vic. She tapped out a message to Nina even though it was the middle of the night in California and there wouldn't be a reply for several hours.

The smell of lemon filled the air as she washed her breakfast dishes. And Trevor's. Not that he had asked her to, but it seemed surly and impolite not to. Her hands itched to clear and wipe down the worktops, but she forced herself to stop. Trevor lived with clutter and had done for some time. The place was clean enough, but there was so much stuff; stuff that she would've chucked away years ago. Still, what did she know after living in a tiny caravan for five years?

In the living room, she grabbed a pair of jeans and a thick sweater. Half an hour later, she returned freshly showered, her hair hanging in damp waves down her back. She dried it in front of the open fire, then reached for her coat, woolly hat and boots, and tugged them on.

The fresh air on her face was bliss after being inside for a week. She leaned against the garden wall while she sucked in one lungful of cleansing air after another, then made her way to one of the fields.

Trevor stood surrounded by sheep, several of which had newly born lambs at their side.

She came up next to him. 'Anything I can do to help?'

He jerked around. 'Should you be outside yet? The sun might be shining, but that east wind is bitterly cold.'

'I'm fine. It's warm enough and it feels marvellous to be in the fresh air. Besides, I've finished the course of antibiotics. Sheila called in before I'd even got up for breakfast to check me out. The chest infection has gone.' She pushed her hands into her pockets. 'I'm ready and willing to work. Need to get back on my feet and out of your hair.'

A knot formed in her stomach as she spoke the words. He hadn't said anything about her leaving. Or staying, come to that. To be honest, she didn't want the conversation, but ignoring it didn't mean it shouldn't happen.

'You could check out the flock down in the bottom corner. See if any of them is about to drop a lamb. If they look in trouble, give me a yell.'

Shannon ambled across the field. Fern followed her. The other sheepdogs remained with Trevor. The sheep were fine. In the past few minutes, one ewe had given birth to twins, but the babies were up and searching for milk already as their mum licked them dry; a welcoming rumble bubbled in the animal's throat as she did so.

Shannon turned around and came face to face with a big ewe, her tummy round and large. The animal stamped her foot at Fern and Shannon instructed her to stay back. The dog circled them both, then lay down several feet away, her eyes never leaving the pregnant ewe.

Shannon spoke softly to the sheep. 'What are you fussing about, you daft thing?'

The animal took a step towards her. The sheep's black face, dark eyes, and Roman nose gave her a superior look. Shannon bent over and whispered silly words of endearment to the creature. With their noses almost touching, Shannon could feel the animal's warm, grassy breath on her face. The mid-morning sun warmed the back of her head. A fizz of happiness ran through her.

'Bloody hell, Shannon, are you kissing that animal?'

Shannon quickly straightened up, but the sheep remained by her side. 'Of course not. I was checking that her eyes were clear and that she was okay. You know, a proper health check.'

'Yeah. Right. I told you before that the animals on Carnmarth aren't pets.' Trevor came up to the sheep, tucked one arm around her neck and ran his hand over her distended belly.

'What's this one called?' asked Shannon.

'I don't name what'll end up on somebody's plate.'

The animal snorted.

'That said, this here is Betsy, one of my best ewes.'

A laugh tumbled from Shannon's mouth.

Trevor grinned. 'Betsy was hand-reared after her mother died. She's a bit special. Guess she'll be around for some time.' Trevor stroked the animal's ear and then stepped quickly aside as if to illustrate that he didn't fuss his sheep. 'Were the ones in the corner all okay?'

'A couple of new lambs, but they were feeding when I left, and the mum looked well.'

Trevor made for the gate in the hedge. 'There's a few more in the next field I need to inspect. I'll bring them into this meadow. It'll make it easier.'

Shannon followed him.

After all the animals had been checked, Trevor stood and cast a final look over his flock. 'I reckon it's time for lunch. You've been out for more than two hours. That's enough.'

Back at the farmhouse, he rested his elbows on the kitchen table and munched on what could only be called a brick sandwich: two huge chunks of fresh crusty bread with a hunk of cheese and pickle oozing from both sides. A large slice of fruit cake, baked by Sheila, lay on another plate. Shannon had the same meal as Trevor but in normal portions.

The chatter flowed between them easily enough, so she took a breath and said, 'Do you ever see your children?'

Trevor stopped chewing and stared at her.

'Well,' Shannon pushed back her shoulders and looked at him, 'I've told you a lot about me. Thought it was time you said a bit about yourself.' She took a bite of her sandwich. 'Since we're sharing food, and that's what people do when eating. Chat, that is.'

'So you say.' He took a huge slurp of tea, swallowed and reached again for the chunky sandwich.

'Well?' Shannon nodded at him. 'Go on.'

'Hell's bells, don't you ever give up?' He dropped his half-eaten lunch onto his plate and leaned back against his chair. 'No, I don't,' he eventually said.

'No, you don't what? No, you don't see them? No, you don't ring them? No, you don't ever contact them?'

Trudie's old sheepdog snores filled the silence.

Finally, Trevor cleared his throat. 'The latter.'

'Why?'

'Bloody hell, Shannon, you're just like the kids were when they were young. Why this? Why that?'

'Bet you miss it?'

'I do, except they aren't kids anymore. They're in their twenties.'

'Blimey, you might even be a granddad.' The image of Trevor gently stroking Betsy's ear came into her mind. 'You'd make a good granddad.'

A flash of pain crossed his face.

'What are your kids called?'

'Daniel and Carla.'

'What happened?'

'Oh, the usual. Me and Ali married too young. Had kids too quickly. She wasn't from farming stock, or even a country girl, so it was all a bit of a shock to her. She hated the quiet, the smell, the animals.' He reached for his mug but didn't pick it up. 'In the end, I guess, she hated me.'

'I'm sure that's not true. You were the father of her kids.'

'Didn't stop her running off with one of the workmen. The bastard took her *and* my kids.'

'Oh.'

Trevor shoved his chair back. The dogs by the Aga got to their feet and fixed their eyes on his face.

'There's obviously more to tell?'

'Yeah, but that's all you're getting today.'

She nodded at him.

He raised his eyebrows in response, reached for his outdoor coat and slipped his feet into the wellington boots he'd abandoned by the front door earlier.

'No need for you to come out again.'

'Have I annoyed you? I don't want to be a nuisance.'

His face creased up. 'Did I say you were?'

'I'm better now. Should I start looking for somewhere else to live? I can't stay sleeping on your sofa.'

Trevor stared at her for a moment, then shook his wellington boots off. 'Come with me.'

They made their way through the living room into the small passageway that led to the back garden. She stood with the door to the shower room on one side and a ton of old boots, shoes and coats on the other wall. Trevor pushed several coats and an assortment of footwear to one side until he exposed a door.

He rapped his knuckles on the frame. 'This here room is full of Ali's stuff, the kids' toys, and a load of other rubbish. Old now, and a load of junk, I guess.' He turned to go. 'If you want to clear it out and get rid of it all, you can use the room for yourself. Paint it up. The heating should work. It used to be the kids' playroom, a happy room once, but ...'

'I don't know what to say.'

'Try yes. Or no.'

'Yes. Oh, yes, please. I'll pay you rent so it's all above board and the like.'

'What, pay intermittently, like before?' Trevor laughed. He had a good laugh. It made his eyes crinkle. 'Besides, you haven't seen the room yet. Could be full of mice and other crap for what I know. Haven't opened the door in years.'

'I'll fix it up.'

'I'm sure you will.' He strode down the passageway. 'Got animals to feed.' At the living room door, he stopped with his back to her. 'I'll stump up for a new bed and a bit of carpet and curtains, seeing as you'll be paying rent.' He closed the door and left Shannon alone in the corridor.

She shook her head and thought how comfortable it had been chatting to Trevor, the man she'd hardly said a word to in the previous five years. Momentarily surprised, she realised it was a good feeling.

Her mobile phone rang and broke into her thoughts.

'Hello, my lovely. I've been worried sick about you. You've not been answering my calls.'

'Sorry, Nina, my phone got damaged and ... well, it's a long story.' She didn't feel the need to saddle her friend with all her troubles over the last few weeks.

'You're okay though? You had an awful cold the last time we spoke. Hope that dreadful landlord is sorting out the heating in your caravan like a proper landlord should?'

'Trevor's been alright. Kind, in fact.'

'Has he had a personality transplant or something?'

Shannon laughed. Nina always made her feel better. 'I got a chest infection and–'

'Are you okay?'

'Yes, yes, it was only a little thing, but Trevor helped me out, you know? Anyway, how are things with you? How come you're ringing me in the middle of the night?'

'Mia's picked up a cough from somewhere. Nothing serious, just keeping us all awake, so I came down to make her a lemon and honey drink. I saw your text and phoned straight away. The text said you wanted my help?'

'It's a big favour.'

'Yeah, go on.'

'One of the people hurt in the car accident was–'

'You still having problems with that troublemaker?' Nina butted in.

'A bit, but nothing for you to worry about. Rosa and I are sorting it.'

'Rosa? Didn't you think she might be the stalker?'

'Turned out she'd been sent the same stuff as me. So, we've called a sort of truce. We need to work together to find out who's getting at us.'

'How can I help?'

'One of the sons was called Paul Whittaker. He was injured in the accident. It seems like he was admitted to Treliske Hospital and quickly moved to Derriford Hospital. He was discharged several months later. Any chance you can find out the address?'

'Gee whiz, not sure if I can from here. Even if I could, the Data Protection heavies would come down on me like a ton of bricks.'

'Oh.' Disappointment shot through Shannon even though she knew it was an outside chance that Nina could help. And she didn't want to put her friend's job with the

NHS in jeopardy; she would need it when she returned to Cornwall later in the year.

'It was a long shot anyway. Chances are he's married and living in Timbuktu or the like.' Shannon tried to laugh.

'Mmm – let me think. Yes, there's a fella I might be able to ask. Someone who owes me a favour.' She chuckled. 'He works in the section where a peek at an old record wouldn't arouse any suspicions. Let me take the details of this Paul guy.'

When the call ended, Shannon opened the door to what Trevor was promising could be her new home. She immediately began coughing. The smell of stale air, dust and goodness knows what coated her throat. She slammed the door shut before the stuff tumbled out into the passageway. Weariness rolled over her. She'd had more than enough exercise and excitement for one day. A cup of tea and a sit down was what she needed.

Settled in a comfortable chair by the Aga, she stroked Trudie's head with one hand and picked up a farming magazine from a pile on the table with the other. Two pages in, her eyes fluttered, then closed.

She woke with a start and glanced down at her mobile phone. Nina again.

'Hi, my lovely. You sound sleepy?'

Shannon looked at the clock on the wall. 'Blimey, I nodded off for over two hours.'

'You obviously needed it.' The line grew silent for a few moments. 'I've found out the information you asked for.'

'That's great.'

Nina's voice grew soft. 'It might not be what you want to hear.'

'Go on.' Shannon's heart raced. Please don't let Paul Whittaker be dead.

'It seems that Paul Whittaker's physical injuries were more severe than you thought. He was permanently disabled.'

'Oh, God, no.'

'I'm sorry, my lovely, that's not all.'

A wave of nausea rolled over Shannon. She clutched the arm of the chair and waited for Nina to go on.

'He also suffered a brain injury.'

A sob escaped from Shannon's mouth. 'No, that can't be true. He was discharged home.'

'I asked my friend to double-check the information.'

'But ... but the newspapers said ...'

'The newspapers don't know everything, and, you know, they don't really follow up stuff once it becomes old news.'

'Oh, my God,' Shannon said again.

'My friend did find out that Paul had been discharged to a specialist nursing home for people with severe mental and physical disabilities. He couldn't delve further and get the address, but he does know it was somewhere in Surrey.'

'The family lived there before the accident.' Shannon's voice trembled as the old, familiar feelings of guilt and shame raged through her body.

'Sorry, I can't ask my friend to find out any more. I can't risk him getting into trouble.'

'I know,' she croaked. 'Thanks.'

'No problem, my lovely. Speak soon.'

The phone went dead.

Shannon steadied her breathing, then punched in another contact. The call was answered immediately.

'I can't speak now. James is out on the patio, and the doors are open. Don't ring back.'

'Rosa. Wait. It's urgent.'

'What is it?' she hissed. 'Be quick.'

Another sob escaped from Shannon's mouth. 'We did a terrible thing.'

'For fuck's sake, Shannon, not this again. I'm hanging up.'

'No,' Shannon shouted down the phone. 'You get your arse over to Carnmarth first thing tomorrow morning. There's stuff I need to tell you. Things we need to sort.'

'James is coming.'

'Tomorrow morning, you hear.'

'Okay,' Rosa snapped before she cut Shannon's call off.

20

Rosa squirted antiseptic spray along the worktops, her jaw clenched. Why had James decided that today of all days he'd linger over breakfast? She glanced up at the wall clock. Only 9:15 a.m., but Shannon had demanded that she came to Carnmarth first thing, and she didn't want another phone call from her. Could she make an excuse about needing supplies for the larder and leave? Or should she wait until James had gone?

The doorbell rang. Shit. Don't let that be Shannon.

She hurried along the hallway and yanked the door open.

Mike Spencer grinned at her. 'Good morning, Mrs Trevail. Is your husband in?'

'Is he expecting you? He's about to leave for the office.' Her voice was more curt than usual, but the last thing she needed was for the owner of Dunmere Security Systems to delay James even further.

'I won't be long. Don't need to see him. A simple check to ensure that the security systems we installed are all working as they should be.'

James appeared at the end of the hallway. 'Hello, Mike. Nice to see you. Come on in.'

Rosa clenched her jaw. She took a step aside so Mike Spencer could enter.

'Are you sure we've not met before, Mrs Trevail?' He peered through narrowed eyes as he drew level with her, an odd smirk on his face. '*Tall Trees* nightclub in Newquay? *William IV* pub in Truro? I'm sure I recognise you from back in the day.'

The knot in Rosa's chest that had formed when Shannon phoned her the previous evening, tightened. She shook her head vigorously. 'Not me.'

James clapped a hand on Mike's shoulder and laughed. 'Darling, it seems like you have a Cornish doppelganger.' He turned to Mike. 'I'm delighted with the system. Come and see for yourself.'

She gulped a glass of cold water at the kitchen sink to calm her racing heart. A bead of sweat trickled down her forehead. After her mum had died, she *had* frequented the clubs and pubs in Newquay and Truro from the age of fifteen until she left Cornwall a year or so later. But she didn't recall Mike Spencer or anyone who would fit his description. Not that she was surprised; presumably, he wouldn't have had saggy jowls and a beer belly back then. Damn and blast. She didn't need this complication on top of everything else. She grabbed her keys and coat. 'James, I'm going out to top up the larder supplies. See you at lunchtime.'

'Drive safely,' James called from his study. 'Love you.'

Rosa crunched the gears in her hurry to leave Curlew House. Good grief, what was the 'love you' all about from James? He normally saved that sort of talk for private moments. Was he showing off in front of Mike Spencer? Jesus, men were so complicated.

Half an hour later, Rosa watched Shannon search the boxes of cereals, various tins, packets, and jars cluttering the worktop at Carnmarth. Eventually, she stopped faffing and found the sugar and coffee. She looked so much better with colour in her cheeks, but why was she so jittery? Her eyes were red as if she'd been crying. Finally, she plonked two steaming mugs and a packet of biscuits onto the kitchen table.

Rosa took a sip and cringed; the coffee was positively awful. She reached for the bag of sugar with a dessert spoon sticking out of the top. Still, the caffeine smell did mask the awful odour of dogs and fried bacon.

'So, what's happened?' she asked.

'Paul Whittaker.' Tears sprang into Shannon's eyes. 'That poor man was badly injured in the car crash and–'

'Yeah, yeah.' Rosa butted in. 'We already know that he was injured but, like I said before, I'm sure a couple of broken bones and a few bruises were soon mended. He probably got a handsome insurance pay out and is living the life of–'

'Listen, for Christ's sake.' Shannon dragged her hand through her hair. 'Paul was more than just injured. He had a severe brain injury. So bad, that when he was discharged from Derriford Hospital he was moved permanently into a care home in Surrey.'

The words hit Rosa like a punch to the stomach. The knot in her chest tightened further. She'd managed to cope with the deaths of their mums and Mr and Mrs Whittaker by placing the blame squarely on Shannon's mum's shoulders. Now Shannon was telling her that another person's whole life had been ruined. She fought for air. Maybe, if she accepted some of the fault for the crash, like Shannon did, then this feeling that her world was about to implode would recede.

No.

She wasn't one to give in. She straightened her back. She mustn't let herself get distracted by the past. They needed to find out who was behind it all.

'Who told you all this?'

'Nina. Through a friend of hers. And she's double-checked the information. It's correct.' Tears welled in Shannon's eyes. 'That poor man wouldn't be capable of harming us in any way.' A tear rolled down her cheek. 'Unlike us, destroying him, like we did.'

'Come on, Shannon, pull yourself together, there's no point dwelling on it, we need to focus on what's happening now.' Rosa stirred another spoonful of sugar into her coffee. 'You know what this means, don't you?'

Shannon nodded. 'His brother, Stephen, might be our stalker. Right?'

'Fucking hell, what is going on? I could sort of understand Paul coming after us, but this Stephen. Why would he come looking for us after all this time?'

Shannon put her head into her hands.

'What about this Zach fella?' Rosa asked. 'He could still be our stalker.'

'I did a load more searches on him.' Shannon straightened up. 'Yesterday, something finally caught my eye on one of the social media pages: a photo taken at a business conference. Smack in the middle of a whole crowd of suits was Zach. I clicked on his name and back-tracked through Facebook and Instagram and, wham-bam, there he was.'

'So, is he a relative of the Whittakers or not?'

'Doesn't look like it. Zach Smith is in fact John Zackery Smitheram. In short, he's on the run from a bankrupt business and a wife he did the dirty on.' Shannon chewed her lip. 'I confronted him this morning and he confessed straight away to everything. I got shirty and told him right out that instead of bothering me he ought to spend the time sorting his own life out. Bit rich, considering I'm not much of an expert in personal relationships.' She reached for her mug. 'Anyway, the bottom line is, it seems that he's just some plonker and not our stalker.'

Rosa shook her head. 'What now?'

Shannon shoved a stack of printed sheets towards her. 'Details and numbers of all the residential and nursing homes in Surrey. I ran them off Trevor's computer this morning. We need to check each home and find out where Paul Whittaker is, what the situation is with him now. That should give us a starting point.'

Rosa flicked through the pages. 'There are hundreds of them.'

For a split second a grimace flashed across Shannon's face. 'Well over three hundred in total and it looks like more than a hundred of those provide care for young adults, which I guess Paul still is. Maybe start with those homes first? I can't think of any other way of getting some of the answers.'

'Okay. We do need to know if he's still alive at the very least.' Rosa lifted her hands in the air. 'And, if so, where he is. If we're canny enough, we might be able to get some information on Stephen Whittaker's whereabouts as well; I'm assuming he'd be listed as next of kin. That man is at the top of my suspects' list now.'

'Mine too.' Shannon put her head in her hands again. 'How do we do this? Nobody is going to give us the information.'

'Easy-peasy. Put on your best accent and pretend to be a financial assessment officer.'

'A what? I … I wouldn't know what to say,' stuttered Shannon.

'Listen and learn.'

Rosa picked up her mobile phone, hit speaker and punched in the first number on the list.

'Good morning, Rowan Nursing Home. How can I help you?'

'Good morning. I'm Sally, Financial Assessment Officer, Surrey Adult Social Care. We're in the process of updating our assessments. I understand that you have a Mr Paul Whittaker as a resident in your establishment.'

'Paul Whittaker?'

'Yes, he's been in residential care for a number of years, and we need to review his financial circumstances.

'Sorry, we've nobody of that name here.'

'At any time?'

'Not that I can recall.'

'I'm sorry to have bothered you. The printouts must have got mixed up. Goodbye.'

Rosa hung up. 'See, easy-peasy. If you have authority in your voice and come over like a know-it-all, it's surprising what people will tell you without checking credentials.'

Shannon's mouth hung open. 'I'm not sure I can do that.'

'Of course you can. I'm not ringing the whole ruddy lot. I need to get back in time for James's lunch.' She punched in another number. 'Listen to me one more time, then you have a go.'

An hour of phone calls later and they'd still had no luck.

Rosa sighed. Trevor would probably be in for his lunch soon and she didn't want to be there then.

Shannon leaned back against the chair and stretched. 'What now? Do we call it a day and check the rest tomorrow? Or should we do half each on our own this afternoon?'

'One more home each now, then I have to go.' Rosa jabbed another number into the phone. The caller answered after two rings.

'Good morning, The Willows Nursing Home.'

'Hello, I'm Sally, Financial Assessment Officer from–'

'We're up to date with all our residents' financial assessments,' the brusque voice boomed into Rosa's ear.

Shit, she wouldn't get anywhere with this one. Still, what had she got to lose? Her number was blocked so there was no way she could be traced.

'Sorry, but our records show that Mr Paul Whittaker's assessment is due for a review. In fact,' Rosa forced her voice to be extra authoritative and commanding, 'it's rather overdue.'

'I can assure you, that's not the case.'

Rosa held her breath. 'You know Paul Whittaker?'

'Of course, that's why you're ringing The Willows, isn't it?'

'Oh …' Rosa forced herself to remain calm. 'Sorry to sound so confused. It's just that a couple of our records have got mixed up. Temporary staff, I'm afraid.'

The woman at the other end tutted.

'Would I be able to see him?'

'Afraid not.' The woman sighed. 'You really do need to get your records straight. He moved to a new home a few months ago.' She tutted again. 'I don't understand why. He'd been in the care of this home for more than twenty years and he was very happy here.'

'May I have his new address please?'

'What do you need that for?'

'To close his client record at this end.' When the woman didn't respond, Rosa rushed on, 'And to make sure that Mr Whittaker has all the benefits he's entitled to.'

She could hear the woman on the end of the phone tapping on her keyboard. A resident began screaming and shouting in the background. Just as well all these people were so overworked that they didn't have time to think about what they were doing.

'Yes, here it is. Nancarrow Nursing Home, St Austell, Cornwall. I hope I pronounced that correctly?' The woman sounded flustered now as the voice in the background grew louder.

'You pronounced it perfectly.'

'Who did you say you were?' The brusque voice was back. 'I need your full name for our file.'

'Sally Smith,' Rosa said before quickly hanging up. She sank back against the chair.

Shannon stared at her wide-eyed. 'Have you found him?'

Rosa nodded and told her everything the woman had said.

'St Austell.' Shannon's face paled. 'That can't be a coincidence.'

'Could you find the number for Nancarrow Nursing Home and ring them, check that he's there.' She pulled a couple of paracetamols from her bag. 'I need to take these.'

'Hello, Nancarrow Nursing Home.'

'Oh, hello, this is Tina, Financial Assessment Officer, Cornwall Adult Social Care. I understand that Mr Paul Whittaker recently moved to Nancarrow from Surrey.' Shannon rushed on. 'It's our policy to undertake a review of his financial circumstances since he's moved into our area.'

'I'm not sure why. He's fully health funded with 'extras' and 'top-up' fees being met by his brother.'

'His brother?' Shannon held her breath. 'Wo ... would you please confirm his name and address to ensure it's the same as the one we have on our records from Surrey.'

'Sorry, who did you say you were?'

'Tina. Tina Smith from Cornwall–'

'Are you new? I don't recognise the name and–'

Shannon quickly cut the call.

Rosa's heart raced. There was no doubt now who the stalker was.

'It's Paul's brother who's behind all the threats, isn't it?' Shannon got the words out before Rosa could voice them. 'Stephen Whittaker.'

'Fucking Stephen Whittaker. He must be in Cornwall.' Rosa tossed the headache tablets into her mouth and swallowed. 'He's moved his brother here so he's close to him.'

'But where? How do we track him down?'

Rosa shook her head. Who was Stephen Whittaker? Neither she nor Shannon knew anybody with that name. Could he be using an alias? Names and faces ran through her mind: that Zach guy; was he truly out of the picture? Mike Spencer? Was he merely some slimeball or could he be Stephen Whittaker? That Vic who Shannon had stayed with; was he being so helpful because he was a family relative of the Whittakers? There was a new postwoman who came to Curlew House most days; was she a spy for the Whittakers? What about all those inconspicuous people in the local shops and restaurants? So many ordinary people who went quietly in and out of their lives. How could she and Shannon identify the person whose heart simmered with rage and revenge underneath so many broad smiles and helpful gestures?

She shivered.

The kitchen door swung open. Trevor kicked off his wellington boots and stepped into the room. His eyes narrowed when he saw her.

Maybe it was Trevor?

She fought to control her breathing. Now she was being idiotic. Trevor had been around for years. The horrible incidents had only started happening since she returned to Cornwall. So why now though, why now? Perhaps they were going totally down the wrong route by focusing on Stephen Whittaker. Maybe it was simply that her moving here had triggered the memory of some chancer who would eventually show himself (or herself) with a demand for money, and the more that person stalked them and frightened them beforehand, the bigger the sum he or she would ask for. Damn and blast, the whole situation was doing her head in. Her brain ached with all the conflicting information, but the name Stephen Whittaker kept coming to the forefront. Why, oh why, had she agreed to come back to this place? She should have outright refused.

'Alright?' Trevor said, looking from her to Shannon and back again.

'Just getting off.' Rosa got to her feet, leaned into Shannon's ear, and hissed, 'The bastard has been watching us the whole time. We have to find him.'

Her bottom had hardly touched the driver's seat before she flicked on the central locking and fumbled for the ignition button.

Stephen Whittaker. Stephen Whittaker. His name banged round and round in her head all the way back to Curlew House.

21

Shannon pushed her empty lunch plate aside and looked through the window into the yard, the image of Rosa's vehicle belting down the lane over an hour ago still fresh in her mind.

Trevor took a sip of his tea. 'How are you two going to find this brother? This Stephen fella?'

'Suppose one of the first things to do would be to check the Electoral Roll in Surrey. Mind you, I reckon, Stephen's so clever he would've already covered his tracks and there won't be any trace of him.' Shannon sighed. The task of finding Stephen seemed enormous, but, on the other hand, it felt good to share with Trevor what she and Rosa had found out earlier. 'It says in the old newspapers that he went to Nottingham University, so Rosa and I could perhaps track him down that way. I'll ring her later to sort out who'll do what.'

'You trust this Rosa?'

'She was my best friend at school.' Shannon shrugged. 'Our mothers were like sisters.'

'Yet you ended up in foster care.'

Her heart raced as unwanted images flooded her senses.

'Is she truly still your friend after twenty-three years of no contact or help? Seems to me she likes her status and wealth a bit too much.'

She shrugged again. 'The Rosa I know is still in there somewhere, hidden beneath that glossy surface. I just wish she would talk about the accident, that's what I honestly want.'

'Maybe that would involve her admitting more than she cares to reveal.'

She ran a hand over her face. Was Rosa hiding something from her, not telling her all she knew about the accident?

Trevor straightened up and leaned towards Shannon. 'You're not fifteen anymore. You've every right to ask her for answers. You shouldn't go on believing she's better than you.'

Trevor's questions unsettled Shannon. She wondered momentarily if she should have told Trevor about Paul Whittaker's life-long injuries and his move to a nursing home in St Austell. After all, Trevor was only her landlord, despite all he'd done for her over the last few weeks. A muscle in her cheek twitched. Should she have told him so much? She stared out the window. Thank God, Vic was striding across the yard to the main door. She got to her feet.

'Vic's on his way to help me clear out the storeroom. Are you sure you don't want to keep anything?'

Trevor stood and reached for his coat. 'Nothing.'

'I had a quick look this morning. Lots of clothes and personal bits, presumably they're Ali's?'

He nodded.

'And the children's things? Are you certain about chucking it all?'

'Should've burnt the stuff years ago.' Trevor opened the door just as Vic must have raised his hand to knock.

'Hello, Boss.' Vic lowered his hand. 'Come to help the maid.'

Trevor nodded, pushed his feet into his boots and made his way outside.

Vic deftly pulled clothes and other bits from the heap in the storeroom. Shannon liked working with him; he didn't talk that much, didn't grumble, and he worked fast. Between them, they'd established a routine: good clothes in black bags for some charity or other; unfashionable, typical nineties-style clothes and magazines in a pile for a bonfire later. An old Walkman and personal items, like a couple of hairbrushes and hardened make-up, would be dumped.

In the corner, Shannon lifted a blanket. She gasped. Stacks of presents, still in their Christmas and birthday wrapping paper, lay piled one on top of the other. Every parcel had a label. She peered at the first one: *To Daniel, lots of love, from Daddy xx*. The next one said the same but was addressed to Carla. By the looks of it, the gifts had been bought over many years but had either never been delivered or had been returned.

Poor Trevor. Poor Daniel and Carla.

'She never fitted in. Never would. We could all see it, but Trevor was besotted with her. In love, and all that malarky.' Vic took off his beanie hat, shook it, and then put it back on. 'Broke his heart when she left and took those kiddies with her. He loved them more than ...' Vic shook his head. 'I don't have the words to describe the state he was in.'

'Poor Trevor.' This time, Shannon said the words out loud.

She took out her phone and took a photo of the first parcel and its label, then unwrapped the present – a pedal tractor suitable for a five-year-old. The next parcel contained a Barbie doll in a riding outfit, complete with a horse and stable.

'The toys look in good condition,' Vic said. 'I'll take them over to Sheila. She might find them useful for the charities she's involved in. Or she can dump them if they're not up to today's standards.'

Shannon spent the next thirty minutes taking more photos and unwrapping presents. By the time she'd finished, she had a catalogue of all the toys and who they were for.

Finally, the room was empty, and she was alone. Vic had left for Sheila's place, having loaded his car with what seemed like a ton of clothes and toys. She stood with her hands on her hips. It was a good-sized room. The walls were clean and, apart from a bit of mould around the window and in one corner caused by lack of ventilation, the place felt dry and welcoming. A thorough cleaning and a fresh coat of paint would finish the job.

Tomorrow, she and Vic would go to B&Q for paint and other bits, then on to Trago Mills in Falmouth to purchase a bed, carpet, and curtains. Trevor had trusted her with his credit card. She smiled; things had certainly changed between them.

Later that evening, she lazed on one of the sofas by the fire in the living room. Trevor lay stretched out on the other sofa opposite her, arms folded behind his head. They watched a film on the TV. When it finished, Trevor rose to his feet and poured himself a whisky.

'Want one?' He nodded towards the bottle.

'I'll have a sherry please.'

Trevor laughed. 'Who would've thought it? I only keep that stuff for one of my aunties when she comes over at Christmas.'

Back on the sofa with his feet up, Trevor turned towards her. 'Vic said you had a successful day.'

'Yep. All cleared. We're off first thing to get the paint, bed, and furnishings.'

'Good. Reckon, I'll ask him to help me clear up the yard next. Might even get around to painting the outside of the main house.'

Shannon sat in silence for a while watching the flames flicker up the chimney. Sooty, the cat, stretched out beside her. Tootsie was asleep on Trevor's lap.

'Now that I'll have my own room, do we need to set ground rules around cooking, using the kitchen and this area? Or should I get a microwave and a small TV for my room?' She ran her hand through her hair. 'Get back to a more tenant-landlord footing?'

'Is that what you want?'

'Not really.' She took a deep breath. 'I'm getting a few offers of work again, so I'll be out most days, but I'll be around for breakfast and in the evening, and it sort of makes sense to share the kitchen and cooking. I could put a sum of money in a housekeeping kitty to cover my food costs.'

Trevor's lips twitched.

She rushed on. 'I don't want to sponge off you. Maybe you would be happier if I paid extra rent for the food?'

Trevor burst out laughing, so much so that he had to put his whisky onto the side table so he could wipe his eyes. The laughter was infectious, and Shannon joined in.

'I *will* pay my rent. Every week. Promise,' she spluttered.

'Like before.' Trevor wiped his eyes again, then turned to look at her. 'I'm sure you can come up with something that will suit us both. I'm happy to go along with whatever.'

He picked up his whisky and leaned back once more.

'You and I will be falling over ourselves in that kitchen. If you want to clear the clutter, you're welcome to. Chuck all the chipped crockery and out-of-date stuff.'

She grinned. 'You'll be going for the minimalist look then?'

'It's time this place had a facelift. It's what you do, isn't it? It's what all that doodling in the sketchbook is about.'

'How do you know what I sketch?'

'Sheila said she asked you to make over – if that's the right word – her kids' bedrooms. You gave her several sketches. She showed them to me.'

'It's really exciting. Sheila asked me to come up with a completely new look for their rooms, in discussion with them of course. I love this sort of stuff. Just never had my own place to ...'

'Yeah, well, I want the same for the kitchen. I'll pay you for your time.'

'How about you do all the cooking for the first week instead?'

He raised his glass in her direction and smiled. 'Now that's the sort of deal I like.'

Shannon turned to watch the flames once again. The combination of the fire and the sherry had warmed her inside and out. She couldn't remember the last time she'd felt so contented.

'You said that Ali took off with one of the workmen. That must have been hard?'

Trevor stared at the amber liquid, took a gulp, got up and refilled his glass.

Shannon pushed on; she wasn't sure why. 'Had he been at Carnmarth for long?'

'Twelve months. Twelve bloody months.' Trevor took another mouthful of whisky. 'I thought the little turd was my friend. Yet all that time he had eyes for my wife.'

Shannon's lips moved. She wanted to say something, but what?

'But she betrayed me as well.' He shook his head. 'Turned out he had a history of pinching other people's wives. A track record as long as your arm. But Ali fell for his patter.'

'That's so unfair.'

'He dumped her after six months. She wouldn't come back, not even for the kids' sakes.' Trevor closed his eyes and rubbed the bridge of his nose. 'I loved Daniel and Carla so much.'

'Where did she and the children go?'

'She found herself another man and effectively pushed me out of the picture, moving addresses and returning all my cards and presents.'

'That's awful. You had rights.'

'Rights!' He thumped the arm of the sofa. 'Men's rights mean shite when the woman does all she can to turn the kids against you. My rights accounted for nothing. Daniel and Carla wouldn't even speak to me when I rang.'

'They were so young; they didn't know what they were doing. Ali would've influenced them.' Shannon took a sip of her sherry. 'You could contact them now, look for them via social media. They'd probably be pleased if you got back in touch.'

'No. I can't take the risk. Would be more than I can bear if they didn't want to know me.'

'But–'

'Look,' he rubbed his eyes with the back of his hand, 'I made the decision long ago to get on with my life at Carnmarth, with the animals and those friends who I knew I could trust. Kept my distance from strangers.'

'Fair enough. Is that why you're so wary about new workers or tenants coming onto Carnmarth?'

'Guess so.'

'If you'd been less cautious,' Shannon said, pulling a comical face as she spoke. 'And I'd been more like my usual full-on charming, talkative self, then we could've been friends for nearly five years.'

Trevor grunted. 'If you say so.'

'You know so.'

'Yeah, you're right. Stupid now, looking back but ...' He shrugged, then stood. 'Time for bed. I'm keeping you from your beauty sleep and boring you with my life story to boot.'

She stood as well. She raised her hand, made to place it on his chest, hesitated and dropped her arm down by her side.

'Thank you for confiding in me.'

He looked into her eyes. 'You're quite a person, you know. Stronger by far than you give yourself credit for.' A smile lit up his face. 'You know, I rather like having you under my feet.'

Unexpected joy shot through her. My God, did she have feelings for him? No, he was her landlord, she was being silly. Still, he seemed to like her. She watched him climb the stairs to his bedroom and basked in a glow of happiness for a few minutes before she made her way to her own bed on the sofa.

22

Rosa stopped midway down the stairs, held her breath and listened. James was in the kitchen on the phone, his voice bright and good-humoured.

'That's right. She's gone out for an early run.' He paused briefly. 'Indeed. You know my wife, mad keen on her exercise.'

She tiptoed down two more steps. Who was James talking to? And what was he saying about her?

'I can take a message, Laura, if that would help?'

Laura? Laura Saville? No, it couldn't be her; she would have rung Rosa's mobile. She pushed her hand into her pocket. Empty. She must have left her phone in the kitchen when she went to bed the previous evening, and James had taken it upon himself to answer it. She moved nearer to the kitchen door and peeked inside, head cocked.

James grabbed a notepad and pen from one of the drawers. 'Join you and Ruth ... lunch at the Hotel St Michaels ... spa treatment beforehand.' James scribbled a couple of words and then dropped the pen onto the worktop. 'Oh, Laura, I'm sorry, I know that Rosa's got a full diary today.' He drummed his fingers on the marble surface as he listened to the reply. 'Yes, I'm sure she'd be delighted to make another date. I'll get her to ring you. Give my regards to Richard and tell him I'll be in touch shortly about that round of golf.'

He tossed Rosa's phone onto the table, screwed up the note and chucked it into the rubbish bin.

Rosa stepped into the room. 'Did I hear you mention Laura's name?'

'Nothing important. She rang me to pass on a message from Richard. Business stuff.'

Did James just lie to her face? How dare he? Liar. Liar. She wanted to shout the words out loud, but they died on her lips. Jesus, what was going on? Why didn't she feel able to challenge him? Her hand shook as she reached into the cupboard and pulled out the breakfast plates and bowls.

'Did ... did I hear you mention the Hotel St Michaels?'

'Oh, that.' He straightened his already perfectly positioned tie. 'Laura was going on about lunch and a frivolous spa treatment, but I told her you were fully committed today.'

James plonked himself into one of the chairs, shook out the newspaper and held it up in front of him, effectively cutting off any further conversation.

Rosa persisted. 'But I don't have anything in my diary.'

He turned a page and gave the newspaper another noisy shake. 'I want you to help me in the study with some office bits. Spreadsheets and other bits.'

'Surely, that can wait?' Rosa placed a plate, bowl, and cutlery in front of him. 'I'd love to see Laura and Ruth. It's been ages since we've got together.'

James folded the paper and dropped it onto one of the vacant chairs. 'They're very lightweight people, darling. Not a good influence on you, spending money on trivia.' He poured a sizable portion of granola into his bowl and splashed milk on top. 'I don't want you seeing them.'

'What?' Did he just say he didn't want her seeing them? She must have misheard him.

'If you want this luxury,' James waved his spoon at the view beyond the window, 'we both have to work hard ... and make sacrifices.'

Rosa's heart thumped as she spread a thin layer of marmite on her wholemeal toast. Thinking about it now,

Ruth and Laura had rung her less and less. Had James intercepted their calls before?

'Don't look at me like that,' he said. 'you've also got to pick up Freya and Marcus from school this afternoon.'

She struggled to keep her voice even. 'Penny's dropping them at the house for me. She's passing the door.'

'Oh?' A muscle twitched in his cheek. 'I do so hate your reliance on others to carry out what is essentially your duty as a mother.'

Rosa dropped her half-eaten toast onto her plate. 'What are you on about? It's only a lift. I'll do the same for Penny's children next week. It works well, and ...'

Her stomach cramped. James's lower lip hung loose. For crying out loud, was he sulking? She held her breath and counted to ten. The last thing she wanted was for the children to endure a dreadful atmosphere during their weekend at home. Again.

She took a deep breath. This could wait. She dumped the rest of her toast in the bin, placed the dishes in the dishwasher and followed him into the study. She spent the next hour and a half formatting the spreadsheet exactly as he wanted, with him leaning over her shoulder the entire time. Then he stood and reached for his case and coat.

'Where are you going? I thought we were going to–'

'We'll have to finish it later. Got a meeting at the office.'

Rosa stared at his back as he made his way out of the study and down the hallway. A few minutes later, his BMW roared past the window and up the drive.

Damn him. It was too late to ring Ruth and Laura now.

She rummaged for a packet of antacid tablets in her handbag, popped two into her mouth and swallowed.

Rosa realised with a start that she felt happy and relaxed for the first time in weeks. She'd met Shannon earlier in one of her favourite villages: Flushing. They'd parked their cars on Trefusis Road and were now walking the coastal path to Mylor Yacht Harbour. The sun caressed her bare legs and arms. She smiled. A perfect Cornish day.

A hundred yards ahead of her on the flat green meadow, Marcus led Fern on a leash. Freya walked on the other side of the black and white collie, stroking the animal's glossy coat at every opportunity. Suddenly, her daughter turned, rushed up to Rosa and hugged her. Then she did the same thing to Shannon.

'This is the best Saturday ever,' she cried before she ran back to join Marcus and the sheepdog.

Shannon grinned. 'They're loving it, aren't they? Fern's such a good dog.'

'Trevor didn't mind you bringing her with you?'

'Well, all his dogs are working animals but they're also his pets. Not that he'd admit it.' Shannon laughed. 'All of them are softies, including Trevor.'

Rosa stopped and watched as Marcus told the dog to sit and Freya took hold of the leash. The dog's eyes moved from Marcus and focussed on Freya.

'They would love a puppy,' Rosa said with a sigh.

'You've got a big enough house and garden. You could get them one.'

'James would never agree.'

'You and the children outnumber him.'

'Doesn't work like that,' Rosa muttered, then turned her gaze onto the yachts making their way up and down the calm waters of Carrick Roads. A speed boat towed a proficient water skier further out to sea. Seagulls, drifting on the light breeze, dotted the cloudless sky. St Anthony's Lighthouse shone brilliant white in the distance.

'It's beautiful, isn't it?' Shannon said.

A long-lost feeling of friendship took Rosa by surprise as she and Shannon stood side by side to admire the view, shoulders touching.

Memories of so many times she'd spent with Shannon flooded her mind. Sisters, in every way but blood; that's what they'd told each other.

'Do you remember that time we pricked each other's fingers with a needle and mixed our blood?'

Shannon laughed. 'We were about ten. Hurt like hell if I remember rightly.'

'Not so much as that time you raced me on my bike, and I came off and broke my elbow.'

The easy talk continued for several minutes, then Rosa froze. Shannon had that look on her face. She was going to ask about the accident again.

'Hey,' Shannon said, 'do you remember those boys we met on our fifteenth birthdays?'

Rosa's shoulders relaxed. Not about the accident after all. Thank goodness.

'Vaguely,' she said.

'We gave our mums the slip and made for the fairground at Marazion. Then they came searching for us and dragged us away like we were toddlers.' Shannon chuckled. 'You got off with one of the lads. What was his name? You went around the back of the vans for a snog.'

'I didn't.'

'You did. Curly-haired guy. You must remember.'

'I don't. Like I've said before, I can't recall a lot of the events that happened back then.'

'Oh.'

Rosa looked down and was shocked to see her hands clenched into fists, the knuckles white. A strange sensation overwhelmed her: a mix of relief that the love she and Shannon had felt for each other during their childhood was coming back, but also a sense of guilt and panic about the accident. Images and thoughts of that day – including some she'd long ago chosen to forget – were becoming more frequent and upsetting,

She pressed her temples in a conscious effort to clear her head before scrambling over a stile, along a narrow footpath and past the big houses leading into Mylor Yacht Harbour. Halfway up the slope into Café Mylor, she turned to check that Marcus and Freya were okay; they were twenty yards or so away taking turns telling Fern to sit, then rewarding her with a small doggie treat. Expensive yachts filled the harbour. On any other day, Rosa would have stopped to admire the view and soak up the holiday atmosphere, but she wanted the so-called safety of strangers and a crowd in the hope of preventing any further interrogation or awkward conversations from Shannon. She hurried up the ramp, but Shannon was hot on her heels, her mouth open.

'Would your dad know if my mum took drugs regularly? Not just on the day of the accident.'

Bile burned in Rosa's throat. She swallowed, ran up the slope, through the café door and headed straight for the toilet. Inside, she hung her head over the basin and retched. Damn and blast, she could cope with the stalker, or her marriage problems and James's mood swings. She could even cope with all the crap that Shannon persisted in forcing her to confront about the accident. But all these issues at the same time?

It was too much.

Eventually, she splashed cold water onto her face, pushed her shoulders back, and went outside on shaky legs to the wooden table where Shannon sat.

'I need to get the children back before James comes home. We should discuss Stephen Whittaker. The kids will be here for their lunch soon.'

'Good change of subject.' Shannon glared at her. 'You have to talk about the accident at some point. You can't keep putting me off. I want answers.'

'I don't remember anything.'

'Really?'

Rosa shivered. 'It's true.' Her hand trembled as she reached for the menu. 'Shame you couldn't find Stephen's name on the Electoral Roll. I'm trying to trace him through the University of Nottingham, but no joy so far.' She lifted her head and stared at Shannon. 'You know the easiest thing to do?'

'What?' Shannon fiddled with the salt and pepper pots. A grey wagtail hopped underneath the table looking for crumbs and bits of discarded crisps.

'For you to take a carer's job at Nancarrow Nursing Home. These places always want temporary staff. You could apply directly or through an agency.'

'Don't be stupid, why would I do that?'

'Because I assume you've done caring work before and got the experience ... haven't you?' The smell of baked potato and cheese on the next table made Rosa feel queasy. 'Besides, it's a good idea.'

'Why don't you do it then.'

'Me? I couldn't do that.'

'Oh, good enough for me though?'

The look on Shannon's face wiped the grin off Rosa's. 'No, it's just that ... that ... well, I couldn't hide something like that from James. I need to look after him. Things are a bit difficult at present and ... You know what relationships can be like at times.'

'Leave me out of this. I'm not getting involved in your marital problems. They're for you and James to sort.' Shannon pushed a strand of hair behind her ears. 'I'm happy with my life now. Got a good place to sleep, a fair amount of work offers coming in, and Bill at The Wheatsheaf wants me for one evening shift every week. I can't let them down.'

'How the hell do we find out where Stephen is then? He's sure to be Paul Whittaker's next of kin. Nancarrow would have his address and contact number. Stephen might even have another name. You could have a look in Paul's file.'

'Oh, yeah, they're going to give it to me, just like that?'

'You'd find a way to get the information. Do whatever is necessary.'

'No.'

Rosa glared at her.

Shannon held her gaze, chin tilted upwards.

Freya, Marcus, and a panting Fern came up to the table. Rosa plastered a smile onto her face and greeted them. Fern shook her head and saliva droplets splattered Rosa's shorts. The children and Shannon laughed in harmony for what seemed like an unnatural amount of time, their arms wrapped around each other. Rosa forced herself to keep the smile on her face.

'What shall we all have for lunch?' she said.

The children poured over the menu.

Rosa turned to Shannon and urgently whispered. 'Nancarrow. It's the only solution. You know it is.'

23

Shannon sat back, rubbed her eyes, and looked through the library window. Tourists and day shoppers wandered in and out of the shops of Truro or stopped to stare at items on display in the windows, while workers on their lunch break rushed through the crowds, their hands full of sandwiches and snacks. Music floated in the air from a busker further down the street.

She looked back at the computer screen. An hour of research and still nothing. She'd chosen to come into the Truro Library to use their machines rather than intrude on Trevor's private space by using his computer all the time. He hadn't complained, but she didn't want to push her luck. She was only his tenant, after all.

Hands poised over the keyboard, she rolled her head from side to side and let out a soft groan. Rosa should be doing this. It was Rosa who'd agreed to try and find Stephen Whittaker via his university records, but then she'd come back saying she'd drawn a blank.

Shannon wanted to give her old school friend the benefit of the doubt but, to be honest, she believed Rosa was so preoccupied with pleasing James and looking after the children that she'd done little more than skim over the surface. So she'd had to allocate *her* whole day to search for Stephen on the computer.

That damn man and his family had taken over and dictated her life for long enough. Not anymore. She had to find him, and if at all possible, she wanted to do it without being dragged into taking a job at Nancarrow Nursing

Home. Anyway, why would they employ her? She'd never worked for a legit agency before. Cash-in-hand jobs and keeping under the radar had served her just fine up to now.

The hunt for records from twenty-three years ago was proving to be time-consuming. Facebook hadn't been invented then, and few people had mobile phones, so the forest of photographic records that today's students took for granted was harder to find. Using Nottingham University as a key, Shannon tried various social media, alumni and classmates sites without luck, until eventually she stumbled upon a string of chats from Stephen's fellow students reminiscing and gossiping about their youth, which revealed that although he hadn't returned to university after the accident, he had nonetheless been awarded a first-class honours degree. Presumably, Stephen had completed his thesis before the accident; not that Shannon knew much about these things, but she was learning fast.

One of his former fellow students had also mentioned that Stephen had taken up an offer of work experience with Shipman and Smith, Accountants, during his last year at university. A quick look on Google revealed the company was still in operation. She noted down the contact details, including the telephone number.

After a while, she massaged the back of her neck, picked up her rucksack and walked across the hallway to the Flying Aubergine café situated within the library. She ordered a coffee and, after a quick check in her purse, a slice of fruit cake. She'd secretly eaten her homemade sandwich in the computer suite earlier in the morning.

Settled on a stool by the window, she resumed her surveillance of the shoppers and workers in the street outside. Seeing a dark-haired woman with two children reminded her of the lovely day she'd spent with Rosa, Marcus and Freya on the coastal walk to Mylor Yacht

Harbour. The children were such bright kids; she loved being in their company. She didn't get why Rosa put that idiot of a husband before her children.

Shannon sighed, then picked up her phone and punched in the number for Shipman and Smith. 'Good morning,' she replied to the warm female voice on the line. 'My name's Alison Brown.' Stone me, she was almost as good a liar as Rosa. 'I'm hoping you can help me find someone who used to work for Shipman and Smith.'

'If you give me the details, I'll see what I can do.'

'I'm wanting to contact a Mr Stephen Whittaker. He helped with a piece of work for my father over twenty years ago. I understand they got on very well. Sadly, my father recently passed away, and it would be in Mr Whittaker's best interests for me to find him. Can you help?'

'Twenty years ago? I'm afraid any employee records from that time would've already been shredded.'

Damn. Damn. Damn.

'Just a moment.' The woman covered the mouthpiece, but Shannon could still hear her muffled words. 'Hey, Frank, you've been here for a long time. Do you remember a Stephen Whittaker?'

Shannon couldn't hear the reply and waited with bated breath.

'Hello, Ms Brown. Yes, Mr Whittaker did work here for short periods of time during his final year at university, but a family tragedy meant he left abruptly without the chance to say goodbye.'

'Did anybody keep in contact with him or have a forwarding address?'

'Frank said he never responded to management about some pay he was due, nor did he reply to personal messages that staff sent to him. I'm sorry, my dear, but we can't help you.'

'Well, thank you anyway.' Shannon hung up.

Another dead end. Why was it so hard to track down this man? She rubbed her eyes. Her brain was fuzzy. She pulled out her sketchpad to clear her thoughts before she resumed her search. On a clean page, she pencilled the outline of Carnmarth Quarry from memory and then began to draw. Ten minutes later, she made her way back to the computer suite.

Lost in what she was doing, she finally stopped and looked at her watch. Another half an hour was all she could bear. The room was too warm, the atmosphere too stale. Hushed voices came from deeper within the library. A couple of schoolchildren barged through the entrance door and ran down the corridor. One of the librarians shushed them. Oh, how she longed to get back to Carnmarth, to stretch her legs and breathe in the cool, clean air.

A search for a central register of accountants revealed there wasn't one. There were, however, several professional bodies with lists of suitably qualified accountants, which she explored in detail for Stephen Whittaker's name, but again she found nothing. A check of Companies House also drew a blank. So, not a hot-shot Director or whatever of some company. She frowned. Stephen Whittaker seemed to have disappeared after the accident. Damn the man, he eluded her and Rosa at every step. A job at Nancarrow Nursing Home was looking to be more and more like the only option.

She reached for the mouse to close the session, hesitated, and then entered another name: Daniel Harris.

Several images appeared on Facebook and she spotted him immediately; the same eyes and dark hair marked him out as Trevor's son.

She clicked on his site. Only a few photographs and no personal details. Not a regular poster of information then.

She clicked onto his *friends* and there she was: Carla Harris. The sister. Trevor's daughter; all grown up and very beautiful. Shannon clicked on her image. Much more information and lots of happy images of someone who enjoyed nights out and holidays abroad.

She was about to click on Carla's *posts* when she removed her hand. Trevor had been adamant that he wanted no contact with his children, so what right had she to probe into what was, after all, his private life? None of it was her business. But ... by sticking her nose in, she now had a problem. Should she tell Trevor that she'd found Daniel and Carla or not? They'd been easy to find on social media and were clearly happy for strangers to access their accounts. Maybe they wanted their father to get in contact.

She could send a personal message to them, couldn't she? They ought to know that Trevor loved them. They ought to know about the years of Christmas and birthday presents that had never been sent or had been returned. She sat back in her chair and looked at Carla's image.

After several minutes, she moved the cursor to hover over the *message* icon and stared again into Carla's green eyes tinged with amber around the irises.

'Tell me, Carla, what should I do?' she whispered. 'What do you want?'

24

Rosa smiled to herself as she watched Shannon stride, sure-footed and confident, along the footpath in front of her. Even Rosa had to admit that the track from Carnmarth Farm to Carnmarth Quarry was particularly beautiful, lined with spectacular granite boulders, yellow flowering gorse bushes, red campions, and other assorted wildflowers.

To her left, the rough moorland rolled away towards ancient patchwork fields, their stone hedges topped with stunted trees. In the opposite direction, a silver ribbon of sea twinkled on the horizon: Falmouth Bay, the gateway to Carrick Roads and the Helford River.

Her house would be nestled over there, overlooking the water. She normally felt a sense of satisfaction that she lived in such an ostentatious property in what was a highly desirable location, but since calling at the farmhouse to collect Shannon, uneasy thoughts had settled on her.

Now that Shannon had cleared the clutter from the kitchen and repainted the walls and the cabinet doors, the place had a clean, modern look that oozed comfort and warmth. Even the dogs and cats in front of the Aga added to its charm. She sighed. No matter what she did to Curlew House, it would never be a real home.

'What are you thinking about?' Shannon said.

Rosa came to a stop next to her friend. 'Just taking in the view. It's so relaxing. Who knew I'd feel like that in your old hiking boots and thick socks?'

'Well, you don't want to scratch those legs of yours and have James asking awkward questions.' Shannon let out a light girly laugh. 'I remember those evenings when you spent hours painting your toenails, shaving your legs, rubbing in tinted moisturiser.'

'You were just as bad. You spilt red nail varnish all over my bedroom carpet. Mum gave me hell.'

'Our mums were a right pair, weren't they?'

'All bark but no bite.' Rosa grinned at Shannon.

'You know, I see a lot of your mum in Freya.'

A warm glow flowed over her. 'I do as well. Sometimes, Marcus gets in a strop, like my dad did on occasions.'

'He was a good man, your dad.'

Rosa stopped smiling. 'The accident changed him. And I can't just forget that he started this whole stalker thing by giving our birthday celebration photo to that so-called journalist.'

'You should make it right with him.'

'You know I can't … what would I tell James?'

Shannon scowled. 'Your dad is your dad. He's family.'

Rosa started to protest, then shrugged. What was the point? Shannon wouldn't understand. 'Maybe,' she said, 'one day.'

They chatted about old times as they walked side by side along the path. For once, she and Shannon seemed to be able to talk about their mums and the good moments they'd shared, without either butting heads or bringing up the car crash.

'You said you found Trevor's children on Facebook. Have you told him?'

'I have. Got an earful for my interfering. Thank God I didn't send a message to either Carla or Daniel. He would've blown a gasket for sure.'

'Has he got in contact with them?'

Shannon shook her head. 'I told him he was being a stubborn cuss. Truth is, he's scared. Scared of being rejected yet again.'

'Aren't we all?'

They walked on in silence.

'I'll need to get back by 4:30.' Rosa pushed a strand of hair from her eyes. 'Before James gets home. Thankfully, I've already prepared his meal for tonight.'

'Trevor and I take turns cooking. It seems to work.'

'You two have become good friends, haven't you?' Rosa raised an eyebrow.

'I rent a room in his house. It makes sense. Nothing else.'

'If you say so.'

'I do.'

The route narrowed and Rosa fell in step behind Shannon. 'Freya and Marcus haven't stopped talking about Fern. I've had to shush them a few times in case James heard.'

'They're super kids. You're very lucky. Great kids, gorgeous house, and a handsome husband to boot.'

'Looks aren't everything,' Rosa mumbled, more to herself than to Shannon.

'Hey, what's up? I thought you had the perfect marriage.'

Rosa shook her head. 'I do ... I have ...' She glanced at the silver slice of sea on the horizon and sighed. 'But ... Well, he's been acting a bit weird recently.'

'Weird?'

'Installing that over-the-top security system for starters, intercepting calls from my friends, and then there's the money thing–' Rosa stopped in mid-sentence. She'd said enough. How could she be so disloyal and ungrateful to James, who gave her everything she and the children could need? What if he did have a few foibles? Didn't everyone? 'It's nothing. Just me being foolish.'

'Maybe.' Shannon shrugged. 'What would I know? My knowledge of relationships or marriage is almost non-existent.'

Rosa gazed at her old friend's back, and the words came out before she could stop them. 'If anything happens to me, I want you to look after the children,' she whispered.

'What did you say?'

'You have to take care of Marcus and Freya if anything happens to me. If Stephen Whittaker ... Well, if anything happens.'

'Happens?' Shannon halted and turned to look at her. 'It won't. We'll find him and put a stop to all of this. But even if it did, you've got James. He might be a bit off for now, but he's your husband, the children's stepfather. Hasn't he got legal rights or joint custody?'

'No. I've not bothered to sort anything like that.'

'But he's loaded. They'll be looked after for life.'

'No!'

'No?' Shannon stared at her.

Rosa took a deep breath and forced herself to speak calmly, as shocked by her own words as Shannon looked. 'No. You're the right person for them, not him.'

'Why? What do I know about children? What's more, I'm stony broke, not even a place to call my own.'

'You and I are the same where it matters, deep down.' Something basic tugged at Rosa's emotions. 'We come from the same roots.' She bit back a sob. 'Promise me. Please. Promise me.'

Shannon kicked a tuft of grass. 'I can't.'

'Why not?' Rosa could hear the tremor in her voice.

'Because it means diddly-squat. Look how our mums' promises to each other came to nothing. It all went to shit from my point of view. Neither your dad ... nor you ... upheld the promise to look after me.'

Rosa's stomach contracted. Her lips moved but no words came out.

'I can understand why your dad might not have wanted me in his house. But you? Why didn't you at least keep in contact?'

'It was complicated. I didn't know where you were, how to contact you.'

'Bullshit. That's an excuse and you know it.'

Rosa dragged a hand through her hair. 'I suppose none of us coped well afterwards.' A voice in Rosa's head screamed at her to turn and run, but instead, she spoke without thinking. 'I ... I'm sorry. If I could turn the clock back to the start of that day, I would.'

She bit her lip as tears sprang into Shannon's eyes, and her friend turned around to resume what now seemed to Rosa to be a very long trek.

'Blooming hell.' Rosa stopped abruptly, then hurriedly stepped back a couple of paces. A terrifying hole had opened up in front of her. 'Is that Carnmarth Quarry?'

'Yep.'

'It's so spooky. How the hell did you sleep in such a place?'

'Had no choice.' Shannon shrugged. 'Besides, it's a beautiful spot. There's only nature and animals, nothing to harm you. I wasn't afraid.' She reached inside her bag and pulled out her sketchbook. 'Look at this.'

Rosa leaned over her and peered down at the drawing and saw not the sinister Carnmarth Quarry in front of her but a colourful sketch showing a transformed landscape.

'What is it?'

'A bit of fun to pass the time.' Shannon pointed out different areas. 'I think the quarry would be ideal for campers.'

'Really?'

'People could pitch their tents in the quarry, explore the place and surrounding trails for wildlife. Proper wild camping.'

Rosa couldn't imagine who'd want to camp out in the middle of gorse bushes and brambles, with foxes screeching to one another all night long, and who knew what else creeping around in the undergrowth.

Shannon ran her hand over the sketched sheet as if seeking confirmation that the plan might work. 'There's a good track from here down to the quarry bottom, and also a road into the site. A bit twisty, but that would add to the fun.'

'If you say so.' Rosa thought of her precious BMW and the potential for dents and scratches driving down a foliage-infested lane in the back of beyond with grass down the middle. 'And you think dyed-in-the-wool Trevor will go for this?'

'I haven't talked to him about it.' Shannon shut the sketchbook and shoved it back into her rucksack. 'Like I said, it's a bit of fun, that's all.' She paused. 'But it's time I did something with my life, just not sure what.'

Rosa looked at the mix of bravado and the need for reassurance on Shannon's face. 'I guess it could be done,' she said. 'If Trevor was up for it. Yeah, sure. It'd be a great place to camp.'

'So, not so spooky after all?'

'Well, not as bad as Halwyn Woods.'

'Halwyn Woods?'

Rosa sucked in her breath. 'A piece of woodland over the other side of Truro. James bought it not long after we moved into Curlew House. He goes there to birdwatch and to get time on his own, he says.'

'Birdwatching?' Shannon snorted. 'Your James?'

For the first time in a long time, laughter burst freely from Rosa's throat. 'Don't. Please don't. I know he doesn't look like the birdwatching type, but he loves to visit the place. More now than when he first bought it.'

'Have you been to Halwyn Woods?'

'He took me to see it once. Bloody awful place. Smelt all mouldy and musty, and the wet leaves ruined my new leather boots.'

Shannon laughed. 'Only you would go traipsing in some woods in posh leather boots.'

'Yeah, well, James didn't see the funny side, I can tell you. He had to fork out for a new pair.'

'Serves him right; he should've got you a pair of wellies.' Shannon wiped her eyes. 'He could afford them. He must spend shedloads on golf equipment and membership fees.'

The word golf sent a shudder over Rosa.

'What's wrong now?'

'James's new golfing buddy is Mike Spencer.'

Shannon grimaced. 'What? The guy who installed the CCTV systems?'

'He's always dropping into Curlew House. Scares me to death. He knows me from the time of the accident, I'm sure of it. When he visited yesterday, he even managed to drop Pengollan Estate into conversation with James. All within my earshot. I could hardly breathe. Thankfully, James didn't pick up on it.'

'There's no reason to think he's our stalker, is there?'

'I don't know. He puts on this horrible false smile when he looks at me, as if he's got one up on me.'

Shannon's eyes grew wide. 'Are you saying you think he could be Stephen Whittaker?'

Rosa shook her head. 'No, I don't think so. Mike Spencer has been trading under that name in Cornwall for decades. I checked his website, along with other social media links and they all seem legitimate.'

'Anybody with a bit of technical savvy can set up a website and that other stuff. Are you sure he has nothing to do with all this?'

'My gut feeling is he's just a slimeball from my misspent youth who wants to yank my chains. Well, he's doing that all right.'

'Nonetheless, it's more than possible that he's related to the Whittaker family. After all, they came to Cornwall for a family occasion.'

Rosa fumbled in her bag and pulled out a pack of antacid tablets; the second lot that day.

'You need to keep an eye on him, Rosa. He could be in cahoots with Stephen Whittaker.'

'You're right.'

Her stomach churned. How much more could she deal with? Her phone rang and broke the silence, then her heart flip-flopped as she glanced at the name displayed: Treloar School.

'Hello,' she gasped. 'Marcus? Freya? Are they okay?'

'Mrs Trevail. The children are fine.' The head's voice sounded calm. 'However, there has been an incident. A very worrying incident.'

'What? What's happened? Mrs Ferris? Please, tell me.'

'A stranger came to the school insisting he had permission to take Marcus and Freya out for a meal. He was not on our records as an authorised person to take the children, so we refused. He became very angry.'

'Who was he?' Rosa's heart thumped harder. 'Did he give a name?'

'No. But he was a most unpleasant man. When I said I was calling the police, he became very abusive before he ran outside and drove off.'

'Oh, my goodness.' Rosa's legs trembled and she slumped down onto a large rock, where Shannon rested a hand on her shoulder and squeezed. 'Are you sure that Marcus and Freya are okay, Mrs Ferris?'

'Quite sure. They know nothing of the incident and are going about their school business as normal.'

Rosa let out a long breath, looked up and gripped Shannon's hand.

'Thank God, they're alright,' Shannon whispered, her eyes brimming with tears.

'Mrs Trevail? Are you still on the line? Mrs Trevail?' Mrs Ferris's voice called from the phone.

Rosa cleared her throat. 'Yes, I'm here.'

'Good. I wanted to let you know that I've called the police. They're on their way. I suggest that you come to the school and talk to them.'

The words galvanised Rosa into action. Adrenaline rushed through her body as she turned and ran back along the footpath.

Shannon kept pace with her. 'Do you think it's Stephen Whittaker?'

'I don't know, I don't know,' she panted as she struggled to draw in air.

In the yard at Carnmarth, she came to an abrupt halt. Two police cars were parked next to the BMW. She shook her head in confusion. Mrs Ferris had said she should come to Treloar School, hadn't she?

She ran up to the first car. A young policeman got out.

'Please tell me they haven't been hurt. Please.'

The officer frowned. 'I'm sorry, I don't understand.'

'My children,' she shouted, 'are they okay?'

'Please calm down, Madam, we're here about another issue. What's this about your children?'

'You're not here about Marcus and Freya?'

The farmhouse door opened, and they all stared as Trevor was escorted to the other police car, a police officer on either side of him.

Shannon stood, white-faced and rigid. She glanced at Rosa, then ran towards Trevor.

'Trevor? What's going on? What's happened?'

One of the officers put his arm out to stop her from getting near, and Rosa realised with a jolt that she wanted to comfort Shannon, but instead, she turned on her heels and raced to her car.

Right now, getting to Treloar School was the only thing that mattered.

25

Shannon pushed the policeman's arm away and rushed up to Trevor.

'What's going on?'

He glared at her. His cheeks were flushed, and a tuft of hair at the back of his head stood on end. The policeman moved between them and forced Shannon to step back. A female officer steered Trevor towards the waiting car.

'Trevor?' She pushed forward and he stopped so quickly she almost tripped into him.

'This is all your fault,' he said. 'I shouldn't have let my guard down.'

Her hand flew to her mouth. 'Don't say that.' She turned to the policewoman, who was opening the car door. 'Why's he being arrested?'

Trevor answered for her. 'I'm being taken in for questioning. Some anonymous turd sent the police a fake photo of me selling illegal drugs at Carnmarth Quarry.'

'No. That can't be true.'

The policewoman eased Trevor into the vehicle, her hand over his head, and the door slammed shut, leaving words unsaid on her lips.

'I've been set up.' He glared through the partly open car window. 'And it's all your doing.'

Her heart pounded against her ribs as the police vehicles slowly left the yard. A jackdaw let out a horrible, harsh call in the distance. Shannon stood there, watching him being driven away.

A hand touched her elbow and she spun around, ready for battle.

'Come on, me girl.' Vic encouraged her to walk toward the main house. 'What you need is a strong cup of tea.'

In the kitchen, she sat at the table, her mind swirling with conflicting emotions.

Vic placed a steaming mug of dark, sugared tea in front of her. 'Drink that.' His gnarled hand pushed a piece of Cornish Heavy Cake towards her. 'And get that down you.'

She stared at the currants that dotted the mixture and poked through the crisscross lines on the top of the flat piece of cake.

'Hevva,' Vic said, nodding at the cake. 'It's what the 'huer' – the lookout – on the clifftop called when he spotted a shoal of pilchards out at sea. The women folk would bake the cake when their men returned with a successful catch. The crisscross marks on the top represent a fishing net.' He cleared his throat. 'Hark at me, rambling on. You'll have learned this at your mother's knee, you being Cornish.'

She nodded. Tears pricked the back of her eyes; her mother had made Heavy Cake most weeks. She looked out of the window. She could hardly breathe, let alone eat.

'You know this'll come to nothing. Trevor's not been involved in any funny business for years.' Vic sniffed. 'In the past, when that so-called wife of his lived with him and sucked him dry, on a few occasions he did turn a blind eye to goings on at the quarry. Even got the odd tenner or twenty quid for his trouble. But he's not been involved in any shenanigans since she left him.'

'I don't understand why this has happened now,' she said.

But, of course, she did. It was the stalker again; bloody Stephen Whittaker.

'I'm out in the yard for a bit. Trevor left the cows and calves half-fed.' Vic patted her on the shoulder. 'You know where I am if you need me.'

He closed the door quietly behind him.

Shannon took several deep breaths and tried to think about Rosa and her children, but fear for Trevor took over. And something else. With a jolt, she realised how fond she'd grown of the gruff farmer, how good he made her feel. He'd given her the chance to be better, to grow. Perhaps in time they might have … A tear tracked down her cheek. That had all been blown away by Stephen Whittaker. One fake photo and it was all gone. More tears flowed. Her fault, Trevor had said. She sobbed. How he felt about her mattered. It mattered a lot.

Suddenly, she thumped the table. If she and Rosa didn't find Stephen Whittaker in whatever guise he had taken on, then what would happen to them? What would happen to their loved ones – Trevor, Freya and Marcus? She and Rosa had to find this Stephen before he took what was most precious to them. But how? She desperately wanted to talk to Rosa. To know that, at the very least, the children were safe.

The kitchen walls pressed in and closed around her. She got hurriedly to her feet and made her way out into the field to join Vic. Together, they checked and moved Trevor's small herd of 'suckler' cows onto fresh grass. She loved that the young ones stayed with their mothers until they weaned themselves or their mums had another calf.

'Trevor and his dad used to have themselves a lovely milking herd once. There were twenty farms hereabouts, each making enough to support a family.' Vic spat onto the ground. 'All gone now. Only the big boys have milking herds these days. They have the same number of cows as all the others once had put together.'

'Did you help them with the milking and such?'

A big grin broke out on Vic's face. 'I loved it. Not sure Trevor did, especially the early morning starts. He likes his sheep and the sucklers.' Vic spat again. 'I'm glad I'm as old as I am, me girl. Seen too many changes for one man's lifetime. What's happening to the countryside turns me stomach, it does.'

'It's progress, I suppose. Every generation must–'

The sound of her phone ringing stopped her in midflow. She plucked it from her jacket pocket. 'Hello? Rosa? Are Marcus and Freya okay?'

'Yes. Yes, they're fine. Look, I'm on the car phone and need to be quick. James is following behind me in his car.' Rosa groaned. 'The school called him as well. He turned up at the same time as me.'

'Oh, that was okay, wasn't it?'

'Bloody hell, Shannon, I didn't know what to say or do in front of him. Then this Detective Constable Blee questioned us both, like, were we aware of somebody who wanted to harm the children? Or know of anybody who wanted to cause us distress?' Rosa talked so fast that Shannon had to strain to hear all the words and sentences. 'Then James put his oar in and interrogated me in front of Mrs Ferris, the school head of all people. He grilled me about my past. But what could I say, Shannon? What could I say? I denied knowing anything.' A sob came down the phone.

'Rosa? You okay?'

'What if something happens to Marcus or Freya because I'm keeping my past from James?'

A car horn blasted into Shannon's ear followed by the screech of brakes.

'Rosa? Rosa? Pull over.'

'Can't. James won't understand why I'm upset. I wanted to bring the children home, but he stopped me. Said they'd be fine. But they won't be fine, will they, Shannon?' Rosa was shouting now. 'They aren't fine while that creep Stephen Whittaker is free to do what he likes.'

'I really think you should pull over.'

'It's doing my head in, keeping everything from James.' Another sob sounded in Shannon's ear.

'Did you find out anything about the man? Was there anything on the school's CCTV?'

'Tall, skinny, but dressed in a dark hoodie so we couldn't see the slimeball's face. What now, Shannon? What do we do now?'

'I think it's time we told the police everything. Maybe speak to this DC Blee?'

'What!'

'Seriously, listen to me. You've been threatened with dead magpies, and my caravan's been torched. That's just for starters. Christ, Trevor's been arrested, and your children's lives are in danger.' Shannon rushed on. 'We can't deal with this on our own. The police could find Stephen Whittaker for us. Question him and … Look, I'm no fan of the police but … it's time.'

'No. I can't … Jesus, I don't know what to do. What if James leaves me once he learns the truth and how I lied to him?'

Shannon could hear Rosa thumping the steering wheel.

'Rosa, please stop. He won't. He loves you.'

'I'll have nothing if he leaves me.'

'Don't be silly, you'll have Marcus and Freya. Get a grip.' Shannon took a deep breath. 'We need to do the right thing.'

'What do I do?' Rosa repeated. 'I can't lose him.'

Shannon sucked in another breath. 'Don't you think you're losing him anyway?'

Rosa's car wheels crunched over gravel. 'Got to go. We're home. James is getting out of the Jag,' Rosa hissed. 'Don't go to the police, Shannon. Don't, just don't.'

The line went dead.

Back in the farmhouse kitchen, Shannon busied herself seasoning one of her favourite meals she'd made earlier: beef stew with dumplings. One of Trevor's favourites as well, she'd recently discovered. She glanced at the clock. Surely, he would be home soon. The police couldn't keep him long on some trumped-up accusations, could they?

As if on cue, a police car pulled into the yard and Trevor got out and slammed the door shut. He stood with his back and shoulders rigid for several minutes as he watched the vehicle make its way back down the lane. Even through the kitchen window, she could see his chest rise and fall as he took deep gulps of Carnmarth air.

She ran outside just as Vic came through the gate into the yard. Zach followed him, stared, and then quickly headed toward his caravan.

'Trevor, thank God,' she cried. 'The police released you.'

He turned his head slowly towards her and growled. 'Why wouldn't they? I did nothing wrong. It's your shit stalker that's the problem.'

'I'm sorry.'

'Sorry? Bloody hell, Shannon, do you know how embarrassing it was for me? This ... this whole thing ...'

'It's not the girl's fault,' Vic chipped in.

'Really? So, if I hadn't let her into my house ... into my home. If she'd gone when I told her, I would still have been dragged into the police station like a hardened criminal?' He snorted. 'I don't think so.'

'You're rightly upset, but don't go taking it out on Shannon, me lad.'

'Vic,' Shannon pleaded, 'there's no need to defend me.'

A glob of spittle glistened on Trevor's lip. 'What is it with women coming in and messing everything up?'

'Don't be a fool, lad. Don't go saying things you'll regret.' Vic stared hard at him. 'She's the best thing that's happened to Carnmarth in years. The best thing that's happened to you.'

'Keep your nose out, Vic,' Trevor snarled. 'I don't need trouble.'

Shannon's stomach clenched. Trevor was right. She was the cause of all this. She was the problem. Why did she think she could make a better life for herself? What her mother did would never leave her; it would always drag her back to that awful day of the car crash and the terrible death of all those innocent people.

'Maybe I should leave?' she whispered.

'What?' Trevor grunted.

'You know, leave Carnmarth. Leave Cornwall even? Like you said.'

My God, she'd said it. Leave Cornwall. It *was* possible, wasn't it? Perhaps that had always been the best thing to do, and she should've done it twenty-three years ago.

Trevor ran his hand through his hair. 'Yeah, maybe you should.'

Shannon's throat tightened. She mustn't cry.

'Don't drive her away, lad,' Vic said quietly.

For a second, Shannon thought she saw a look of confusion – or was it regret? – on Trevor's face, then he looked at her properly for the first time since the police had dropped him off.

'Okay. Okay, I'm sorry. I know I'm being a right jerk.' He ran his hand through his hair again. 'I'm tired and dirty. I need a shower and something to eat.'

'I've made beef stew and dumplings,' she said.

Trevor nodded, then turned on his heels. The farmhouse door slammed shut within moments.

'Fool,' Vic muttered before plodding across the yard towards his caravan.

Shannon stared at the kitchen door. Her eyes filled with tears at the thought and promise of what could have been. Standing stock still, she heard none of the usual animal noises in and around the farmyard, nor the birdsong in the trees. Fear for the future overwhelmed her senses. Her mind was blank. Beef stew and dumplings? Was that all she could say to him when he apologised?

Eventually, she rolled her head from side to side and flexed her fingers. Yes, she would move out of Carnmarth and probably Cornwall, but not until she and Rosa had found Stephen Whittaker and, with any luck, had him locked up.

There was only one thing to do, only one logical place to start: Paul Whittaker.

She opened her phone and punched in the number for Nancarrow Nursing Home.

26

Rosa applied a coat of bright red lipstick, looked in the dressing table mirror and forced a smile. Freshly showered, hair washed and blow-dried, and in full make-up, she looked every inch the successful wife that James wanted. So why didn't she feel like it? Why didn't the smile reach her eyes, no matter how hard she tried or how many happy thoughts she conjured up?

The diamond studs that James gave her as a birthday present twinkled in the artificial light, and she wore his favourite cream cashmere sweater; too hot for an evening meal, but she hoped if she looked her best, it would shake him out of the awful moody silence he'd adopted since they'd got back from Treloar School several hours ago.

At the thought of Treloar School, the face of the young police officer came into her mind.

After they had finished with all the questions and note-taking inside the school, DC Blee had walked with her to her car. James had stormed ahead and was already at the wheel of his Jaguar.

'I thought you might've taken Marcus and Freya home with you,' DC Blee said. 'Seeing as you were so upset about what's happened.'

'I wanted to, but James felt it was best they stayed. The children weren't aware of the incident, so ...' She shrugged. 'He's probably right.'

He looked at her oddly. 'Oh, I don't know. Most fathers would jump at the chance to spoil their kids with a nice

201

surprise. Wouldn't you and Mr Trevail enjoy taking them to McDonald's for a special treat?'

Rosa snorted. 'James wouldn't be seen dead anywhere near a McDonald's, and he doesn't do surprises or, at least, not those types of surprises.'

DC Blee shook his head. 'Pity. Anyhow, I hope you have a friend you can confide in.'

'Oh, I do. Shannon at Carnmarth Farm.' She clamped a hand over her mouth. Why the hell had she blurted out Shannon's name, to the police of all people?

'Good.' He reached into his pocket. 'Take this, just in case you remember something else.'

Rosa looked at the official card giving DC Blee's contact details and mobile phone number.

'It's a direct line. The quickest way of getting to me,' he pushed the card into her hand, 'should there be another problem.' He turned away and headed towards a police car parked nearby.

James had revved the engine of his Jag several times. Rosa, in response, had hurried to her vehicle and had pulled out in front of him, aware of his presence in the rearview mirror the whole way home.

A door slammed downstairs. Despite the cashmere sweater, Rosa shivered. James was still in a mood then. She shivered again. Jesus, what if that dreadful man had managed to take Marcus and Freya? What would he have done to them?

Tears filled her eyes for the umpteenth time since leaving the school. She blinked them away and stood abruptly. Pushing her feet into high-heeled shoes, she tugged at the waistband of her trousers, which had slipped down to rest on her hip bones. Her hands fitted easily between the band and her concave stomach. She'd lost weight, too much weight. The stress of everything was clearly getting to her.

Her phone bleeped. Shannon. Rosa scanned the brief text message. Thank goodness, the police had released Trevor and – relief shot through her – Shannon had got an interview at Nancarrow Nursing Home. Maybe they would finally track Stephen Whittaker down.

She patted her hair and made her way downstairs. There wasn't much to do but steam the vegetables and cook the meat; she'd prepped everything earlier.

In the kitchen, she placed a couple of sirloin steaks on the grill, then popped both English and French mustard onto a tray – she was sure James would insist on eating in the dining room – along with various other relishes and condiments she thought her husband might want with his meal.

James sat at one end of the kitchen table with a large scotch in his hand, a newspaper laid out in front of him, and his cheeks flushed.

'You disappointed me today,' he said.

Rosa jumped as his deep voice echoed around the kitchen. 'Disappointed you?'

'Yes.'

'In what way?'

'You know I don't approve of you wearing jeans, but today's outfit went a step too far.' He roughly folded the newspaper. 'You looked like a tramp.'

Rosa's heart rate quickened. 'What?'

'What in damnation did you have on your feet? You looked … cheap. Like someone had dragged you through a hedge backwards. In front of that frightful Mrs Ferris, of all people.'

Blood pulsed through Rosa's temple. Shannon's walking boots: she'd forgotten to take off the old boots and socks she'd borrowed in her rush to get to Treloar School.

'I …' she faltered.

'Who would own such atrocious things? How did you come by them? You could never have bought them?'

'One of the parents at the school invited me for a walk. She loaned them to me.' Rosa could hear the tremble in her voice and forced herself to remain calm. She knew what he suspected: that she'd worn the boots on some tryst with a lover. And how could she defend herself when she couldn't tell him the truth?

'That Penny woman, I suppose. The one you use to bring the children home on a Friday evening.'

'I don't use her. We help each other out. Me one week and Penny the next.'

'So it was her?'

'No.' Rosa's head was spinning, trying to keep up with the lies. 'It was a friend of hers.'

'A friend of a friend. How intriguing.' James snorted. 'What's her name, this mysterious new hiker friend of yours?'

'Jane.' Rosa noisily pulled out the grill pan and made a fuss of turning the steaks and putting the pan back into its slot with a clatter.

James returned to reading the newspaper, and Rosa stared through the window at the yachts serenely tacking across the river. The early evening light glinted off the water.

The steak tasted like leather in her mouth. She pushed most of it to the side of her plate and nibbled on a green bean. She'd never really understood the saying 'the silence was deafening,' but she did now.

'I've been looking at schools.' James spoke quietly but the words still echoed around the barren, soulless dining room.

'Schools?'

'There are excellent boarding schools in Devon that would be ideal for Marcus and Freya. They might need to go to separate establishments to get the best education for each of them, but I judge that to be a good thing. It would make them more independent. Twins can get terribly clingy with each other.'

'Separate schools for Marcus and Freya?' Her heart started to thump again. She couldn't comprehend what James was saying.

'Treloar School is plainly incompetent.'

'Incompetent?'

'Do you have to repeat my every word? It's becoming rather irritating, darling.'

She flinched at the term of endearment, then rallied. 'I don't think they're incompetent. The school staff stopped the man from getting anywhere near the children. They followed all the right protocols and procedures by calling us and the police.'

She sucked in a deep breath. Panic clawed at her throat. Marcus and Freya couldn't go to school in Devon. They just couldn't. She'd miss them so much. And, more importantly, how would she protect them in another county? Stephen Whittaker was so cunning; he would find them wherever they were. She had to stop James from embarking on this terrible plan. She tried to speak but her throat was too dry. She swallowed hard and tried again.

'I don't understand why you think they need to go away. They're doing well at Treloar School. They like it there.'

'My prime concern is for their safety. I assume, as their mother, you'd want the same thing.'

'But I ... I wouldn't see them at weekends.'

'They'd come home for half-term and holidays.' James wiped his mouth with a napkin. 'As I said before, I believe it would be good for them.'

Damn him. 'But–'

'You'd do well to remember that I'm your husband, the children's stepfather, and,' he arranged his knife and fork precisely side by side on his empty plate, 'as I pay the school fees, I've every right to have the final say on which one or ones I spend my money on.'

Rosa's heart beat so fast that for a moment she thought she would faint. She reached for her glass of water. Droplets splashed over her hand as she lifted it to her lips. Had she been kidding herself this whole time, thinking she and James were working as one in some sort of wonder marriage-cum-partnership? Now, the minute things had got tough, the moment he thought she wasn't performing her role to his satisfaction, he'd pulled rank, leaving her in no doubt as to where the power in their relationship really lay.

'Of course, the concerning question is, who wanted to take the children out of Treloar School in the first place?' He glared at her, one eyebrow raised. 'Well?'

'I've … I've no idea,' she stuttered.

'But you must have some clue? An old flame? Ex-husband? The children's father, perhaps?' He smirked. 'You never did tell me anything about your past, did you … darling?'

Her chest felt so tight she pressed her hand against her rib cage.

'Mike Spencer.' The words rushed from her mouth without rhyme or reason.

'Mike Spencer? He's the father of Marcus and Freya?'

'No, no, of course not.' Her hand fluttered in front of her. 'He's so creepy,' she gasped. 'He's always around here. Leering at me, and–'

James's sudden laughter shocked her.

'My darling, I think you're losing it. Mike's a harmless idiot. An uneducated and self-taught yokel who happened on a good idea and built himself a business.'

'Then why invite him to Curlew House so often and play golf with him if you don't like him?'

'Because he's a darn good golf player, helping me improve my handicap until I can find somebody more suitable.' James pushed his plate towards her. 'The steak was wonderful, but I'll skip dessert. The Jag needs a clean and polish; the mud from your tyres made a right mess of the bodywork. You drove so fast back from Treloar School, I had a job to keep up with you.'

'My fault … again.' She stood and followed him into the kitchen.

'Stop being paranoid, Rosa. It doesn't become you.' James picked up his car keys, turned and kissed the top of her head.

Involuntarily, she pulled away. Damn, James, she would send Marcus and Freya to the local comprehensive school before she'd send them away.

He laughed, and a sudden anger replaced the panic that had gripped her.

She stood and faced him. 'You need to listen because I want to make it crystal clear that I've no intention of allowing Marcus and Freya, *my* children, to move to a school in Dev–'

The sound of his fist slamming onto the kitchen table ricocheted around the room.

She took several steps backwards.

He followed her, his red face only inches from hers, his every word punctuated by his finger poking into her chest. 'Don't. You. Ever. Talk. Back. To. Me.'

She came to a halt, her back pressed against the worktop, cold marble seeping through her sweater.

'Do you understand me?' He raised his hand, fist clenched. 'I said, do you understand me?'

She flinched. He was going to hit her.

'Do you?'

She nodded.

His hand whizzed past her face and slammed, palm down, onto the worktop right next to her. 'Good,' he said, then picked up his keys and phone and strolled out of the kitchen.

Rosa slid to the floor, her body shaking with sobs.

27

Shannon smoothed her red tunic top down over her navy trousers, then straightened her name badge. Today, she'd been paired with Meg, a care assistant who'd worked at Nancarrow Nursing Home for what seemed like forever. This morning, Meg was teaching Shannon how to hoist and manoeuvre the residents from their comfortable beds into their custom-made wheelchairs and get them dressed for breakfast.

Everything about Nancarrow oozed opulence and wealth, from the luxurious hotel-style dining room – pristine white tablecloths crisscrossed over blue ones, quality crockery and cutlery – to the sumptuous bedrooms, tastefully decorated, with individuals or families encouraged to add their own touch with the introduction of personal pictures, photos and furniture as they wished.

Whoever was paying for Paul's fees was shelling out a shedload of money. Even if he were fully health funded, the 'extras' this place incurred would be draining somebody dry. Stephen Whittaker? Or did Paul have enough compensation from the accident to fund his own care? Shannon hoped it was the latter as she held the door open to Room No. 10 so Meg could push a large white hoist into Paul's bedroom.

'Good morning, Paul,' Meg said in a jolly voice. 'How are you today, my luvvie?'

Paul's head shook from side to side as he gurgled a sleepy hello. His body lay in a foetal position, his left forearm curled across his chest, the hand limp and useless.

Shannon sucked in her breath. Would she ever grow used to seeing him like this?

Meg glanced at her. 'It takes a while to get your head around some of the stuff we see here, especially when bad things have happened to the younger residents. You'll cope.' She turned and smiled at Paul, then back to Shannon. 'You have what it takes. I've seen enough staff come and go over the years, and I can tell. Helping them is what we can do to make their lives better.'

Shannon wasn't sure that what she was doing would make Paul's life better, and neither, she expected, would Meg be so sure if she knew why Shannon had really taken the job. Shannon had been working at Nancarrow for ten days now, and each time she saw Paul, her heart raced, and the horrible guilt she'd held onto for all those years rose to the surface. Guilt for what she and her mum had done to cause the terrible sight in front of her. Guilt for Paul's promising future having been so brutally replaced by the physical and mental prison he endured every day. Was he aware of his prison? She couldn't answer that, but she did understand now why his brother wanted revenge.

'Shannon, give me a hand to roll him, then we can hoist him into his wheelchair. Just watch what I'm doing and follow my instructions.' Meg continued to talk to Paul as she worked. 'Bathroom first, then breakfast, my luvvie. Bacon and eggs again this morning? Or is it going to be cereal and toast?'

'Ba ... bacon and eggs.' Paul's words were slurred, but his voice was stronger and clearer now that he was awake.

'Green sweater or navy sweater, Paul?' Shannon asked.

'Gre ... green.'

She wondered how well he could see her; one eye constantly drifted into the corner socket and out again. She hurriedly gathered his clothes and followed Meg and

Paul, now in his wheelchair, into the en suite to attend to his personal care needs.

'So, what brought you to Nancarrow?' Meg asked.

Shannon jolted. For a split second, she thought the canny older woman had sussed her, but Meg smiled and said, 'There must be carer jobs nearer to you. Nursing and Residential Homes are crying out for staff.'

'I …I wanted to work in an establishment for residents with learning disabilities, and Nancarrow's the best.' Blimey, when had she become such a good liar? 'And, I'm afraid to say, the money this place pays made the decision easy as well.'

'I know what you mean; this establishment pays a higher rate to keep their staff, which in turn pleases the families. Still, the money doesn't compensate if you don't like the work.'

Shannon understood that. She was still getting over the shock that an up-market place like Nancarrow had employed her. Rosa had coached her on what to say at the interview, and Mrs Martin had come good with a reference, presumably to salve her conscience. Thankfully, all the criminal checks came back clear and, hey presto, Shannon had got herself a properly paid job – with the need to open a bank account – for the first time in her life.

Shannon eased Paul's arm into his green sweater and brushed his hair. There was hardly any grey for a man nearing forty years of age, and his face was surprisingly wrinkle-free. Perhaps it was the lack of worries that kept him so young and innocent-looking? She took the metal clipboard from the end of his bed and updated his care notes. Unfortunately, only Paul's name had been entered on the top. In the last ten days, she'd found out nothing about Paul's next of kin or any information about Stephen Whittaker. It seemed that the care staff only really knew the residents' names and brief backgrounds, together with whatever their family members told them. The nurses on the premises knew about their health and medication requirements, but their personal files were kept in the manager's office, which was always locked whenever she was absent from the room. The nurse on duty was the only other person who had a duplicate key.

Eight hours later, Shannon pulled her car into the layby between Tresillian and Truro and parked behind Rosa's BMW. Rosa got out and climbed into Shannon's vehicle.

'Crikey, Shannon, call this a seat? It's hard as a board and lumpy.'

'Sorry, Madam, not all of us can drive a new car smelling of leather and polish.'

Rosa thumped her lightly on the thigh. 'Don't be cheeky, I don't have the time. Did you find out anything?'

'Nope.'

'Nothing from the other staff?'

Shannon shook her head. 'They know very little about Paul. Just that he was involved in a car accident years ago, and he used to live in Surrey.'

'You have to get to his file.'

'I've been trying, but the manager has all the personal records under lock and key. I don't think I'm going to find Stephen Whittaker this way.'

'You must.' Rosa's voice was loud in the confines of the vehicle.

Shannon stared at her. Christ, she looked awful; thin, pale, a slight tremor in her hands. James and that failing marriage of theirs had taken its toll on her old friend. Why didn't she leave him? She'd been a strong, independent woman before she'd met him. What was stopping her from packing up and walking away? Still, what did Shannon know? She'd lived in a broken-down wreck of a caravan for five years and only quit because somebody burnt it down.

'You can't give up. You can't,' Rosa said again.

'What can I do? Break into the office?'

'Yes.'

'What?'

'That's exactly what you've got to do. Break into the manager's office and find Paul's file.'

'You've got to be joking. I'd never get away with it. There's always loads of staff about.'

'Not at night, surely?'

Shannon sighed. Rosa was right. She already knew she had to do this if she was ever going to be able to move on with her life. Since his arrest, she and Trevor had settled back into the routines they had established before, and the initial anger he'd shot her way had been replaced with a tense truce of sorts. Sadly, the easy-going relationship that had begun to develop between them had soured somewhat. Neither of them, it seemed, could talk about their feelings or worries, and it saddened her.

'I'll do it,' she whispered. 'On my next night shift.'

Nancarrow was a totally different place at night. The lights in the corridors were dimmed, and apart from the occasional call bell ringing, or a resident shouting, it was pretty much like any other old house with its unexplained creaks and groans.

Staff numbers at nighttime were very much reduced, but there was still plenty to do: helping residents who needed to be turned several times to prevent bedsores, giving comforting words to those who woke from nightmares, along with regular checks to each room to see that all was well with its occupant. Shannon found herself working the night shift with Frank and Joan. She'd only seen Frank a few times around Nancarrow but knew Joan better.

Her stomach churned as she and Frank changed Dan's pyjamas and bed sheets in Room No. 25. Tonight, she planned to get into the manager's office. She had tried the previous evening, but an emergency with one of the residents had scuppered that. She had to find some excuse to be on her own if she was to have any chance of getting into the office. As she tucked the clean sheets around Dan's sleeping body, she knew it was now or never.

She took a deep breath and winced.

'You okay?' Frank asked.

'Bad cramps.' Shannon pulled a face. 'You know … that time of month.'

'Whoa. Too much information.' Frank's brown eyes widened as he raked his hand through his hair.

'I need to get a couple of paracetamols from my rucksack in the staff room.' She rubbed her abdomen and winced again. 'And, well, you know … attend to other things.'

'Go.' Frank held up his hand, palm toward Shannon. 'I can manage here.'

Running down the stairs to the ground floor, Shannon glanced at her watch; she reckoned she had about fifteen minutes at most before she had to get back to Frank.

In the kitchen, she grabbed a large piece of chocolate pudding left over from the residents' evening meal. She loved that there was always surplus food for the staff if they wanted it. Holding the bowl, she walked towards the nurses' station – a grand name for what was, in fact, a room not much bigger than a cupboard, furnished with a couple of chairs and a tiny desk. The walls of the cupboard were lined with cabinets that held all the prescribed medications, lotions and creams that the residents needed. Joan was busy taking boxes down from the shelves and counting medication into various dispensing containers. But it was the small rack off to one side that Shannon had her sights on because dangling from one of the hooks was the key to the manager's office.

'Hey,' she said as she moved into the room, squeezing behind Joan and placing the bowl of chocolate pudding on the tiny office desk in the corner. Joan twisted around to stare at the pudding. As soon as she turned her back, Shannon grabbed the office key from the rack and slipped it into her pocket.

'Goodness, Shannon, don't tempt me,' Joan said. 'I don't have enough 'syns' left on the Slimming World plan this week to eat that.'

'Oh, sorry. I fancied something sweet and thought you must be getting peckish too.'

'You weren't wrong.' Joan grinned at her as she picked up the bowl and spoon.

'Enjoy.' Shannon smiled back at Joan's round face as she tucked into the pudding. 'Can't stop. I'll come back in my break for a longer chat.'

A few minutes later, Shannon's hand shook as she pushed the key into the office door. She checked her watch again; ten minutes left.

Inside, she quickly locked the door behind her, pulled out her phone and punched the torch symbol. Holding the light close to her chest, she scanned the long, narrow room. Two office desks, clutter-free apart from a printer and two telephones, fitted against one side. Shelves, which lined the wall above, held near-empty wire baskets, envelopes, a red hole punch and a stapler. On the other wall, the torch light picked out a tall, cream filing cabinet. Shannon quickly leant down and tugged at the handle of the roll-up front.

Locked. Damn.

She glanced at her watch; eight minutes.

Her breathing quickened as she tried the desk drawers, looking for the small key that would open the cabinet. Two drawers later, she'd found nothing but a box of tissues, a wrinkled apple and a load of pens and paperclips. In the third drawer, Shannon found a small tin hidden beneath a bag of mint humbugs and yet another box of tissues. She lifted it out and prised open the lid. Eureka! Two small keys. She hurriedly knelt and tried the first key. The lock clicked and sprung free from its fixings. The front started to roll upwards with a loud rattle. She gasped and clamped her hand on it to stop the noise, then hesitated with head cocked. Surely, Joan would come running at any moment, but the only sound was Shannon's breath rasping in her throat.

She took a couple of deep gulps of air and slowly eased the front upwards to expose the bottom two rows of records. She saw his name tag immediately. Three very large files of a different colour and quality – presumably from the previous nursing home – were stacked one on top of the other. Next to them, in its allocated slot, was a thin wallet file like all the others for the Nancarrow residents.

She pulled the record out and opened it up on the floor. Inside the cover was exactly what she was hoping for: a detailed information form containing all the essential data on Paul Whittaker: his full name, date of birth, and, please, sweet please, next of kin.

A bead of sweat trickled down her neck.

Three minutes.

Just enough time to take a photo of the information. She and Rosa would read and check everything later. She switched her phone from torch to camera mode, turned on the angle-poise lamp on the office manager's desk, placed the open file underneath the light, and took several photos.

'Hi, Joan. Have you seen Shannon?' Frank's voice.

Shannon fumbled to switch off the angle-poise lamp. In her haste, she knocked the file onto the floor. Papers scattered across the carpet. She froze, hand pressed against her chest. Breathe in. One. Two. Three. Breathe out. One. Two. Three.

'Saw her ten, maybe fifteen minutes ago. She brought me a pudding.'

'Said she didn't feel too good, but she's been gone an age.'

'Oh. Come to think of it, she was a bit pale and anxious.'

'You don't look so well yourself, Joan. Everything okay?'

'Yes, well, no. I've lost the key to Mary's office. I've got to find it, or she'll fire me.'

The knob on the office door rattled and twisted. Shannon's heart thudded in her chest. Fortunately, she'd remembered to lock the door from the inside.

'Can't have gone far. Have you checked your pockets? Look, come and check out the ladies' loos for me, make sure Shannon's okay, and then I'll help you look.'

The voices in the corridor slowly faded as Joan and Frank moved away.

Shannon switched her torch back on. She had to get a move on, slip the key back into the office and catch up with Frank, spin him some tale. She needed to keep this job until she found out where Stephen Whittaker was. She tidied the contents of Paul's file but stopped for a moment to check the photos she'd taken against the information sheet. The last thing she needed was blurry data. Besides, the urge to see the content overwhelmed her; this information could change her life.

Her eyes settled on the next of kin box: Stephen Whittaker. No surprise there. She looked further down for his home address and emergency contact number. She swallowed. This was it. Now she would know where he was. Her eyes widened. A lump came into her throat almost choking her. She forced herself not to cough.

No. No. This couldn't be happening.

In the address and emergency telephone number boxes was a neatly typed message: '*All contact to be made via Philips, Smith and Lawrence, Solicitors.*'

Shannon's eyes blurred with tears as she collapsed back onto her heels.

Damn him. Damn Stephen Whittaker. He'd outwitted them again.

28

Rosa pushed herself harder and harder as she sprinted flat out across the beach. Her eyes watered, each breath a struggle. Finally, when her gasps became peppered with the odd squeak and her throat was hoarse, she stopped and bent over, arms folded tight across her chest. After a few minutes, she forced herself to straighten up and ran her hand over her protruding ribs. She flinched, and when she rolled up her lycra top, shock once again sent a tremor through her body at the sight of the black-grey bruises tinged with yellow. Was it only last week that James's unpredictable moods had turned to violence? Rosa leaned against the cliff face, then slid down onto the sand.

She'd walked on eggshells all that evening as James's mood swung from a terrible silence to downright rudeness. Everything about her was wrong: her hair, her clothes – usually his favourite things – her food. When the evening meal had finished and she was loading the dishwasher, he'd elbowed her as he slammed his coffee cup into the sink, causing her to grab the worktop to avoid tripping over the open dishwasher door. She had dared to mumble something under her breath and in an instant, he'd shoved her to the floor, bent over and punched her in the ribs until she cried out and begged him to stop.

Afterwards, he himself had begged: begged for her forgiveness, kissing her face and whispering loving words into her ears, like he'd done in those first months after they met. Later still, after they'd made love, he'd told her over and over that he loved her and would never do it again.

But he had.

She rolled up her sleeve and looked at the fresh fingertip bruises on her upper arm. A sob rushed up from deep within her chest. How had it come to this? How had she not seen it coming? Why didn't she just pack up and leave him? In the past, her confident persona had deterred any sort of abusive men from getting within half a mile of her. On the rare occasion that one did get too close, she simply walked away. Immediately.

She pushed a strand of hair back from her face. If only she could get a decent night's sleep, then maybe the constant headaches and the tension in her neck would go, and she could think more clearly. But where would she go with two children in tow? Leaving would put their education and futures at risk. Who else would want her, now that she looked so scrawny and worn down with life, just like the middle-aged women on the Pengollan Estate? Men with money wanted to be seen with a bit of fluff or a looker on their arm, and there were plenty of young, beautiful women under thirty who would oblige in exchange for the lifestyle that James offered.

Another sob rocked her body. Damn James. Logically, she knew his behaviour was that of a classic bully. But … he had a hold over her. What she couldn't understand was how she had let her defences down, how she'd allowed him to have such control over her. Was it love?

Questions rattled round and round in her head. Where would she go if she did leave? Shannon? No, she was only a tenant at Carnmarth Farm. She couldn't help her. Her dad? She knew deep down that he would come good and help in an instant, but the thought of moving back to live on the Pengollan Estate was more than she could bear. She couldn't inflict that future on Freya and Marcus.

She stood up and brushed the sand from her clothing and hands. No, she was being over dramatic. James hadn't meant to hurt her. He was stressed with work. To be fair, it must be hard to establish a new financial consultancy business in Cornwall. And on top of that, he knew she'd been lying to him. What else was he supposed to think, given his history and her complete inability to tell him the truth? No wonder he was going out of his mind. No, James provided her with a wonderful house and life. The children were well looked after, and he hadn't said any more about moving them to different schools in Devon. She shivered and hurriedly pushed the thought away that he still might be planning the move behind her back, and she might yet find herself spending week after lonely week with only James for company.

She jogged on the spot to warm up her stiff muscles.

James had sent her an enormous bunch of white roses earlier in the morning, with a card declaring his love for her. That was enough. He wouldn't hurt her again. She would try harder and do everything she could to keep him happy. This thing with the stalker would be over soon, and they could go back to how things were.

Rosa stared at Shannon as she walked across the decked area behind the Beach Café and placed the tray on the table. It had been some time since they'd met at Chapel Cove, and how things had changed. This time, it was Shannon who had bought the coffee and cakes, and she was the one who looked healthy and well-dressed. The ludicrous pigtail had gone, and her shiny hair tumbled over her shoulders. Rosa shuddered inwardly. Was she the one who now looked drawn and pale?

'I've never been so scared in my life.'

Rosa took a sip of coffee as Shannon repeated her story about breaking into the office at Nancarrow, and how a couple of the staff had nearly caught her.

'What the hell do we do now?' Rosa groaned.

'I'm going to stay on at Nancarrow for another month. See if I can discover any more about Paul or Stephen from the staff. Also, Meg, one of the care assistants, mentioned that Paul has had a couple of visits from someone. She didn't know if it was a relative or a guardian or legal rep.' Shannon took a big bite of chocolate cake. 'But I thought if he turned up again, it might give me a lead to Stephen.'

'At least it's some sort of plan. I had another go at checking out Mike Spencer but if he's anything but a CCTV expert, he's covered his tracks well.'

'Like Stephen Whittaker, you mean?'

'Who knows.' Rosa swallowed. 'Mike Spencer will be at Curlew House later this afternoon to undertake maintenance checks on the security system. He knows James won't be there, but he insists on dropping in anyway.' She shivered. 'He gives me the creeps.'

'I feel the same about Zach.'

'What? Is he still hanging around Carnmarth?'

'In no hurry to go back home and face the music, according to Vic.'

Rosa sat upright.

'Maybe he's waiting until he's got some money.' She gasped. 'Maybe he's hoping to make a quick buck to fund his failed business and get back in his wife's good books.' She grabbed Shannon's arm. 'Maybe the whole social media thing is a cover and he's Stephen Whittaker.'

Shannon blew out her cheeks. 'And maybe he's just a pillock.'

Rosa flopped against the back of her chair.

A seagull flew low over their table. Rosa grabbed her plate, broke off a piece of sponge and popped it into her mouth. It tasted like sawdust and she almost retched. When had she last eaten?

'Don't you find it hard working at that place and seeing all those people with ... you know ... difficulties?' she asked.

Shannon smiled. 'Truth is, I'm loving it. Those people with difficulties, as you call them, are brilliant. For the first time in my life, I feel that I'm doing something worthwhile.'

'Isn't it hard seeing Paul?'

Shannon shrugged. 'I've been caring for him nearly every day. Beth, who works at the home as a counsellor-cum-activities manager, saw me sketching in my break and asked me to sit in on an activity session and show the residents my drawings of the farm animals and wildlife.' Shannon took another bite of cake. 'Paul loved my sketches of Trudie and Fern. He laughed out loud and was clearly happy. I felt great, thinking I'd helped him feel better. Beth reckons he probably had a pet dog before the accident because he'd also lit up last month when somebody brought in a PAT dog for the residents to stroke.'

Rosa stirred her coffee. Perhaps she should take up Shannon's offer and visit Nancarrow to see Paul? At the same time, wouldn't it be a good idea if she faced up to what she'd done and owned up to her role in the accident? It might stop the conveyor belt of grisly accident scenes and grey newspaper images of the Whittaker family that rolled through her head for most of her waking moments.

It's all my fault, it's all my fault. The words suddenly intruded into Rosa's thoughts, overriding everything else. No. No. She wouldn't go there.

She straightened up and lifted the cup to her lips. 'You look happy,' she told Shannon.

'It's a great job. Having a regular salary coming in is a welcome change as well.'

'I've found in life that money generally helps. A lot.'

'Money isn't everything,' Shannon replied.

'Isn't it?'

Shannon reached for her hand. 'You okay? You don't seem like yourself. Is James treating you as he should?'

Rosa pulled her hand away and scrambled in her bag for her lipstick. A bit of make-up would make her look less wretched. She didn't need Shannon feeling sorry for her.

'You can talk to me,' Shannon said softly. 'I'm becoming a good listener.'

Rosa looked at Shannon, tempted to spill the lot, but how could she tell her oldest friend that everything in her life was a lie? How could she confess that James had been violent more than once, and yet she'd still made the decision to stay with him? No, she was used to hiding secrets; what was another one?

She applied a coat of lipstick. 'DC Blee rang again. He says he's just checking there's been no more incidents.' Rosa forced herself to smile. 'I think he knows I've not told him everything and he's pumping me to say more. It's another thing to stress me out.'

'Don't worry about DC Blee. You can handle him. I'm more worried about you. You know you can tell me if there's anything wrong?'

'Everything's fine.' Rosa flapped a dismissive hand in the air. 'James and I are good. Freya and Marcus will be home later today for the weekend. We'll have fun.'

'Rosa?'

'Yes.'

'I hope you still have a Plan B if things don't turn out right. From memory, you always had one.'

'Of course I have. If it all goes belly up, I'll divorce James and take him for half of all he's got, including Curlew House.' Rosa laughed out loud.

A couple at the next table turned to look at her.

Shannon touched her hand again. 'Just remember that whatever happens, you'll still have the most precious gifts in the world.'

'What?'

'Marcus and Freya.' Shannon's eyes fixed on hers. 'They're the most wonderful human beings. You'll still have them no matter what happens with James.' Shannon squeezed her hand. 'I hope you realise how incredibly lucky you are to have them, with or without the money.'

Rosa turned and studied the waves rolling back and forth on the shoreline. What did Shannon know about luck? How could anybody consider themselves lucky if they didn't have either power or money? And these days, she had neither.

Rosa opened the cooker door, lifted out the joint of pork, basted it and returned it to the oven. The meal was on track. She made herself a cup of Chamomile tea and stood with her hands wrapped around the hot mug, staring at the array of happy photos on the kitchen wall: her and James's wedding photograph taken a little over twelve months ago, Freya and Marcus in their neat school uniforms, and the large headshot of James. A handsome man, Shannon had called him when she saw the picture on her only visit to Curlew House a few months ago. Little had Shannon known – and neither had she back then – that behind the smiling face and crinkly blue eyes hid a bullying, coercive husband.

Rosa moved to the kitchen table, rested her elbows on the surface and let out a sigh. Shannon's comment about her Plan B rattled around inside her head. At the very least, she ought to check her financial security to confirm that she *would* have money from Curlew House if she and James did split up.

Unfortunately, while James had his faults, being disorganised with all his paperwork wasn't one of them; everything he dealt with would either be password-protected on his computer or in files under lock and key in his office.

The tea was doing nothing to relax her. She wouldn't be able to calm down until Mike Spencer, who was in the basement checking the system, had left the house.

A thought rushed into her head. Tea sloshed over her hand in her hurry to stand. Would she be able to do it? Did she still have her old skills? She briefly smiled, then nodded.

Minutes later, she placed a freshly made mug of coffee and a piece of cake on the bench slightly inside the entrance to the basement; it was the closest she wanted to get to the creep below the stairs.

'Another coffee and a piece of cake here for you, Mike.'

'Thanks, Mrs Trevail.' He craned his neck and looked up the stairs at her. 'You're always so kind to me.'

'I was wondering how long you're going to be. I need to go out for a few bits of shopping.'

'Ten minutes, and then the system will be back on again. In the meantime, if any burglars break in, I'll be here to protect you.' He grinned again, his eyes half-closed as he looked her up and down.

She hurriedly ran back up the basement stairs, grabbed a thin metal skewer from one of the kitchen drawers, and rushed into James's office. Her heart thumped in her chest. Eight minutes max before the cameras were back on. She could do it, couldn't she?

With a few twists and turns, the lock to James's metal cabinet clicked and the drawer popped open. Still got it, girl, Rosa smiled to herself.

She ran her fingers along the name tabs until she found the one she wanted: Deeds – Curlew House. Her hands shook as she opened the wallet file, laid it on James's desk and started to read.

The words swam before her eyes and her vision darkened at the edges. She fell into James's leather chair. James had already taken control of her bank account, and now it was clear that the only name on the Deeds was James's. Fuck, if she divorced him, she would have nothing.

Shannon's words pounded into her head: 'Whatever happens, you'll still have the most precious gifts in the world.' Well, that may be so, but what sort of gift was she to her children if she couldn't provide for them in any shape or form?

She stood and looked through the window at the sea, then pressed her palms flat against the cold surface and banged her forehead against the pane. There was no escape. She was trapped in this bloody glass prison.

29

Shannon ran her hand through the white curls on the calf's face, then scratched the spot between its ears. The summer sun caressed her body as she watched Trevor finish erecting an electric fence in the next field. He gripped the wire with one hand and jumped with exaggerated jerks as the rhythmic shock pulsed through him. She laughed at his good mood and the silly game he was playing for her benefit. Time really did heal, thank God, and over the weeks since his arrest, Trevor had shrugged off his anger and hurt and was back to his old self.

She felt a tug and looked down. The calf had grabbed the end of her blouse and was sucking it into one soggy mess. 'Yuck, leave off, you monster.' She gently pushed the animal's head away and ran her fingers over its soft red-brown coat.

Trevor came up to the gate. The cows and other calves had shifted into a tight group against the metal bars, clearly eager to taste the new grass.

'That's a Hereford, and those black ones are Aberdeen Angus.' He undid the latch as he spoke, a smile spreading across his face.

'I do know what they are.' She grinned at him.

'Thought you might have forgotten with all the hours you've been working at Nancarrow.' He pulled the gate aside, and the animals rushed through into the new pasture. Shannon followed them.

'It'll only be for a short while longer, until we can find Stephen Whittaker.'

'You haven't had any trouble from him recently. Maybe he's given up?'

'Maybe, but him doing nothing scares me.' Shannon shivered. 'I've a gut feeling he's got something big up his sleeve. Why else go to all the trouble of moving Paul to Cornwall?'

'Why can't the git show his face? The man's a right coward and screwup if you ask me.'

Shannon stared at the cows, munching at the grass. The calves gambolled and played together in small groups. She didn't want to think any more about Stephen Whittaker and ruin this perfect scene.

Trevor pinned the gate open with a large granite boulder to give the animals the run of both fields. He leaned against the newly trimmed hedge. The collies, Flo, Fern, and Kim, fixed their black and white faces onto Trevor's, waiting for his next instructions, their tongues lolling. Trudie ambled over to sit next to Shannon, while Whisky plonked his fat Jack Russell bottom onto her foot. Happiness flooded through her; she, Trevor and the dogs were like a little family.

A few white clouds scudded across an otherwise perfectly blue sky. A kestrel fluttered over a patch of grass in the far corner of the field. She glanced at Trevor and her heart thumped at the sight of his clean-shaven face and neat hair. He'd certainly smartened up in recent months, but then, so had she.

'Are you at Nancarrow tomorrow?' Trevor took out a tube of mints from his pocket and offered her one.

She shook her head. 'Got an early shift, but I can help to bring in the hay bales after I finish if that's any good.'

'You'll be knackered.'

That would be true, but the physical work on the farm was different to the work at Nancarrow. The clean air and the quiet pace of life at Carnmarth calmed her. How would she cope if she had to leave … or, rather, when?

'Take my car.'

'What?'

'Take my car in the morning. Yours is a wreck. I'm surprised it's lasted so long. It'll let you down soon.'

'I can't, what if I ding yours?'

He laughed. A good sound. 'Well, that's a real risk if the number of dents on your old banger's anything to go by.'

'Why lend me your car, then?'

'Just being selfish. Reckon you'd only call me or Vic if your old thing breaks down in the middle of the night or whenever. Call it damage limitation.'

'Thanks.'

'I'll cook tonight, if you like,' Trevor said.

'I would like.'

'And you can tell me about those sketches you've done of the quarry.'

Shannon pushed away from the hedge with a jolt. 'You've seen them?'

'If you will leave them lying around, what do you expect?'

'It … it was only a bit of fun.'

'Really?'

Her cheeks grew hot. 'I thought if you had a few campers in the quarry, it would earn you some extra money, and I could pull my weight by getting the punters in and organising everything. Make life easier for you.'

Trevor waved his hand towards the cows lined up along the electric fence, their tails swishing as they pulled chunks of grass into their mouths. The young calves now lay around in little groups, chewing their cud.

'What's hard about this?' he said.

'You're always working. I know small-time farmers don't make much. Besides,' she thumped him gently on his arm, 'you're not getting any younger.'

He dropped his stick, put up his fists and pretended to play-fight with her. 'Don't be cheeky.'

In return, she bunched up her hands and threw a few mock punches into the air. The dogs barked and ran in circles around them. Trevor stopped and looked at her. They both laughed.

'Seriously, though, people would pay to camp somewhere quiet and peaceful to relax and explore the surrounding trails for wildlife. You could even think about putting yurts or good quality caravans in the quarry for people to rent.'

'Just a bit of fun, you said.'

She shrugged.

'So, you're staying around to organise all this and to help me run it?'

'That was the original idea when I did the sketches. But …. now …' Shannon kicked the earth with the toe of her boot. 'Once we've found Stephen, then I probably ought to move on.'

Trevor turned and walked off in the direction of the farmyard. 'Wouldn't want to do it without you,' he grunted.

She stared at his retreating back. What the hell did that mean? Did he want her to go, or did he want her to stay? Was he offering more than a job? Her heart raced, then she shook her head. Getting Trevor to admit his feelings for her, if he had any, seemed to be a step too far. Any sort of future was up in the air anyway, what with Stephen Whittaker still out there somewhere, no doubt plotting both her and Rosa's downfall. What she did know was that she couldn't return to the way she'd lived for the past twenty-three years; she could never go back to that small and invisible life.

She bent down and stroked Trudie's ears, and then they both moved off to follow Trevor back to the farmhouse. One of the cows let out a soft moo as she walked by. A pair of buzzards drifted on the thermals, their soft peep-peep calls echoing over the peaceful scene. At that very moment in time, all was well with her world, and that was enough.

She carried the tray into the lounge and began to hand each resident a cup of tea or coffee together with a piece of cake on a china plate. Frank, on an early shift for a change, followed her and helped those who needed it.

Stopping next to Paul, she knelt beside him. 'Cake or drink first?' she asked.

'T … Tea. Thir … thirsty.' He took the plastic beaker with his good hand, and she helped him guide the drink to his mouth.

'Did you enjoy seeing Bruce, the black Labrador that Christine brought in this morning?'

Paul grinned and nodded his head several times. 'Liked me,' he said.

She held the plate while he took a couple of bites of cake. For several minutes, he seemed happy to chat and answer her questions.

The lounge started to fill up with visitors dropping in to see their relatives. Laugher and chatter filled the air.

'Does anyone come to see you, Paul?'

He shrugged and looked away.

'What about your family, do they visit? Like your mum or dad…' She knew she was being a total cow mentioning his dead parents, but she couldn't stop herself. 'Or your brother?'

Paul flung his arm out and pushed her back onto her heels. The cake fell to the floor. Grunts emanated from his throat. Shannon got to her feet, picked up the cake and tried to straighten the cushion behind his back, all the while talking softly to him about Bruce and the dogs on the farm to calm him.

Meg came over. 'Is everything okay?'

'I think I've upset him by asking if he had family visiting.'

'Oh dear.' Meg bent down and stroked Paul's arm. 'It's okay, luvvie. Everything's fine. The folk singers will be here soon. You like to sing along with them, don't you?'

'I li … like my brother. Wh … where is he?' Paul shouted. 'Wh … Mum?'

Meg frowned and glanced up at Shannon, whose heart thumped against her ribs. How could she have been so callous?

'I'm so sorry,' she whispered to Meg.

'Don't worry, it happens sometimes. An odd word reminds them of something that they'd forgotten about until that moment.' Meg smiled at her. 'It might be best to leave Paul with me until he calms down. Go and give Frank a hand with the other residents.'

Shannon moved into the far corner, near the door to the TV room, and helped Lily with her food and drink. Paul's voice broke through the general chatter and noise in the room. Startled, Shannon looked in his direction.

'My … my brother,' he yelled. 'Ste … Stevie.'

Shannon swung around in the direction that Paul was pointing.

Oh my God.

She stepped back a few paces until she was in the TV room, hidden from the main lounge. She peered around the edge of the door.

Paul continued to shout. 'St … Stevie.'

Stevie? Stephen? The man walking through the door had to be Stephen Whittaker, Paul's brother. Shannon gasped. She recognised his face … but from where?

The man strode with confidence across the lounge towards Paul. Several of the relatives and staff glanced in his direction, but his handsome face was firmly fixed on Paul's.

Suddenly, Shannon remembered a photograph. She shook her head and slunk away from the door to lean against the cool wall next to the TV. Gunfire from a Western roared in her ears. No, it wasn't possible. No. No. It couldn't be him, a voice screamed in her head. She peered around the door again.

It *was* him.

James Trevail was holding Paul's hand and smiling.

Rosa's husband and Stephen Whittaker were one and the same man.

30

Rosa's head was spinning, Shannon was shouting down the phone at her, something about Stephen Whittaker and James.

'Rosa? Rosa, do you understand what I said?'

Rosa shook her head. 'No. What are you on about?'

'Stephen Whittaker came to Nancarrow today. To visit Paul.' Shannon was saying every word very slowly this time. 'Stephen is James. Or rather, James, your husband, is Stephen Whittaker. Do you understand?'

Rosa's head buzzed. How could James be Stephen Whittaker? How could James and Paul be brothers? James was an only child; he didn't have a brother. He … She realised with a jolt that as far as James knew, she herself was an orphan. Had they both lied?

'Rosa? Rosa, say something.'

'You've never met James. How would you know if it was him?' Rosa's voice took on a defiant tone as she spoke. It couldn't be James. They'd made love that morning and he'd kissed her body with such tenderness.

'I saw that photograph of him in your kitchen that time, remember? I'm pretty sure it was him.'

'I'm sending you another picture of him over the phone. Check it again.' Rosa tapped the most recent snap of James and pressed the 'send' button. 'Is that who you saw?'

'Like I said, I'm pretty sure, yes.'

'For crying out loud, Shannon, pretty sure isn't enough.'

'Sorry, but my phone is old, and the screen is scratched.'

'You've got it wrong.' Rosa ran her hand through her hair. 'For heaven's sake, James married me. Why would he do that if he was Stephen Whittaker?'

'I don't know what the shite thinks, Rosa. But I know what I saw, and I saw your husband talking and laughing with Paul.'

'I can't believe …'

'I think you should get Marcus and Freya and come to stay at Carnmarth for a few days. The children can have my room and we can sleep on the sofas.' Shannon cleared her throat. 'Seriously, listen to me, Rosa, you need to leave Curlew House. It's not safe.'

'Did … this man … see you there?'

'I had my back turned to him when Paul started shouting. I don't think James … Stephen, saw me.'

'But he could have? If it was James, surely he would've confronted you there and then?'

'I'm pretty sure he didn't see me, but …'

That blasted phrase again: pretty sure. Why wasn't Shannon certain? Rosa's heart raced and she fought to push the panic down. Who could she believe? Shannon? James? What if Shannon had got it wrong? Thousands of people in Cornwall were tall and dark-haired. Besides, James was so loving to her when things were good between them. They were married and he paid for the children's education. Why would he do that if he was out for revenge?

'I need to go. I must pick up Marcus and Freya, they're home for the weekend.'

'Oh, Rosa, please listen to me. At the very least, promise me that you'll come to Carnmarth if things don't feel right when James gets back later. I'll square it with Trevor.' Shannon sighed. 'I'm finishing my shift shortly and heading back to the farm. I wish you'd just pack and leave. I'm afraid for you. I know that James and Stephen are the same person. Please.'

Tears unexpectedly welled in Rosa's eyes. Why was she so afraid to walk away? Why wasn't she listening to her friend's advice? Was it the thought of leaving Curlew House and all it represented, to sleep on some old worn-out sofa on a farm in the back of beyond? She stifled a sob. Everything was falling apart, and she felt powerless to make a decision. What had happened to her?

After finishing the call with Shannon, Rosa paced the kitchen from one end to the other, passing the wall of glass with only a cursory glance at the yachts and small boats in the Helford River. Finally, she stopped in front of the montage of photos on the wall: her and James's wedding photo, the large picture of James that Shannon referred to, and various other happy snaps of them as a family. In all of them, James's blue eyes twinkled, and he was laughing and smiling. No, he couldn't have made that up. One final look and she made her decision; she would not leave.

She would collect the children from Treloar School as normal and then wait for James to come home for his evening meal. Chances were, everything would be fine, and Shannon had got it wrong. But ... if James did act strangely, she would be able to tell he was lying, and she would leave in the morning with Marcus and Freya. In the meantime, she had food to prepare for the family to eat later.

No matter how hard and furious she chopped the vegetables and diced the onions, the knot of disquiet in her stomach refused to be driven away.

Rosa drove through the gates into Treloar School, parked her car and rushed towards the main door. Children streamed out of the building, hauling large bags and talking to parents, grandparents, or others tasked to ferry them home for the weekend.

Mrs Ferris stood in the doorway supervising the handover of each child to the relevant responsible adult.

Rosa quickened her pace. She was later than usual. The traffic had been heavy, and she'd had to remake the sponge pudding she'd made for dessert. Her head was all over the place, and on the first attempt, the mixture had sunk in the middle.

The school head frowned at her as she stepped toward the entrance.

'Hello, Mrs Ferris. Are Marcus and Freya ready to leave?'

Mrs Ferris's frown deepened, and she shook her head. 'Marcus and Freya have already left, Mrs Trevail.'

'Left?'

'Your husband collected them over an hour ago. He said he wanted to take them out of school a little earlier as he had a special weekend planned for the family.'

Gravel scattered in all directions as Rosa braked hard and brought her car to an abrupt halt outside Curlew House. She shoved the door open and called out for Marcus and Freya. Inside, she checked all the downstairs rooms and then upstairs. The house mocked her with each shout and door bang; the place was empty.

In her head, she tried to control her panic by chanting: they were safe, James was not Stephen Whittaker, James would not hurt them. There would be a simple explanation when they eventually arrived home; they'd been to the beach, or James had taken them for a surprise fish and chip supper. But … James didn't do surprises.

Rosa ran into his study and grabbed the filing cabinets' handles, but they were all locked. Damn it, she needed evidence. She no longer cared that the CCTV cameras recorded her every move.

With trembling hands, she rammed a paper knife into the first lock. The drawer sprang open. She yanked several files onto the desk and searched through them, then she caught sight of the name tab on one of them and gasped. The words, neatly written in James's handwriting, burned into the backs of her eyes – Nancarrow Nursing Home. She opened the file and stared at the invoices for Paul Whittaker's care fees.

Bile surged into Rosa's mouth. She swallowed it back down. Her throat stung with residual acid. She flopped into James's chair, put her head into her hands and sobbed.

A few minutes later, she blinked and forced herself to stand on wobbly legs. Then she saw it. Her heart thudded against her rib cage.

The door to James's gun cupboard was ajar. She nudged it open.

Empty.

31

Shannon's knuckles were white as she gripped the mobile to her ear. Outside the farmhouse window, life was going on as normal, but there was nothing normal about the hysterical voice at the other end of the phone.

'He's taken them,' Rosa screamed. 'From school.'

Shannon didn't need to ask who had taken Marcus and Freya. It was as though, on some deep level, she had always known it was what he would do. 'Where are you?'

'At home.' Rosa wept. 'But they aren't here, Shannon. Marcus and Freya aren't here.'

Shannon attempted to speak, but she couldn't find the words.

'What if he's taken them to those schools he mentioned in Devon or … worse.' Rosa's sobbing grew louder. 'He's taken his gun. The cabinet's empty.'

'Gun?' Shannon's stomach flip-flopped. Trevor had a rifle for use on the farm, so she wasn't afraid of firearms, but in James's hands? Dear God, the very thought made her feel sick.

'I should've listened to you earlier. He wouldn't hurt them, would he?' Rosa spluttered and coughed. 'It's us he wants, not them.'

'I'm on my way.'

Shannon accelerated down the drive to Curlew House, skidded to a halt next to Rosa's BMW, and rushed in through the open door.

'Rosa? Rosa, where are you?'

A strangled sound came from further inside the house. Shannon hurried through the clean, bright kitchen and into another corridor. She followed the odd noises to the downstairs wet room, where Rosa knelt on the floor, head hung over the toilet, retching. She looked up. Mascara ran down her cheeks.

'Rosa? Talk to me.'

'Terrible images of Marcus and Freya keep flashing before my eyes,' she wailed. 'Their still bodies and blank eyes staring at nothing. Nothing.' She retched again. 'Everything's tainted, splashed with blood.'

'He's been a father to those children for years. He won't harm them. Even he wouldn't sink that low.'

'Only eighteen months.'

'What?'

Rosa's head shrunk down into her hunched shoulders. 'We've only known James for eighteen months,' she whispered.

'Christ, you can't be serious?' Shannon stared at her, then grabbed a towel from the rail. 'You've got to pull yourself together. Now. We need to find him. It's the only way we'll find Marcus and Freya. Try not to worry, there's still no reason to assume he would hurt them.'

'He's hit *me*.' Rosa rolled up her sleeve. Livid fingertip bruises dotted her arm.

'Christ, Rosa.' Shannon pulled her into a hug. 'Has he hurt you before?'

'Several times ... recently,' Rosa whispered. 'Before that, he was always so loving and ...' Rosa bent over and clutched her arms across her stomach.

Shannon straightened, jaw clenched. Why hadn't her friend confided in her? If she'd left James when he'd first been violent, maybe this tragic situation wouldn't have happened.

'Has he ever hurt Marcus and Freya?'

Rosa shook her head, and the sudden anger and panic that Rosa's confession had stirred in Shannon subsided a little. She reached out and touched Rosa's shoulder, but she jerked away and slumped against the tiled wall, her head rocking from side to side.

'You need to get up, Rosa. Getting the children away from him is our only concern; everything else we can deal with later.'

Rosa gazed at her, stood, and then stumbled to the basin.

Shannon glanced around the luxurious wet room. The space had no window, and the artificial overhead light gave the area an eerie glow. Everything was magazine-style perfect: the gold taps, the double shower with its giant showerheads, white towels, matching bespoke soap and moisturiser containers.

All of it gave Shannon the shivers. 'I'll wait for you in the kitchen.'

A few minutes later, Rosa sank into the kitchen chair opposite Shannon, skinny arms hanging loose at her sides. She'd aged ten years since the last time they'd met. Was that only a few days ago?

'Have you called the police? Rosa?'

'He wouldn't hurt them, would he?' Rosa asked again, her red eyes fixed on Shannon. 'You were right. James is Stephen Whittaker. I found several invoices from Nancarrow Nursing Home in his office.'

'We've got to call the police. We need their help. Now.'

'I've got contact details for DC Blee. He gave me his card that day he came to Treloar School. The number's on my mobile.' She scanned the worktops.' I must've left it in the wet room. I'll get it.'

'Wouldn't it be quicker to ring 999?'

'He said to call him direct if I had any further problems.'

While she waited for Rosa to return, Shannon took out her phone and punched in Trevor's mobile number. No answer. She briefly smiled; he often left it on the kitchen table when he was out in the fields, which, of course, was the very time when he should have a mobile with him. She left him a message, telling him briefly what was going on and where she was.

Rosa returned to the kitchen, sat down, and scrolled down her contacts list. 'Here he is.' She pressed his name and put the call on speaker phone. The ringtone echoed around the room, followed by a bleep-bleep sound indicating another caller. Rosa jerked forward. 'It's James,' she shouted. 'On WhatsApp.'

'Hello.' DC Blee's deep voice boomed into the room. Rosa cut him off and swiped the screen to accept the incoming call from her husband. 'James? James, where are you? Are Marcus and Freya okay?'

Shannon shifted next to Rosa and peered over her shoulder. James's face filled the small screen. He was laughing.

'My, my, it's so lovely to see you both together.' He leered at them, perfect white teeth on show. 'How are you enjoying your day? Good, I hope.'

'James.' Rosa wailed. 'Please, please don't hurt them, I beg you.'

'Don't call me that,' he snarled. 'I hate that name. I'm Stephen. Stephen Whittaker. But then you know that already. What clever things you are.'

Rosa placed a hand over her mouth. Shannon fought the urge to throw up. Stephen laughed again, then stopped abruptly.

'You're going to know what it's like to suffer the loss of loved ones.' His mouth twisted in a hard line, and his voice was cold when he said, 'Like I did when you killed my parents and destroyed my brother's future.'

'Where are Marcus and Freya?' Shannon shouted down the line. 'Where are they, you bastard?'

'Find *me*, find *them*.' Stephen leered back.

Rosa's eyes widened as her phone bleeped for a second time. 'It's DC Blee. What shall I do?'

'Answer it,' Stephen snarled. 'Tell him everything's fine, then get rid of him. I don't want the police snooping around. Remember, I can see and hear it all.'

Shannon glanced around the room, wide-eyed, looking for the cameras. Rosa had been right all along to be paranoid.

'Hello,' Rosa said, her voice sounding hoarse.

'Mrs Trevail?'

'Yes.'

'This is DC Blee. You tried to ring me a few minutes ago, and I wanted to check if everything was okay. Mrs Ferris from Treloar School contacted me earlier. She told me that Mr Trevail had taken Marcus and Freya out of school early, without your knowledge, as I understand it. She was very concerned about the situation.'

'Oh, what a scatterbrain I am. There's no need for Mrs Ferris to worry. I should've rung her. James and the children arrived home shortly after I did.'

'So, no concerns? No problems?'

'I overreacted, I'm afraid. James treated the children to a McDonald's.'

'McDonald's? I –'

'Yes, he wanted to surprise them. So like James. Anyway, everything's fine here. Thank you so much for calling.' She hung up.

'Well done, Rosa.' Stephen clapped. 'What a good little actress you are.'

A shiver ran down Shannon's spine.

'Mind you, I've been a great actor too. Worthy of an Oscar, I think, for playing the best husband and lover in the world, reeling you in like the sucker you are.'

Rosa stifled a sob. Shannon clutched her trembling hand. Her friend was close to the edge.

'No point in crying, Rosa,' Stephen said. 'You had a good innings with me. Besides, it was fun while it lasted, wasn't it?'

'Please don't,' Rosa cried.

'Don't let him get to you,' Shannon hissed in her ear. 'It's what he wants.'

'What I want, dear Shannon, is to get this show on the road, but first, you have to find me. Are you up to the job, ladies?' Stephen glared at them. 'Now, come and find me, but make sure you leave your mobiles on the table. I don't want either of you ringing that nice DC Blee nor anyone else from the police after you leave the house. I warn you, if you put a foot wrong, it will be Marcus and Freya who suffer.'

The screen went blank.

Shannon stared at the silent phone, struck momentarily powerless by the man's words; he was clearly capable of doing anything to the children. A rush of love for Marcus and Freya surged through her. The thought of anything happening to them filled her with dread. Her heart thumped hard against her ribs. Where would they even begin searching for him? For the children? Suddenly, she needed to hear Trevor's voice, even though the CCTV system, or rather, Stephen, would pick up on her every word. Trevor still didn't answer. Where was he?

Her hand froze.

Stephen had said they would both suffer. A blanket of fear rolled over her, and her breaths came in short gasps.

Had he got Trevor as well?

32

Rosa collapsed into the rattan garden chair, leaned over the matching table and put her head into her hands. How would they be able to find Marcus and Freya? James – Stephen, whatever his blasted name was, was playing with them. All the time, words pulsed in her head: *It's all my fault, it's all my fault.* She wiped a blob of saliva from her chin with the back of her hand.

'Come on, Rosa. Think.' Shannon placed a glass of water in front of her. 'Is there somewhere he might've taken them?'

Rosa got to her feet. White spots, like wriggling tadpoles, swam in her vision. She forced herself to walk up and down the patio. Damn Stephen and his bloody cameras; she felt as trapped outside as she had indoors.

'Is there a place that only James …' Shannon slapped her forehead. 'Dammit, Stephen, goes? What about those woods you mentioned once?'

'Halwyn Woods?'

'Does he still go there?'

'Yes. Yes. He goes birdwatching. He owns the place. Says it's peaceful and private, the way he likes it.' Realisation hit Rosa and she strode towards the kitchen. 'We need to go there.'

'Do you know the way?'

Rosa momentarily faltered, then rushed to the sink and splashed her face with cold water. She had to remember. Shannon was right, she had to get her act together long enough to find the children and get them away from that madman. Grabbing her car keys, she tossed her mobile phone onto the table beside Shannon's and rushed outside.

Brambles and twigs scraped against the sides of the BMW as it hurtled towards Truro and then out into the countryside. In no state to drive, Rosa cowered in the passenger seat, her teeth clattering. By the time they came to the entrance to Halwyn Woods, everything she'd fought so hard to forget about the car crash and her mum's death was bombarding her brain: the crunch of metal, the screams, the silence.

Her body shook. She'd been duped. Not by James, she realised, but by Stephen Whittaker. How had *she*, streetwise Rosa, allowed it to happen? The answer, when it came, made her want to throw up again, but she swallowed the bile back down.

This was happening because she was selfish and greedy. Because she'd put her own needs for status and wealth first. Bottom line, she'd put her wants before Marcus and Freya's, and now … now they were paying the price for her stupidity. She moaned. Had she ever loved him? Maybe. Had he ever loved her? She moaned again. Don't be stupid, Rosa.

'Left? Right?' Shannon shouted.

She pushed herself upright. 'Right. Here, just here.'

Shannon wrenched the wheel, slammed on the brakes, and brought the car to a halt. Rosa's body shot forwards and then back again in the passenger seat. Shannon leapt out of the car. Rosa followed right behind her.

'So where's Stephen's hidey-hole, his bird hide thingy?' Shannon cried.

The trees rustled in the wind as Rosa scanned the area for familiar landmarks; James had only taken her there once – damn it, would she ever think of that man as Stephen? She rubbed her eyes. She had to, for the sake of her sanity.

A large boulder at the start of one of the paths suddenly triggered a memory, and she broke into a run. 'This way.'

Five minutes later, she'd convinced herself she'd gone in the wrong direction. Twigs snapped under her feet and the thick canopy of branches overhead blocked out the sun. Her heart raced, but she forced herself to keep moving, to push aside the horrible images that threatened to overwhelm her. Branches snagged at her arms and top before she broke through the undergrowth into a secluded clearing and came to a halt. Shannon took deep breaths next to her.

Tucked away in the corner was Stephen's woodland sanctuary.

A brand-new metal shipping container, its door locked with a large shiny padlock, had replaced the broken-down hut that Rosa remembered. A generator hummed in the background. An earthy, dank smell clawed at her nostrils.

'His car's not here.' Tears pricked the back of her eyes. She blinked them away, she had to concentrate. Her children's lives depended on her.

'Look, there's fresh tyre tracks. He's been here. He must've used another entrance to this part of the woods.'

A primitive urge to hold her children flooded through her, and she rushed to the container and banged on the door, yanking frantically at the padlock.

'Marcus? Freya?' she yelled. 'Are you in there?'

The only answer came from a woodpecker, tap tapping in a nearby tree.

Shannon picked up a large stone and took a swipe at the padlock. Rosa picked up another rock and did the same.

Clang. Clang. Clang.

After what seemed forever, the padlock gave way. Rosa wrenched the door open, stepped inside, and stopped in her tracks.

Shannon moved past her, walked further into the musty space, and stood with her mouth open. Newspaper clippings, hand-written notes and diagrams of the car crash covered the walls. Pictures of Rosa, her children, and Shannon were plastered on another wall, alongside snaps of Carnmarth farmhouse, Shannon's old caravan, and Curlew House. In the far corner, a bank of four computers, their screens blank and still, stood on a small desk.

There was no sign of Marcus or Freya. Or Stephen Whittaker.

Shannon broke the silence. 'It's like a military command centre.'

'What now?' Rosa forced the words through her chattering teeth. 'What do we do now?'

It's all my fault, it's all my fault.

As if in answer, the computers flashed into life and Stephen Whittaker's face filled each screen: four identical depictions of the man she hated. Rosa lunged at the machines as if she could physically drag her nails across the grotesque faces.

Shannon grabbed her by the arm. 'Don't, we need to hear what he's got to say.'

'My, my, what clever things you are. You found my headquarters. Impressive, isn't it?'

Blood pounded through Rosa's ears, and she grabbed the edge of the desk to stop herself from crumpling to the floor. Shannon wrapped an arm around her waist, and she leaned against her.

'Please don't hurt them. Take me instead. Please,' she whimpered.

'Oh, I'll take you,' he sneered at her. 'I want both of you.' He laughed, then burst into song, his eyes wide. 'One for sorrow, two for joy … la, la, la … six for gold, seven for a secret never to be told.'

'He's fucking mad,' Shannon whispered. 'He's led us on a wild goose chase.'

The singing stopped abruptly. 'You caught me off guard when I saw you at Nancarrow, diving through the doorway into the other room, looking just like any old carer.' Stephen's lip curled. 'Oh, yes, dear Shannon, I saw you.' He shook his head. 'Nancarrow disappointed me, employing the likes of you.'

'Where are they? Please, James … Stephen. … Please tell me.' Rosa sobbed.

'Where do you think we might be?'

'Please tell me, please.' Rosa rubbed her face with the end of her top.

'What's my favourite place in the world?' He laughed. 'The place where I'm the centre of such a happy family.'

'Cur … Curlew House?'

'Hooray, my darling. Yes, we're back home.'

A shiver swept over her body at the sound of the once loving word he'd used so often.

'Home, Sweet Home,' he hummed in a sing-song voice. 'I needed to get everything ready for you. It's all set up now.' He chuckled, his four faces filling the screens. 'It's time for the show to begin.'

The screens flickered and four new images replaced Stephen's faces, all identical.

A scream surged from Rosa's mouth. No. No.

The bright red bonnet of Stephen's E-Type Jaguar filled the shipping container. Marcus and Freya were slumped in the passenger and driver seats, their faces deadly pale, their eyes closed. A hosepipe ran along the floor, the end wedged into a narrow gap in the driver's window. She stopped breathing. Presumably, the other end would be attached to the exhaust pipe.

She cocked her head. Was the engine running? Were they dead? Drugged? Dying? Her teeth clattered again. She put a hand to her mouth.

'Is that the garage at Curlew House?' Shannon nudged her. 'Rosa, is he at Curlew House?'

Rosa stared, then nodded. 'It's the double garage at the back of the property that he uses for his Jaguar only.

'My, my, this CCTV system works a real treat. I must thank Mike Spencer for such an excellent job when all this is over. He's a man after my own heart; will do anything for money.' Stephen's disembowelled voice throbbed over the images of the too-still children. Then the screens changed, and Stephen's faces glared for the second time from the computers.

'Come to me.' He beckoned at them with his forefinger. 'Now. Don't be long.' His face had turned to stone. 'Remember, no tricks or stops along the way to ring the police. There's a tracker on your BMW, Rosa, so I'll know if you stop.' Stephen's mouth twisted into a grim line. 'Obey, or the children will pay.'

Behind her, Rosa heard Shannon shout, 'We're coming.'

She was already running out of the shipping container.

The journey from Halwyn Woods to Truro seemed to take forever, even though Shannon broke all the speed limits. And, damn and blast it, Truro was only the halfway point to the Helford. The narrow road and high hedges flew by in a blur. Neither of them spoke. What could they say?

'Fuck,' Shannon suddenly shouted.

Another vehicle was heading straight towards them. Rosa screamed. There wasn't a gateway or wide bit in the road for either of them to pass safely. Shannon kept going, her mouth a tight line. The BMW momentarily rocked as it knocked against the wing of the other car.

The sound of metal hitting metal blasted Rosa's senses. She wrapped her arms across her stomach in a futile attempt to stop the shivers that ran up and down her body. Hideous images and sounds bombarded her thoughts again, and she couldn't push them away. But then, this was nothing more than she deserved. *It's all my fault, it's all my fault.*

Shannon kept her foot hard on the accelerator until she reached Curlew House. Rosa leapt out of the BMW before the vehicle slewed to a stop, ran to the back of the house and banged on the garage door. Shannon came up beside her and did the same. A click sounded and the door slowly rolled from the ground upwards. They ducked under the widening gap.

A scream filled the air. Rosa realised it came from her as she ran towards Marcus and Freya, who still lay motionless inside the Jaguar. Every fibre of her body wanted to rip the hosepipe from the driver's window, open the door and hold her children tight, but Stephen stepped in front of her. He held a gun in his hand.

'Stay where you are.' He leaned into the vehicle and switched the engine on. Exhaust fumes pumped into the interior.

Rosa screamed again.

'My, my, it's all been worth it just to see your faces.' He raised his hand and pointed the remote at the garage door. It closed with a clunk, cutting off their only chance of escape.

Rosa shivered. 'Please. Not my children.'

Stephen snorted, then reached into the Jaguar and switched off the engine. 'Try anything stupid or come any nearer and I'll turn it on again … for good.'

Rosa dropped to her knees. This man she thought she'd loved was insane, and murderous. How could she have been such a fool?

'What do you want from us?' Shannon asked.

'Information. I want to know every detail about the accident.'

'But–'

'Shut up. I'm doing the talking.' Stephen pointed the revolver at Shannon. 'I know it was your mother who was driving that day and that she was drugged up to her eyeballs.'

Rosa put her head into her hands; tears seeped through her fingers. *It's all my fault, it's all my fault* banged around and around inside her head. No, she wouldn't listen. She couldn't. She looked up, fixed her gaze onto Marcus and Freya and frantically searched for the rise and fall of their chests or the twitch of an eyelid to reassure her they were still alive.

Stephen's voice pierced her vigil. 'Which one of you two supplied the driver with the drugs?'

Shannon gasped. 'What do you mean, which one of us two? You're mad.'

'I know it was one of you.'

'You're crazy. Why would you think that?'

Rosa stumbled to her feet, her heart thumping against her ribs.

'It was me. I gave her the drugs.' She kept her face turned to Stephen, away from Shannon. 'I spiked her drink.' She couldn't look at Shannon. 'It's all my fault. It's all my fault.'

Finally, she'd said the words out loud.

33

Shannon blinked several times. Had Rosa just admitted to supplying Shannon's mum with drugs? No, she must have misheard.

'Go on.' Stephen's hand, steady as a rock, pointed the revolver at Rosa's chest. 'Tell me everything.'

Rosa's body shook with uncontrollable spasms. 'Please don't hurt the children for what I did. Please,' she begged.

'Stop fucking crying. Tell me what happened that day.'

Had Rosa been lying all these years? Shannon shivered. Had she been the fool of all fools? Had she carried all that guilt and shame for something neither she nor her mum was responsible for?

'It was all my fault,' Rosa said again.

'Yeah, yeah, you already said that. Get on with it,' Stephen snarled.

'It … it was our fifteenth birthday celebrations. Our mums took us to St Michael's Mount and Marazion for the day. After we'd had lunch and done the tourist bit, we gave them the slip and … Well, we met these guys at the fairground.' Rosa gulped for air. 'It was all meant to be just a bit of fun. A snog and then back to find our mums.'

Images and sounds floated into Shannon's mind: the brightly painted carousels, the music, stalls filled with candyfloss, and the rich aroma of cooked burgers. A group of lads, no more than kids really, flashed into her head. If the day had ended differently – normally – then she would've forgotten those boys years ago, but their faces had always lurked at the edges of her memories. Why? She held her breath and waited.

'I ...' Rosa cleared her throat. 'I got off with the ringleader. We went around the back of one of the caravans. Kissed a bit. My first real kisses. Then ... then ... Shit, this is so hard.' She rubbed a hand across her mouth. 'He offered me some tablets from a plastic bag. Only a few quid he said, and you and your mate will end your birthday celebrations on a high.' Tears spilt from Rosa's eyes and rolled down her cheeks. 'I don't know how I could've been so stupid. I bought two of the vile things for me and Shannon.'

Rosa pushed her hair behind her ears. 'Our mums found us and dragged us away from the fairground. We had a final drink at the Red Lion pub. That ... that was when I ... I went into the toilet and crushed the tablets into a powder. Fuck, what was I thinking?' Rosa shook her head. 'I ... I then offered to get the drinks from the bar. It was easy to drop the powder into my drink and Shannon's before I returned to the table.'

Shannon gasped. Was Rosa really saying that she'd doctored Shannon's Coca-Cola without telling her? Was that the reason she'd acted like an idiot in the back of the car, laughing and joking, arms flailing everywhere? She shook her head in bewilderment before a blast of anger replaced all other feelings and thoughts. For all these years, she'd felt responsible for causing the accident after her uncontrollable arms had knocked the back of her mum's head, and that was the moment when her mum had lost control and ... everything changed forever. Anger burned in her throat. Not only had she put her miserable life on hold, but, even worse, over the years, she'd grown to hate her mum for being a druggie. Shannon ground her teeth. She wanted to scream. Her mother had been innocent.

'Stop stalling.' Stephen waved the gun at Rosa.

'Shannon's mum picked up the wrong glass,' Rosa cried out. 'She picked up my glass.' Wide-eyed, she stared directly at Shannon. 'What could I do? I ... I thought it would be okay, that your mum would be okay. I would've been in such trouble if my mum had found out what I did.'

'How could you?' Shannon gasped.

Shannon felt sick to her stomach. The car accident would never have happened if only Rosa had knocked that glass from Shannon's mum's hand. If only she'd done something. Anything.

'How could you?' she repeated.

'What's the matter with you?' Stephen shouted as though he'd read Shannon's mind. 'Why didn't you stop the fucking woman from driving?'

Rosa bowed her head.

Damn her, she was acting like some child who'd been told off for a minor indiscretion. Rage built inside Shannon. Rosa had betrayed her yet again. During the last six months, Rosa had loads of opportunities to tell her the truth. Christ, she'd even begged Rosa on several occasions to say what she remembered about the accident, even asked her who she thought might have supplied the drugs. Shannon clenched her fists. She'd allowed herself to trust Rosa and to fall in love with Marcus and Freya. God, she'd let her emotions run free and her guard down, like she hadn't done since the accident. Her nails dug into her palms. It had all been for nothing.

'I'm so sorry,' Rosa whispered. 'So sorry.'

Shannon turned away from her and glared at Stephen. 'Why now? Why torture us now, after all this time?'

A grin flashed onto Stephen's face. 'The torture bit has been fun, hasn't it?'

The bastard was mocking her. She wanted to smash his face to smithereens. She wanted to smash Rosa's face to smithereens. Her nails dug deeper into her palms.

'Okay. Okay.' He glared at her. 'I only discovered that one of you caused the accident two years ago. A new bloke joined the tennis club where I played, who just happened to be an ex-policeman with a runaway mouth. Over drinks one lunchtime, he started to talk about the first case he ever attended as a young police constable in Cornwall. To be fair, he never mentioned any names, but I knew he was talking about the accident that killed my parents and ruined Paul's life.' Stephen waved the gun again at Rosa. 'Paul was the best of us. You might as well have taken him too, for all the life he has.'

'I'm sorry. Please,' Rosa wailed. 'Please let Freya and Marcus go.'

'Don't worry about them. You'll all be going to the same place soon. Suicide, by carbon monoxide. Very fitting that everyone will believe that neither of you could deal with the guilt anymore and decided to end it all. I will play the bereaved husband bit by saying that you couldn't cope after you came back to Cornwall. The move triggered what was obviously some sort of post-traumatic stress.' He laughed. 'It's right that both of you, and the children, should end this way. An eye for an eye and all that.'

'You're mad. A bloody psycho.' Shannon spat the words out.

'Maybe. But what fun I've had with you two.' He shook his head. 'After the chat with the mouthy policeman, I researched every detail about the accident. The police suspected that one of you two had supplied the drugs, and one of you had also taken them. But they didn't act on the information because they concluded that you'd both already lost so much.' He paced a few steps one way and then the other. 'Fucking police, they didn't care about what *I'd* lost, what *Paul* had lost.'

'So, you came for revenge. Tracked us down like animals.' Anger burned in Shannon's chest; she didn't care anymore about what either Stephen or Rosa thought, didn't care if she upset them or not.

'Hit it on the nail, Shannon. You were easy enough to find, living in that hovel. It hardly seemed I needed to take revenge on you, you'd done it all by yourself.'

Shannon's breaths came in gasps as the truth of what he was saying hit home. She'd been her own judge, jury and executioner.

'Still, burning your caravan to the ground was a good feeling.' He chuckled. 'One flick of a match and, whoosh, you had nothing.'

She took a step towards him.

'Rosa, dear Rosa. Now *you* were altogether something different. It took me a while to find you. It was worth the wait. You were gagging to find a man like me, weren't you?'

'No. No.' Rosa covered her face with her hands.

'Reeled you in with sweet talk and money.'

'You said you loved me.' Rosa screeched at him. 'For heaven's sake, you *married* me.'

He laughed again. 'Good, wasn't I? The only tolerable thing that came out of my parents' deaths was the money I inherited from their estate and my father's business. That, with the compensation and their life insurances, made me very, very wealthy. I invested well in the stock market, so I've never had to work.' He moved his gaze between Rosa and Shannon. 'It gave me the freedom to find you dear ladies and to pay whatever schmucks I needed to help me.'

He tilted his head towards Shannon. 'Maybe I should thank your mum's dangerous driving for my good fortune?' He tilted his head again, this time at Rosa. 'Or you, my darling, for spiking her drink?'

'Fuck you,' Rosa sobbed.

Shannon inched forward.

'Indeed,' Stephen replied with a grin. 'I knew if I offered you everything you'd ever dreamed of – money, a beautiful house, clothes, jewellery – you would fall for my charm. I even played the doting dad to those brats there.' He gestured to the car.

Shannon took another step. There was no way she was going to allow this shit of a man to hurt Marcus and Freya without a fight. Nor was he going to have the pleasure of setting up a suicide scene with all of them as unwilling participants. She wasn't going to lose her new life. What had happened hadn't been her fault. It wasn't fair. None of this was fair.

Stephen raised his arm and pointed the revolver towards the car. 'Get in.'

'No,' Rosa said.

Shannon ran the last few feet, barrelled into Stephen, and knocked him to the ground. She scrambled on top of him, her hand gripping the gun's cold metal muzzle. He threw her to the floor, and they rolled back and forth, but she still held onto the revolver. So did Stephen. But he was so much bigger than her. He punched her in the ribs with his free hand and tossed her to one side. She gulped for air. He stood and kicked her hard in the stomach.

She doubled over.

He attempted to walk away, but she grabbed his leg. He couldn't kill Marcus and Freya, he couldn't. He swung his arm back, then down, and hit her on the head. She let go and slumped onto her side.

'Try that again and the children will get it. A slow and painful death for them, from some well-placed bullets, would suit me just fine.'

Through her pain, she watched him turn and walk calmly to the garage door, open it and go outside.

It closed behind him with a resounding thud, trapping her, Rosa and the children inside.

34

Rosa stared at the closed garage door, then at Shannon who was scrambling to her feet, blood running from a gash on her forehead. *It's all my fault, all my fault.* She put her hand over her ears in a futile attempt to block both the words still pounding in her head and the terrible threats Stephen was screaming through the door. She stood rooted to the spot, her mind a fog.

A mumbled sound pierced through the nothingness.

Instinctively, she swung around, her hands coming to rest on the bonnet of the Jaguar. Shannon was dragging Freya out of the passenger seat. The children! Rosa's brain and body galvanized into action. She yanked the hosepipe from the driver's window, flung open the door, and lifted Marcus out. She placed him gently onto the floor behind the vehicle, next to Freya, as far away as was physically possible from the maniac outside.

'Marcus? Freya? Can you hear me?' She shook their still bodies. 'It's Mummy.'

Her heart raced at the sight of their pale faces. What had that monster done to them? She shook them again. Their lips weren't blue, so maybe not carbon monoxide poisoning. Some sort of drug or sleeping tablets? She gasped. The sleeping tablets she'd been taking on and off for the last few months?

'Mum ...' Marcus mumbled.

'Marcus. Marcus. Sweetheart.' She rolled him into her arms and hugged him tight. How had she ever thought that money or status was more important than the love she felt for her son at this moment? She'd lost her so-called husband, her precious Curlew House, and Shannon – the only real friend she'd ever had. But she knew now, without any doubt, that if Marcus and Freya died, then she might as well die too. Nothing else mattered as much as them.

Shannon patted and squeezed Freya's hand. 'Freya. Freya.'

Freya's eyelids flickered and she let out a little moan.

Rosa reached across and wrapped her other arm around her daughter in a fierce, protective grip. They were beginning to come around.

'Thank God,' she whispered, looking at Shannon for confirmation that all would be well with the children. But Shannon avoided her gaze, her lips twisted into a sharp line, every muscle in her face set like stone. 'Shannon?'

Shannon got to her feet, marched to the door and pummelled it with her fists. 'Let us out, you bastard. You won't get away with this.'

'Oh, I will, I will,' Stephen shouted back. 'I'm coming for you.'

Shannon stopped beating the door and leaned her head against it, her arms hanging loose at her sides. The garage fell into an awful silence. Head cocked, Rosa got to her feet and moved nearer to Shannon. Stephen's sing-song voice crept under the door. 'One for sorrow, two for joy … la, la, la … seven for a secret never to be told.' Then, silence again. Rosa strained to hear what he was doing out there.

A click broke the silence.

The garage door rolled slowly upwards, causing Shannon to jerk upright and step backwards. Rosa shuddered as Stephen strode into the garage, gun raised.

'Your time is up.' He grinned. 'It's time to put my plan into action.'

Shannon made a move towards the open door.

'Don't,' he snarled. 'Unless you want another clout on the head. Or a bullet.' He stared at the empty seats in the Jaguar and shook his head. 'You can't save them. Or yourselves.' He laughed, pointing the revolver at Rosa's chest as he did so. 'My plan is suicide, but ... shooting the kids ... now that, dear Rosa, that might be fun. I could work on that scenario before I called the police.' He snorted. 'A few fake tears. A sob even, as I tell them how you so obviously couldn't bear to see them slowly die, so you did the decent thing by shooting them first.'

'No,' Rosa croaked.

'No? Well then, make it easy for them. Suicide by carbon monoxide poisoning is what I wanted all along, and surely that's the least you can do for them? Let's get on with it, shall we? All of you get in the car. Time for sleepy-byes.'

'I can't ... I can't,' Rosa sobbed. 'Not my children. I can't ...'

'Oh, I think you can.' Stephen's finger twitched on the trigger.

Rosa looked from Stephen to her children, her head spinning. He would do it, wouldn't he? He'd shoot them in cold blood. She couldn't let him do that. She couldn't. Sobbing, she lifted Marcus and laid him in the space behind the driver's seat. Shannon's face was ashen as she did the same with Freya.

'Now, you two, get in.'

Rosa lowered herself into the driver's seat next to Shannon.

Stephen picked up the hosepipe and shoved the end back through the gap in the window. 'Switch the engine on,' he shouted to Rosa.

Rosa, numb, blinded by tears, fumbled around and felt for the key in the ignition. The engine roared into life and fumes started to seep out of the hosepipe.

'No tricks. No trying to escape,' Stephen growled.

'Fuck this,' said Shannon as she grappled with the door handle.

'Don't test me, Shannon. I can shoot you first if you'd prefer.' Stephen aimed his revolver at Marcus's head. 'Or them.' His crooning voice floated into the vehicle 'Three for a girl. Four for a boy.'

Shannon collapsed back against the seat, eyes closed.

Rosa lowered her head. For a moment, she'd thought that Shannon would come up with some miracle plan, but how could she? What could either of them do against a madman with a gun? She coughed and covered her mouth with her hand. Shannon pulled her top up over her nose and mouth.

'Oh, this is so enjoyable. Watching you suffer.' Stephen slapped his thigh. 'Oh, I love it when a plan comes together.'

'Bastard,' Shannon hissed.

Stephen cleared his throat and spat on the ground. 'Time for me to step outside. Best to watch your demise from a distance. Don't try to get out. I'll be watching you. This is too much fun to miss.' He hesitated for a heartbeat, then said, 'Remember, I'm doing this for my parents and Paul. You deserve everything that's happening to you.'

Stephen strolled outside onto the gravel. Curlew House sparkled in the sunlight behind him. The world was going on as normal, while they were about to die in this nightmare; her children ending their short lives in this dreadful place. *It's all my fault.* She bowed her head. Tears brimmed in her eyes. Everything was lost.

'Mum?' Freya's weak voice filled the silence. Rosa swung around. Freya's eyelids fluttered open, revealing wide, unfocused eyes. 'Mum,' she mumbled again.

Some animal or maternal instinct took control of Rosa's body. She had never believed it when people said they saw red, but red was what she was seeing right now, flooding her vision. She turned back. Stephen stood out on the driveway, watching them, an insane grin on his face. She gripped the steering wheel, released the handbrake, and rammed her foot down on the accelerator.

The Jaguar leapt forward. Stephen stood stock still, eyes wide, as she drove his beloved vehicle straight for him. A gunshot blasted off; the wing mirror shattered.

She bumped forward and backwards in the seat as the car smashed into Stephen. The impact threw him to the ground, and then the vehicle rocked again as it lurched over his inert figure and out onto the drive. Shannon thumped into the dashboard with a grunt and then slammed back against the seat. The engine cut out and the vehicle rolled to a stop. Rosa slumped over the steering wheel, blood pounding in her ears, her vision edged with a reddish blur.

'Oh, my God,' Shannon cried.

Everything came back in a rush: Shannon's voice, the tick of the engine, seagulls squawking overhead. Slowly, Rosa pushed the driver's door open, got out and walked to the rear of the car. Stephen lay flat on the ground, arms spread wide, eyes closed. Had she killed him?

Suddenly, all her senses were blasted at once. Blue flashing lights and sirens shook her back to life. A police car, followed by an ambulance, raced down the drive to Curlew House.

Shannon yelled, 'Rosa?' She yanked the passenger seat forward, lifted Freya from the car and placed her on the lawn. 'Rosa, you need to get Marcus out.'

Rosa rushed to Marcus and pulled him free.

The police car came to a halt. DC Blee was at the wheel. The paramedics got out of the ambulance; one hurried to the children and the other to Stephen. The woman paramedic leaned over him, felt his neck, and slowly shook her head.

When the paramedics finished treating the children and giving them oxygen, Rosa knelt on the ground, clutched Freya's hand and stroked Marcus's hair. Their eyes were clearer now. Overwhelmed with love, she kissed them both on the cheek. The paramedics busied themselves getting the children into the ambulance. Rosa stepped forward to join them, but a hand stopped her.

'I'm sorry, Mrs Trevail, but you need to come to the station.'

'What?' She stared at DC Blee in disbelief.

'Miss Reid will accompany Marcus and Freya to Treliske Hospital. Don't worry, the paramedics are happy that they're recovering well and are out of danger.'

She scanned the area for Shannon, who stood on the once immaculate grass, now churned up with yet more police cars. She leaned against Trevor; his arms were wrapped around her, and her head was pressed into his chest. Where had he come from?

'But I'm their mother,' Rosa said.

'Mr Trevail, um, Mr Whittaker is dead. You need to be formally interviewed under caution.'

'No,' Rosa cried. 'He was going to murder us all.'

DC Blee gripped her arm. 'Then it will all be fine, and you can go to your children once we're finished, but right now you need to come this way.'

Rosa pulled herself away from the young officer and rushed over to Shannon, who'd now moved and was about to climb into the ambulance.

'Please, Shannon, tell them it wasn't my fault. I had to do what I did.'

Shannon glared back at her.

'He would've killed us all. Tell them.' Rosa could hear the hysteria in her voice. 'I need you to tell them the truth.'

Shannon turned away and hauled herself up into the ambulance. 'Keep away from me, just keep away. I never want to see you again.'

Rosa's shoulders sagged. DC Blee took her arm again and steered her towards the waiting police car. A hand protected her head as she bent down, got into the vehicle, and slumped against the seat. Would she end up going to prison because she'd killed Stephen? Perhaps it was what she deserved for all the deaths and ruined lives she'd caused. Was it her turn to pay now? Now that she'd lost everything, including her children.

Out of the police car window, she saw Shannon sitting in the ambulance with Marcus and Freya. She would care for them, like Rosa had asked her to do on that day walking to Carnmarth Quarry. Like their mums had promised they would do if anything ever happened to either one of them.

Rosa groaned. Except she had made sure that her mum's promise got broken, by blotting out every last detail about the accident and the good life before it. Including, she realised with a physical ache, the love she'd felt for Shannon all those years ago. The same love that flooded through her body now for the slip of a woman who had stepped in without hesitation to look after Marcus and Freya, even after all the hurt and harm that Rosa had inflicted upon her.

Rosa put her head into her hands. She had no right ever to expect Shannon to forgive her. No right at all.

35

Shannon tucked a kitchen roll under her arm, picked up a bowl of coleslaw and made her way across the yard and into the meadow. She placed the items on a white plastic table next to a couple of quiches, savoury snacks and other salad dishes. Underneath the table, wine and beer cooled in a black bucket filled with ice. Assorted picnic chairs and straw bales were dotted here and there.

She smiled at the sight of Vic overseeing the BBQ in an oversized chef's hat and saucy apron. Bill, from The Wheatsheaf, stood chatting next to him, happily swigging down a bottle of beer. Trevor was with his cousin, Sheila, her husband, and two of the local farmers that Shannon had worked for. Ada Martin and Maisie sat in a couple of the better chairs, shaded by a large, orange-coloured garden parasol that Trevor had dug out from somewhere. She would even have invited Zach if he'd still been around, but he'd recently slunk back home with his tail firmly between his legs.

Everything looked neat and tidy, the yard cleared of all rubbish and the farmhouse newly painted; all Trevor's handiwork, with a little bit of help from Vic. A buzzard drifted lazily overhead. In the next field, most of the cows were lying down, chewing their cud. A few lambs in the other pasture bucked and played chase-me around their dozing mothers.

A giggle bubbled in Shannon's throat at the happiness that flooded through her. It was hard to believe how such a wonderful feeling of optimism and love had replaced the knot of misery and shame she'd carried around for decades. Thanks largely, she knew, to Trevor coming into her life.

The events of the last six months leading up to the death of Stephen Whittaker had been horrendous, but now, four weeks after Rosa had killed him, she and Trevor believed it was the right time for a small get-together to thank those who had stood by them, to draw a line under the past and look forward to the future.

Shannon would have loved it if Nina and her family could've joined them today, but Jake's contract in California had been extended for another three months. What a reunion it would be when they eventually returned to Cornwall, even though Shannon knew she'd get a rollicking from Nina when she heard the whole story about what had happened.

A car pulled into the yard. Shannon walked towards it. The first two occupants tumbled out of the vehicle: Marcus and Freya. They immediately ran over to Fern, who lay in the shade with the other collies, and began patting her before finally shouting, 'Hi, Auntie Shannon.'

Auntie Shannon? That sounded good.

During the last few hours of Stephen's life, when he'd given them the runaround and held them captive, she'd realised how much she'd grown to love these children. It was good to see them looking so fit and well.

The last occupant got out of the car.

A mix of emotions hit Shannon at the sight of Rosa. It was the first time they'd seen or spoken to each other since Stephen had been killed.

Armed with a bottle of wine, Rosa stood in front of Shannon. 'Thanks so much for your text inviting us today. I thought that maybe …' She shifted the bottle from one hand to the other.

'We need to talk. Come with me.' Shannon returned to the meadow, dragged a couple of canvas chairs off to one side, poured two large glasses of white wine and handed one to Rosa. 'I need one. You probably do too.'

Rosa nodded and took a sip.

'We need–' Shannon began.

'No, please. There's something I have to say first,' Rosa butted in. 'Thank you. Thank you for making that statement to the police.' She took a deep breath. 'If you hadn't, I'm sure they would've charged me with Stephen's murder, or at least manslaughter.'

Shannon took a sip of wine and stared into the distance. A lot had happened in the twenty-four hours after Stephen's death. She had gone with the children to Treliske Hospital, where doctors had confirmed that Stephen had drugged them with sleeping pills. After they'd been discharged, she and Trevor had taken them back to Carnmarth, where they'd cuddled up to Fern and Trudie for comfort. DC Blee had visited the farm later that evening to provide an update.

He advised them that his suspicions had first become aroused when Rosa told him that Mr Trevail had taken the children for a McDonalds as a nice surprise. Then, when a very angry driver had called into the police station to report his car being hit on the Truro to Halwyn road by 'a mad woman driving a BMW', which turned out to have Rosa's number plate on it, bells started ringing. When he'd failed to reach Rosa on her mobile, he'd remembered her mentioning a friend and he'd rung Carnmarth, where Trevor relayed Shannon's telephone message to him, sending them both rushing over to Curlew House.

DC Blee had also needed a general statement from Shannon giving her version of events leading to the death of Stephen by Rosa's hand.

At the mention of Rosa's name, loathing mixed with anger had flared in her stomach, but, if she was honest with herself, Rosa had done the only thing possible to save all their lives. And that was what she told DC Blee.

'I'm glad that the police dropped any charges,' Shannon finally said.

Rosa let out a long breath. 'Oh, Shannon, you're the best of us two. You always were. You gave that statement clearing me despite what I did to you following the accident and how I've treated you these last few months.' Rosa fiddled with the stem of her wine glass. 'I don't know how I could've been so awful to someone I cared so much for ... cared for like a sister.'

Shannon continued to stare into the distance.

'I know I buried my head in the sand, blotted it all out. It was easier to forget my part in all the deaths and blame the accident on your mum ... and you. I was also so angry with Dad. He was alive. Mum wasn't.' Rosa pressed the cold glass against her forehead. 'It was only when I saw you again that the memories started to come back to me.'

'I guess we both ran away, in our own different ways,' Shannon eventually said.

'Can you ever forgive me for abandoning you?' Rosa placed her drink on the ground and pulled a tissue from her bag. 'If my mum could see me, she would be so mad at me for what I did.'

Shannon shifted in her seat, turned and looked at Rosa properly for the first time since she'd arrived. 'Look, Rosa, I'm not sure if I can forgive you completely. I spent years living a half-life because of you. But you were only fifteen, full of mischief. We both were. Your mum would forgive you, I'm sure. It's what mums do.' She lifted her hand towards Rosa, then let it drop back onto her lap.

'We've both wasted so many years running from something we did when we weren't much more than children.' Shannon drew in a deep breath. 'Perhaps it's time that we should at least forgive ourselves.'

A watery smile appeared on Rosa's face. She lifted her glass in the air. 'Maybe it's also time for these to be topped up.'

Shannon did the honours.

Rosa raised her glass. 'To Marcus and Freya.'

'I'll drink to that,' Shannon said.

Rosa pointed her drink in the direction of her children. 'It wasn't until I nearly lost them that I realised how much I loved them, and that material wealth means nothing. I would've laid my life down for them at the end if it had come to it.'

'You nearly did.' As she said those words, Shannon realised that she would have laid her own life down for those children too. She felt tears welling up at the thought of the danger they'd been in. Time to change the subject. 'I hear you've moved into Primrose Cottage in Cribba Village.'

Rosa tipped her glass towards Shannon again. 'Thanks to you, again, for putting in a good word with Ada Martin.'

'Will you get anything from the sale of Curlew House?'

'No. Everything goes to Paul Whittaker, which I'm glad about. At least he will be financially secure. Besides, it wouldn't feel right to benefit from that so-called marriage.' She gave Shannon a lopsided grin-cum-grimace. 'Except, I did keep the few pieces of jewellery he gave me. I flogged them to pay the deposit on Primrose Cottage and to buy new uniforms for Marcus and Freya. They're at Cribba School, which they are loving, by the way.'

'What about you? Will you need to get a job?'

'Absolutely. But that's nothing new. It was only when I met James-bloody-Stephen, that I got out of the habit of looking after myself.' Rosa glanced at Shannon. 'When I get a job, I might need someone to help with Marcus and Freya. A friend, to pick them up from school occasionally, babysit now and then.'

'I'd like that. They're good kids.' Shannon got to her feet. 'I need to mingle a bit and check that Vic isn't burning all the sausages and burgers.' She waved in the direction of the yard. 'It looks like Fern might need rescuing. There's only so many 'sits' and 'downs' one dog can do in a day. Come on.'

For the next hour or so, Shannon served food and chatted with her guests. Out of the corner of her eye, she could see Rosa in conversation with Sheila's husband and Bill. Trust Rosa to be chatting up the men; would she ever change?

On her way back to the farmhouse for puddings and cake, she caught sight of Trevor, mobile phone clutched to his ear. He mouthed 'Carla' as she drew nearer. She nodded and gave him the thumbs up. He had finally taken the plunge and contacted Carla and Daniel through the Facebook accounts she'd found that day in the Truro Library. Carla had replied immediately and seemed pleased to hear from him. Since then, he'd talked to them both on several occasions, and a plan was in place for them to visit their dad soon.

Shannon stood in the kitchen, up to her elbows in soap suds, and recalled the conversation that she and Trevor had had in the corridor at Treliske Hospital while they waited for the children to be discharged.

'You were pretty brutal with Rosa,' he'd said.

Shannon had clenched her jaw tight and stared out of the window at the cars parked outside.

Trevor gazed down at his feet. 'Whatever she's done, that seems a bit uncalled for in the circumstances. Not like you at all.'

Shannon turned towards him. 'She admitted she was responsible for the car accident that killed both of our mothers,' she spat. 'Admitted she spiked my mum's drink with drugs.'

'Bloody hell.'

'Still think I was too harsh? Her lies made me hate my mum as well as myself.' Shannon's voice cracked. 'I detest her.'

Trevor glanced in her direction, his eyes wide. 'That's a hell of an admission, but it's her burden to carry, not yours. Her actions killed her own mother as well as yours. She has to live with that.'

'So, she'll know what it's been like for me, then.'

'Don't make the same mistake I made, Shannon, spending even more years of your life wracked with guilt and shame, hating instead of living.' He put his hand on her arm. 'I did that with my ex-wife, and I lost Daniel and Carla because of the way I acted.'

Shannon shrugged. Rosa's words were still so raw. How could she ever move on from what that woman had done?

'Think about it, Shannon. Try and make peace with it. Maybe, even forgive Rosa? For your sake.'

Forgiveness? That was a step too far.

She glared at him. 'Maybe, you should make peace with the past and contact Daniel and Carla, seeing as how you're all into this forgiveness malarky.'

'Clever. Very clever,' he'd muttered, and he'd tapped his fingers on the window before adding, 'Yes, you're right. Maybe I will.'

She was so glad that he had put those words into action. And so glad she had listened to him. She had to make peace with the past or her future would be blighted too.

Fern let out a bark and Shannon looked out of the window. Rosa was bending down, speaking to Marcus and Freya. A ball lay at Fern's feet. Shannon wiped the suds from her hands with a tea towel. Could she do it? Could she truly forgive Rosa for everything?

When she returned to the meadow with the puddings and cake, Rosa was seated by herself, so Shannon spooned two good helpings of trifle into bowls and went over to join her.

Rosa took the bowl and smiled. 'Just like your mum used to make.'

Shannon savoured the sweet taste on her tongue.

'What about you?' Rosa turned towards her. 'Are you still working at Nancarrow?'

'I've got a new job at Lamorne Nursing Home in Falmouth.'

She smiled to herself. She'd completed one last shift at Nancarrow. Seeing Paul again had been hard. Between her and Rosa, they had been responsible for wrecking his life in every way possible, but he seemed happy and content. Like Nancarrow, Lamorne Nursing Home primarily cared for people with learning disabilities, and she loved it. They wanted her to undertake training in counselling and become a qualified carer; things couldn't be better.

'Tell me, did your idea of using Carnmarth Quarry for a campsite come to anything?' Rosa asked.

Shannon glanced over towards Trevor, who was in a huddle with Sheila and others. Her stomach flipped with love. What a different person he was from that grumpy old man of six months ago. Had his love for her done that? Was love the reason why he'd come to Curlew House to search for her that day after he'd got her telephone message, and the call from DC Blee? Was it why he'd held her in his arms while she cried into his chest? Why he'd shielded her from the sight of Stephen's mangled body? She thought he loved her, but he hadn't said it out loud, nor had he made any sort of promise or commitment to her.

'Trevor's going to fund a couple of caravans to start the project off. Wants me to manage it part-time to fit in with my work at Lamorne.'

In some ways, she couldn't wait to get started. It could be so exciting running the two jobs together and she had lots of ideas, like the vulnerable people from the home using the site for activities, or even holidays.

'You and Trevor?'

'Mmm.'

'What does that mean?'

'I'm not sure if I'll be staying at Carnmarth.'

'Now you're being ridiculous. You love Trevor. You're one of the most together couples I've seen in a long time.'

Shannon's heart raced. Was she being stupid wanting more, when only a few months back, if she'd had only a fraction of what she had now she would've been delirious with joy?

'We get along great and, yes, I love him. But … but he hasn't told me how he feels.' She looked up at her old friend. 'And I can't accept that I might be the runner-up or consolation prize in comparison to his ex-wife.'

She knew Rosa would find it hard to understand this, considering what she'd been through in the last couple of years with her fake marriage, but staying in a comfortable situation with Trevor, with no commitment from him emotionally, would seem like exchanging one prison of low self-worth for another. Perhaps she had to come to terms with the fact that he was too damaged by what his ex-wife had done to him. Perhaps she needed to move on.

Rosa frowned. 'Give it time. That man loves you, any fool can see that.' She bent over and scrabbled in her bag. 'Look what I found.'

A light green stone sparkled in the sun.

'Mum's necklace,' Shannon murmured. 'Oh, my goodness, where did you find it?'

'Dad had it all the time. The police gave it to him after the car crash. He thought it was Mum's and packed it away with all her other stuff in the attic.'

'You've seen your dad again?'

'I took Marcus and Freya. He was over the moon, and they were delighted to discover they've got a grandad. Flipping hell, I've got so many mistakes to make up for.'

Shannon clipped the necklace around her neck and fingered the stone. Happy images of her mum pulsed through her mind, wiping away the last vestiges of hate and bad feelings. Memories of the mum she knew before everything became tainted by the dreadful accident came flooding back. Her mum had been a good person, doing the best she could, and from now on, those were the only memories that would count.

At the same time, she knew, like Trevor had, that it was time for reconnection and forgiveness. She reached over, grasped Rosa's hand and squeezed it. 'Thank you,' she said.

Rosa gripped her hand hard in return. They sat for a few moments in silence looking at each other; no further words were needed.

Trevor walked towards them.

Rosa got to her feet. 'I think I'd better rescue Fern again from my two.'

'Vic's still cooking up a storm.' Trevor smiled at Rosa. 'Please keep tucking in or we'll be eating sausages for the next week.'

He stood next to Shannon. 'That looked a bit intense. Are you okay?'

'All good. We're getting there.'

Shannon stared into the distance. Laughter and voices filled the air. The fields and hedgerows were bathed in sunshine. She was standing next to the man she loved. Surely, that was enough.

'What're you thinking?'

'How much I love Carnmarth and would miss it if I ever had to leave.'

'Why the hell would you leave?' Trevor stepped back a pace and ran his hand through his hair.

'Well, I am just your lodger.'

'Is that all you think you are? For God's sake, Shannon, you're everything to me.' He moved from one foot to the other.

'You've never said.'

'You know I'm not much good with words.' He glanced at her, sighed, and then took a deep breath. 'I know you can do what you want, go where you want, but ...' He ran his hand through his hair again. A tuft stood up on end. 'But ...' He took her hands in his. 'Please stay. I need you.'

Why was she being so silly, so stubborn, when her feelings for him were so simple? She loved him. Wasn't that all that mattered? Wasn't that enough?

Suddenly, he stood still, cupped her face in his hands, and looked deep into her eyes.

Happiness and love overwhelmed her. She stepped closer to him and rested her hands on his chest. She no longer needed him to say the words; his beautiful green eyes told her everything she wanted to know.

But he said them anyway.

'I love you, Shannon Reid.'

Her heart soared. It was enough, more than enough.

It was everything.

Acknowledgements

Thank you to Grosvenor House Publishing Ltd for helping me bring this book to print.

Special heartfelt thanks to Kath Morgan (mentor and editor) and Wendy Mason (fellow writer) for their help, advice and constructive criticism. I wouldn't have done it without you.

Many thanks to Jill Dyer, Gillian Moyes and Liz Wever for taking the time and effort to read my draft manuscript and for providing invaluable feedback.

Also, thank you to Millie Light for her eagle eye at the proofreading stage.

To those of you who have read, and liked, my debut novel, *Sisters of Vellangoose*, well, you made my year. Thank you. I hope you like *Daughters of Pengollan* just as much.

My biggest thanks must go to my husband, Adrian, for his unfailing support and for always being there on the good days and the bad. Love you.

9 781803 817965